TATIANA
AND THE
RUSSIAN
WOLVES

Stephen Evans Jordan

Clovercroft Publishing

To my parents, Edwin and Marguerite,
for encouraging my literary pursuits.
And to my wife, Susan, for being my
cheerleader and Jill of all trades.

Tatiana and the Russian Wolves

©2018 by Stephen Evans Jordan

Published by Clovercroft Publishing, Franklin, Tennessee

Edited by Christy Callahan

Cover and Interior Design by Suzanne Lawing

Printed in the United States of America

ISBN: 978-1-948484-10-7

ACKNOWLEDGEMENTS

- Cindy Birnes of Cindy Birnes Public Relations for her enthusiasm and creative thinking
- Christy Callahan for her careful work as Copy Editor
- Cambridge Center for Adult Education for the initial guidance on creative writing
- Craig Carpenter for his patience with the website design
- Larry Carpenter for his guidance and wisdom
- Donna Cousins for her very early review of the manuscript
- Elizabeth (Betty) Daudelin, Leslie Keeley, and Marie T. (Terry) Sullivan for their super careful proofreading
- Chris Guillen Photography for setting me at ease during the author photo session
- Brian Harms for his terrific design work on the bookmark and poster
- Dr. Janet Harris for her thoughtful assessment of the story and marketing strategy
- Mike (Houli) Houlihan for his endless list of resources
- Suzanne Lawing for the splendid cover design and layout
- Janis Long Harris of Tyndale Momentum for her enlightenment on the world of publishing
- Michael Madigan for his inspiration and encouragement
- Jerry McGlothlin of Special Guests for the book trailer that captured the essence of the story
- Christy McGlothlin of Easy as Pie Consulting for her wealth of knowledge on social media
- Tim Mersch and Bill Wooten of Relevant Radio for the excellent recording of the book trailer narration
- Oak Park Writers Group for their helpful critiques

PROLOGUE

The stories of Russia my mother told me as a young boy were like fairy tales, verging on the grotesque but fascinating too. So I read about Russia and discovered the mysticism that joins Russians to the land they call Rodina—Motherland. In my young mind's eye, Russia became a supernatural force in a woman's form—with a troubled past and the darkest of secrets. As an adult confronting my mother's shadowy past, I would discover that her secrets and Rodina's were layered so that each held yet another.

In 1941, Adrian Mikhailovich Romanovsky and Alexander Valentinovich Trepoff left Paris and returned to Russia. The older man must have been seeking vengeance; the younger might have been escaping. I'll never know—both men perished in Rodina's frigid embrace. Against the backdrop of World War II, their fates were unimportant, but returning to Russia was so consuming, so headlong that they deserted my mother in German-occupied Paris. Years later in California, and forsaken once again, her past consumed her, and she abandoned me—her only child.

Memories of my mother often take me back to the garden behind our home in Berkeley, where we took afternoon tea and considered my Americanization. Her advice was simple: "Do what you have to do." She was preoccupied; my adjustments impeded our wanderings. We were travelers. Art books and museums were departure gates. Her incredible imagination allowed her to walk into paintings, explore the settings, and talk to the subjects. When I was a boy, I followed her; but after she died, I put away such make-believe.

Chapter 1

June 1985

Moscow

My first trip to Russia started on a bright summer day. I was drawn to Red Square, the Kremlin, and the massive Spasskaya Tower, its electric red star dominating Moscow's evening skyline. Below the Kremlin's walls, St. Basil Cathedral's multicolored onion-shaped domes were more vivid than I had imagined, their gold Russian crosses shimmering in the summer light. Perhaps reflecting Russia's recent past, Spasskaya Tower seemed to glare down at St. Basil's standing its ground in ancient serenity.

The Russia I had imagined as a boy did not stand up to the Moscow I encountered as an adult. A few blocks from Red Square, the buildings were shabby and needed a good scrubbing; broken windows were replaced with plywood and cardboard, and broken concrete showered down from the exteriors. The people were shabby too: their clothing was often dirty; some smelled of old food and older sweat; stumbling drunks were common any time of day. Dressed in an American business suit, I stood out and felt watched.

Late one afternoon, I was outside the Bolshoi Ballet looking at the posters when an old woman—a street sweeper, *babushkas* they're called—and three of her friends approached. They were dressed worse than most Russians, with traditional kerchiefs (*babushkas*) over their heads and lumpy sweaters in warm weather.

The approaching woman had once been tall but was now hunched; her glasses were mended with black tape, and she was still wearing winter boots. She asked, "Why are you here?"

I shrugged as if I didn't understand.

She winked at her friends. "You, all dolled up like that, we've no use for you people." With a shooing motion, she said, "Get out of here. Now. Understand?" As I walked away, she called me a vulgar name.

I turned and said in Russian, "Why, you horrid old creature. Tell me, did you kiss your mother with that filthy mouth of yours?"

She was surprised. Her friends shuffled in their boots.

I stepped toward her; she didn't retreat. "I was minding my own business, not bothering a soul until you strolled up and called me the foulest name."

She seemed amused.

"Why don't you and your friends just totter off and leave me alone?"

"Where are you from?" She grinned. "Where did you learn Russian like that?" She bowed a little. "Come on, tell me." She looked to be at least seventy, but Russian women of her type looked older; it was the endless drudgery. What teeth she still had were bad, her skin was splotchy from exposure to the cold, and years of vodka hadn't helped either. I admired her, a tough Russian.

"I'm an American, but Russian is my first language." I smiled at her.

I could smell the onions on her clothes and alcohol on her breath as she stepped toward me. "Your family ran away after the Revolution?"

"Otherwise they'd have been shot or sent to the gulags."

She agreed with a nod. "Your Russian's old-fashioned and southern." She cocked her head. "Buy vodka for my friends and me? What do you say?"

Poor thing, what she had lived through: the Revolution and the Civil War; the forced collectivization of the farms during the late '20s and early '30s and the resulting famines; Stalin's purges of the late '30s, the horrors of World War II, followed by more of Stalin's infinite brutality. Surviving all of that, she ended up a street sweeper. Well, God bless her; I gave her enough rubles for a liter of vodka and then some.

Taking the money, she said, "You're a gentleman, a real gentleman.

Sorry for the name I called you." Backing away, she added, "Olga, Maria, Anastasia, and I will drink to your health." She paused. "To do so, we need your name."

"Alexander."

"All three, please."

"Alexander Andreivich Romanovsky."

"God bless you, Alexander Andreivich," she said, waving the money to her friends.

"Your name?"

"Tatiana," she said over her shoulder. I didn't catch the rest.

Tatiana was my mother's name. "God bless you, Tatiana," I shouted as she faded away.

Thinking about our exchange, I wondered if Tatiana was somehow connected with my feeling of being watched. If I were being watched, giving an old woman money for vodka was harmless, even in Russia. After all, I had been told for several days that Russia was changing for the better; perhaps it was. Or maybe I was sensing the fear that ran throughout Russian history and still stalked the people.

***

Earlier that year, I had been promoted to Vice President and Eastern European Area Manager at Universal Bank. Based in San Francisco, it was one of the world's largest commercial banks. Soon after my promotion, the Soviets invited the world's leading banks to Moscow to discuss financing a natural gas and oil pipeline to Western Europe. I spoke Russian and French as well as English, and Universal had sent me to kick the project's tires. An easy assignment, since Universal's senior management was determined to be the project's lead American bank.

I spent a week in Moscow, attending presentations by Sov-Gas (the Soviet entity that would borrow the funds) and studying their projections. The Soviets hosted an elaborate dinner the first evening. Subsequent evenings offered numerous possibilities, including the ballet and the symphony.

I was staying at the cavernous Hotel Ukraine. Built during Stalin's reign, from the outside the hotel looked like a high-rise concrete pastry. The rooms were comfortable, and the antiquated fixtures worked. The formal presentations were over, and I was scheduled to leave Moscow early the next morning on an Aeroflot flight to New York. Reviewing my notes in the lobby near the bar, I saw Boris Izmailov approaching and waved.

Boris was one of the Soviet Foreign Trade Bank's senior officers; his bank would coordinate much of the project's borrowing. We got along well during the brief time I knew him. Speaking English, Boris told me that he had business to discuss and escorted me to a conference room off the main lobby where he introduced me to an elderly watery-eyed man, Ivan Alexinsky, whom I remembered from the Sov-Gas presentations. Ivan had stayed in the background, but he stood out. It was his clothes; his baggy suit was forty years out of date. He looked liked one of Stalin's men.

I introduced myself in English. Without standing or offering his hand, Ivan grumbled in Russian. I sat down. Neither Ivan nor Boris spoke. After a long moment, I asked Ivan in Russian about the pipeline project. Boris answered with a quick rehash of earlier presentations. Since Boris and Ivan wanted to see me, I decided to wait until they explained why. They didn't. Boris looked at Ivan, who stared at me. I folded my hands and looked away.

Ivan leaned forward and asked, "Where were you born?"

"Paris. Why do you ask?"

"But an American citizen?"

"Yes."

"Naturalized?"

"Yes."

There was a knock on the door; I jumped a little. As Boris opened the door, a man from the hotel said that I had a call from San Francisco that would be sent to my room.

"It's early morning in California. Must be important," I said. "Excuse me."

Ivan seemed surprised, Boris relieved.

In my room, I was asking a confused hotel operator for my overseas call and sensed someone behind me. It was Boris.

"*Izvinitrye pazhalsta* (excuse me), *Alexander Andreivich.*" His statement struck me as odd, since earlier introductions had been in English, and I had introduced myself as Alexander Romanovsky, without my patronymic, Andreivich.

I stood up. "Yes?"

Boris continued in Russian, "Sorry, but the door was open. Ah, there's no call from the States. I set this up. We must speak." Boris and I resembled each other: in our late thirties, we were both tall, fair, with Russian light-blue eyes. Boris's Russian was educated with a clipped, big-city accent that sounded northern, probably Leningrad. Compared to his, mine was outdated and drawly with my mother's southern accent.

I thanked the operator and hung up. "What do you want?" I said in Russian.

Boris looked around the room. I followed his eyes; Boris nodded. My room was bugged. He asked, "How does Ivan strike you?"

"Lately I've had the feeling of being watched. Perhaps Ivan has something to do with that?"

"Your Russian name attracted the police." Boris's tone was blasé; his eyes weren't.

"And?"

"The police found some odds and ends about your grandfather. Then they called in Ivan—he's a retired KGB general—and he remembered your grandfather, Adrian Romanovsky, from the old days. Checking files that had been stored away for years, Ivan found out that your grandfather returned to Russia with the Germans during the Great Patriotic War." Russians call World War II the Great Patriotic War.

"That was ages ago," I said.

"According to Ivan, those old files say that Adrian Romanovsky was a war criminal. Ivan thinks the American authorities would come after you if they found out."

"Under American law…"

"What if the American authorities did a complete background check on you and your family? Problems?" Boris nodded yes.

"Yes, there could be repercussions." My voice had fluttered.

"And there's Universal Bank to consider." Boris motioned as if he were tying a knot—my grandfather and Universal Bank.

As a trainee, I was told that, in the event of a bank robbery, I was to cooperate. I hoped that policy extended to blackmail. "I will see to it that Universal participates in the Sov-Gas loans so long as the information about my grandfather is not disclosed to Universal or the American authorities."

Boris circled his thumb and forefinger. "Well, that's settled," he said. "Let's go downstairs and tell Ivan the good news."

Instead of the elevators, Boris took my arm and guided me into a stairwell. "Nice work, you sounded sincere and frightened."

"I was and am. What did we just do?"

"I am professional, a banker like you. I have principles like yours, Western. Ivan believes you can be forced to make Universal approve the Sov-Gas financing. I told him that Western banks don't work that way, and you can't force Universal into deals. But he's drunk all the time and won't listen. So we're doing it his way." With a giddy laugh, he added, "One more thing: I'm scared."

"Then I'm terrified." We blinked at each other. "Does your bank know about this?"

"My bank has nothing whatsoever to do with this...this stupid blackmail," Boris sputtered. "If they knew I was involved, I'd be in big trouble. However, Ivan could make far more trouble if I told my bank that he had forced me. If you help, maybe we can get out of this mess." He grabbed my jacket. "Please, help me."

"This is moving far too fast."

"Don't you see? Ivan has you," Boris said.

"Well, I don't think so. For one thing, I was born two years after the war ended and never knew Adrian Romanovsky. As for the American immigration authorities, even if they checked my records, I'd deny knowing anything about my grandfather returning to Russia with the Nazis. But here's where it may get tricky for you: Universal's policy states that any attempt to blackmail or bribe its officers must be reported in writing. I'll write a report telling them exactly what happened."

"I can't stop you reporting this," Boris said. "Ivan's a survivor. He made it through Stalin's purges, the war, and the dangerous time after Stalin's death. He knows where all the bodies are buried." Boris laughed a little. "Ivan is one of the freest men in Russia; no one gets in his way."

"I see."

"Ivan can make trouble for you. Maybe a passport problem. You were born in France but travel under an American passport. Sorting that out might take a day or two. Given the way you dress and talk with that fancy accent, a few nights in police custody might be tricky."

"Okay, I'll go along with Ivan since Universal's management is eager to be the lead American bank in the pipeline project."

"Why didn't you tell me this before?" Boris said.

"Being blackmailed pushed everything else aside. And until now, Universal's credit decisions were none of your business."

"Yes, of course," Boris said. "I'll tell Ivan that you'll see to it that Universal approves the deal. Our taped conversation in your room will prove that. Then all that is left is to listen to Ivan. He always goes back to the old days before the war when he was coordinating actions against the Whites in Europe." The Whites were royalists who fought the Communists during the Russian Civil War that followed the Revolution from 1917 to about 1922.

Boris offered me a cigarette.

I had quit years ago but took it.

"You're one of the lucky ones," he said. "Your family got out. My grandparents were sent to the gulags because they were landowners— kulaks, enemies of the people. But they were peasants with a few hectares of land and some livestock."

"Lucky? Out of two very large families, I'm the only one left." I tried the cigarette and was dizzy.

Boris said, "Adrian Romanovsky was captured toward the end of the war. According to Ivan, when the Germans retreated, Adrian Romanovsky went to an estate his family owned before the Revolution and waited. He told the Red Army interrogators that he was a czarist officer, then a White officer."

"And?"

"An officer, he demanded to be shot. Ivan said that Adrian Romanovsky was hanged. The hanging was slow."

"Why in God's name…"

"I don't like this any more than you do." Boris shook his head. "Ivan is my ex-father-in-law; that's a primary reason why this is happening." Boris studied his cigarette. "This is all about Ivan's hatred; I'm afraid you're going to listen to it."

I ground out my cigarette. "You may tell Ivan that I have no intention of listening to his odium."

"Odium?" Boris said. "Have you thought about updating your Russian?"

"I have. What else does Ivan know?"

"After the Whites were defeated, Adrian Romanovsky and his young son, Andre, fled to Turkey. A year or so later, they reached Paris. Adrian became the leader of a White émigré group that assassinated Soviet agents operating in Europe. The young boy, Andre, was a child prodigy and would become an important mathematician. When the Germans invaded France, Andre was evacuated to England and worked breaking German codes. Your mother, Tatiana, worked for a major Parisian art gallery; she came from one of the original boyar families—princes, going back to Kievan Rus. Her family name was Trepoff. The files end when Andre and Tatiana, his wife, left France and went to the University of California with their young son, Alexander Andreivich—you."

"What else did Ivan say about my mother?"

"Not much, but I know the Nazis used Parisian galleries to plunder museums and private—that is, Jewish—art collections. German terms were: take it or leave it. Should you leave it, we'll take it and send you to the gas."

"What did Adrian Romanovsky do for the Germans?"

"Counterpartisan work."

I wondered about my mother's brother, Alexander Trepoff, who returned to Russia with Adrian Romanovsky and vanished.

Vanishing—a theme that runs through Russian folk tales and history:

Olga was gathering mushrooms in the forest and vanished,
Must have been the wolves.

A knock on the door one night and Sergei vanished,
The wolves again.

Since Boris hadn't mentioned Alexander Trepoff, neither would I. Perhaps his file never existed, or perhaps he and his file had vanished. "The Germans were killers back then," I said.

"People who assisted them had various motives. However, some were as bad as the German, others even worse."

"I've read that Russians are possessed by Russia. My grandfather going home to die was quite Russian, wasn't it?"

Boris's smile was tenuous. "You should keep him in your mind that way."

"I hope you're as honest as I think you are."

"Thank you, thank you," Boris gushed. We clapped each other's shoulders and brushed cheeks. "You're ashamed of being Russian?"

I didn't know many Russians. My parents had avoided the Russians in Paris. The only Russians I met in California were at the Russian Orthodox church in San Francisco that my mother and I attended. Most of the parishioners were émigrés bewildered by the upheavals that flung them to the other side of the world. They clung to one another, but my mother refused to socialize. When I asked why, she said they weren't our type; we were special Russians who'd become quite rare. I missed her point and thought the two special Russians lived in the intimate world my mother and I had created.

Descending in an elevator, I hoped that I had read Boris right; if not, things would get far worse, and soon. Boris asked me to arrange appetizers and vodka while he spoke to Ivan. I greased the concierge with a pack of Marlboros, an unofficial currency that was better than rubles or dollars. The concierge called the bar, then minutes later, a waiter and I entered the conference room.

I filled the short-stemmed glasses with icy vodka and said, *"Za vashe zadarov ye!* (to your health!)" We downed the vodka.

Helping himself to the pickled mushrooms, Ivan asked, "How do I address you? Your Honor or Your Radiance?" Czarist terms of address for the aristocracy. I didn't answer, and Boris poured another round.

As he was about to repeat his question, Ivan's cigarette cough rumbled into a phlegmy spasm, his skin went rusty-scarlet, and his eyes watered. Probably a formidable man in his youth, Ivan was in his seventies, and his lungs were racing his liver to see which went first. He lit a cigarette and gulped the vodka. His high Slavic cheekbones made his blue eyes look small. A common complaint among Russians: small eyes.

Russian eyes had fascinated me since I first saw them on television news. Always in the winter, the cameras caught the smallish eyes set in square Slavic faces as Russians navigated the snow with a slow rolling gait, arms tight to their sides. I was told that they walked that way because they had been bound in swaddling clothes as babies. Or perhaps they were balancing themselves on icy streets and a slippery society.

Ivan caught me staring and wheezed, "Your Radiance; yes, that fits."

"That was a long, long time ago," I said. "Anyway, as Boris may have told you, I'll see to it that Universal Bank participates in the Sov-Gas financing. That's conditional, of course, on you not telling Universal and the American authorities about my grandfather."

"I'll see to it." I detected an ember of satisfaction in Ivan's damp eyes. "But tell me, Your Radiance, does it bother you that your grandfather was a war criminal?"

A Soviet secret policeman calling anyone a criminal was preposterous. "I never knew my grandfather. On the other hand, the French and the British gave my father medals for his service during the Great Patriotic War." I stood up. "But why, in heaven's name, are we discussing my grandfather who died more than forty years ago?"

Ivan yelled, "He was hanged. Now, sit down."

"I'll stand."

Boris's eyes widened.

Ivan glared. "People like your family…" Coughing stopped him.

"People like you killed most of them," I said.

"Obviously, we missed a few." Ivan gasped after several shallow breaths. "My father's family came from the south, where your accent is from. White cavalry squadrons took his village. Those fancy officers—like your grandfather—declared the village Red and nailed the men to a barn. My grandfather, an old man, hands nailed, freezing to death."

"What does that have to do with me?"

Ivan tossed back another vodka. "My father was Red Cossack cavalry, a squadron leader, in the south. His troopers came across one of those big estates. The men had gone with the Whites and left behind the women and old men. My God, what those women went through." Ivan drifted off into his thoughts; from his expression I couldn't tell if they were pleasant or troubling. Then he refocused. "Your grandfather got what he deserved."

"Why are you doing this?"

Ivan said, "Your grandfather—"

Boris took over. "Ivan, all of our grandfathers are dead. Awful deaths…yours, mine, his."

"The aristocrats," Ivan said, "I've never seen any in person. Only their pictures, like you in fancy clothes." I was wearing a summer-weight, gray-striped Brooks Brothers suit. "And talking with that aristocratic drawl, you're one of them, a pampered lap dog. You're a banker pandering to rich capitalists, like your mother pandered to the Nazis."

"She did not." I glanced at Boris, who seemed surprised.

"The French resistance was Communist," Ivan sneered. "They didn't miss anything and reported everything. And why would our informants lie?"

"Communists believed that aristocrats were capable of anything."

"They were right. But that's between you and your mother."

"She's dead."

"Sorry," Ivan said.

"You're not."

Pointing to me, Boris said, "He's one of the few left; their time ended years ago." Taking Ivan's shoulder, he said, "Let's go."

Ivan staggered and pointed at me. "You're a ghost. A damned ghost." Clapping his hands, he said, "Boo, go to hell, where you belong."

Returning to my room, I was drawn to the window. Northern cities come alive in the summer, releasing energy the winter had muffled under heavy wraps. Lines were forming at the theaters. In the parks children were playing, young couples were flirting, older folks reminiscing accompanied by the balalaika's fluttering cords. I thought of joining them for the homemade pirozhki and sausages blistered over open fires; the beer would be fresh, the vodka clean. More vodka was tempting, but I had a report to write.

Exhuming my grandfather and my uncle in a memo to Personnel was demeaning for my parents and the relatives I had never known. They were gone, along with the millions that Communism had consumed. Not mourned then, they had become ciphers in the history books. As Stalin himself once said, "A single death is a tragedy, a million is a statistic."

I sat down and wrote the report.

Stretched out on the bed, I waited for my mother. Early that morning, she would emerge from dawn's frail light; we would talk, as we had before she became ill. About to leave, she would ask if I loved her more than anyone; I'd say yes. When I asked if she had loved me, she would fade away without answering.

Chapter 2

June 1985

New York City

I arrived in New York City early in the evening, checked into a hotel near the airport, and phoned Fiona Sinclair in San Francisco.

Fiona had been my mother's closest friend. I was seventeen when my father died, and my mother never recovered. Her grief was diagnosed as acute depression, but the doctors had it wrong. She had become insane.

I can't imagine what would have happened to us without Fiona; she moved us into her home and arranged for my mother's care. Fiona became my legal guardian and sent me to college. My parents' money didn't cover my mother's care, let alone my education. When I asked for an accounting, she refused to discuss the matter.

Fiona picked up on the second ring. "Fiona, I'm in New York. I need your help."

"What went wrong in Russia?"

"A retired high-ranking policeman who knew of my mother and Adrian Romanovsky questioned me. He said that mother pandered to the Germans during the occupation."

"Tatiana sold some art to the Germans. I'm sure you know that."

"I do, but the policeman used the word *pandered*."

"Pandered, how?"

"He didn't say; I wasn't about to ask."

"Why don't you tell me what you know," Fiona said, "and I'll fill in any gaps. On second thought, why don't we discuss this tomorrow when you get home?"

"I'd like to get this cleared up now…if you don't mind?"

Fiona said, "Before the Revolution, Tatiana's family had an incredible art collection. Your maternal grandmother, Olga, did the purchasing and oversaw the collection. Olga passed her talent to your mother; both of them had *the eye*. Why don't you continue, Alexander?"

"As you probably know, after the Civil War, the Communists coerced Olga to catalogue and appraise confiscated art—much from her family's collection—and were selling to Westerners for hard currency. In the early 1920s, Olga, my mother, and her brother were allowed to leave Russia and went to Paris, where Olga found a job as a nanny and art advisor to a Jewish banker. The banker was a kind man and let my grandmother set up a home in his townhouse's basement."

"Keep going," Fiona said.

"Before the war, an important Parisian art gallery employed my mother as a catalogue clerk until the owners discovered that she had *the eye*. *The eye* knew which pictures held the money and, as the war approached, which held the lives. Just before the war, the Parisian art market became increasingly predatory. The gallery became a conduit for quick sales as Jews flooded the market with paintings. After the German occupation, highway robbery became the norm. Mother was disgusted and quit."

"Then what?"

"Mother and the banker negotiated his family out of France by selling his collection to representatives of that fat Nazi. What was his name?

"Herman Goering," Fiona said.

"Yes, him. The banker and his family went to Brazil or Portugal. Mother was quite proud of that."

"I could have found work for her at one of the galleries here in San Francisco, but she refused to have anything to do with buying and selling paintings." Fiona paused. "Then what did Tatiana do?"

"She took some kind of job with a large French construction company," I said.

"Right, the company needed Russian translators."

"Russian translators? Why?"

"Oops!" Fiona gasped. "Spilled my tea." She put the phone down for a long moment. "The construction company—I forget its name—employed Russian volunteers."

"Volunteers? You mean Russian prisoners of war?"

Fiona didn't answer.

"What did this construction company do?"

"I believe they did work for the German military authorities," she said.

"And the Russian POWs?"

"Tatiana said that they were farm boys who volunteered, so to speak, to get out of the German prison camps, where they were being starved."

"So—"

"Look, Alexander, Tatiana didn't join the Resistance or anything like that. She was alone in Paris. Her mother died right after the war started, your grandfather and uncle returned to Russia, and your father had been evacuated to England. Technically she may have cooperated with the Germans; so did a lot of French. Bear in mind that Tatiana's feelings about France were ambivalent: the French were contemptuous of the Russian émigrés, and she was never allowed French citizenship. In short, she survived."

"I see…"

"You're upset?"

"Mother was so evasive about those days."

"Did the policeman say anything else about Tatiana?"

"No, he was more interested in my grandfather. I'll tell you about that later."

"If I may have been less than forthright, well, I didn't want to harm your memories of Tatiana," Fiona said. "You understand, don't you?"

"I do, I guess."

"I'm afraid Tatiana will never let go of you."

"I don't deserve to be let go of."

"My dear boy, so harsh on yourself." Fiona brightened. "I'll pick you up at the airport tomorrow afternoon; we'll have a lovely supper."

"I'm looking forward to that."

"And so am I, Alexander."

CHAPTER 3

JUNE 1986

SAN FRANCISCO

A year later, we were going to the opera on a Friday evening, and Fiona picked me up in her Mercedes. I didn't care for opera, but escorting Fiona was a small repayment for all that she had done for my mother and me.

On the way, I was telling Fiona, "Universal has decided to send me to their Moscow representative office on an interim assignment. I don't think I'll be in Moscow too long."

"When did you find out?"

"Oh, it's been off and on for a month or so. The bank thought they'd found a replacement, but that fell through. Now I'm going for sure."

"Your first trip was hardly auspicious, was it?"

"Unnerving, that's for sure."

"Could your grandfather still be a problem?" Fiona asked.

"I attached a letter to my visa application explaining my grandfather. The visa came back with a short letter thanking me for my candor and assuring me that my grandfather was no longer an issue for the Soviet government."

"Shouldn't you have explained that Tatiana's brother returned with the Germans too?"

"I'm pretty sure they don't know he existed."

Fiona gripped the wheel to navigate a busy intersection and started up Pacific Heights on her shortcut to the Opera House. "Why are they sending you?"

"The bank's office was opened only six months ago. The representative was fired for black-market dealing. Everyone uses the black market for one thing or another, but an internal audit found that he was using bank funds to speculate."

"When are you leaving?" She had stopped at a red light.

"Next Saturday, I'll fly to New York and Sunday to Moscow."

"I wish you'd have told me sooner." Fiona's formidable temper seemed about to detonate. "Perhaps your candor could have applied to me as well as the Russians?"

"Fiona, the light turned green." We crossed the intersection. "I didn't want to upset you, like I just have. You're angry or worried?"

"Of course, I'm worried. Oh, there's something else too. We'll talk about it later."

"Come on, don't do that."

At the next light, she said, "Fred Imhoff, you know, Drew's…ah, consort. No, that's not the word. Well, you know, Drew's companion has full-blown AIDS."

"And Drew?"

"I don't know. But one has to assume," Fiona said. "Fred and Drew have been, as you know, together for some time."

Andrew Faircloth (Drew) was Fiona's son from her brief and only marriage. I thought that Fiona was avoiding the word *lovers* since I had fallen in love with Drew when my mother became ill that summer. I felt myself blush as we turned into the parking garage. Squealing tires on the concrete brought me back. "What are you going to do?"

Fiona parked and sat back. "Don't know. For years, I've told myself that while I've always loved Drew, I don't like him. But how can you love someone you don't like? I suspect it's the same for Drew."

"Let's skip tonight's Wagner and go back to my place. I'll fix something for supper, or we can go out."

"I'm hosting a supper afterwards, remember?" Fiona looked out the window and said, "Funny, isn't it? My family forced Drew and me into a de facto alliance of sorts. If Drew does have AIDS, how will my family take that? Sorry, rhetorical question. That pack of jackals will bay at the moon."

"Mother said that you have the heart of a saint and the family of a true martyr. Given the circumstances, might reconciliation with Drew be in order?"

"I wish my maternal instincts, such as they are, would surface. Anyway, Drew and I have business to sort out; maybe I could begin there." She started to get out.

"When did you learn about Fred?"

"About a week ago."

"Why didn't you tell me then?"

Fiona slid across the seat. "I have to be careful with you." She put her hands to my face. "You're like Tatiana: so delicate, so fragile."

"You're embarrassing me."

"In front of whom?" Fiona's smile was forlorn.

That evening's performance, *Parsifal*, was Wagner's most tedious opera. The knight Parsifal dealing with a witch in a magical garden was as far as I got before my thoughts turned to Drew.

After having walked out on Drew years ago with no real explanation, it was remarkable that we got along as well as we did. We had become cordial over the past several years, and I wanted to see him before I left for Moscow.

By the intermission, I had no idea what Parsifal was up to. In the large hall, Fiona and her friends dissected the evening's performance; most were unhappy with the lead, who seemed distracted or bored—I couldn't blame him. Once we were in our seats, the music came up, and I tried thinking about Moscow. It almost worked.

Fiona shook my arm as the seats were emptying. "Overwhelmed by the Wagner?"

"Caught me daydreaming."

"About Russia?"

"And Mother too."

"Guests are coming; we must hurry."

That Saturday morning, I left a message on Drew's answering

machine, telling him about my assignment, and promised to write from Moscow. I tried his office and was told that he was in Dallas, tending to clients. Thinking about it, my message on the answering machine was perfunctory. Drew and Fred lived eight blocks from me, and I walked over.

Their Tuscan-inspired home on Marina Drive overlooked the Marina Green and the San Francisco Bay. From Drew's front window, Alcatraz was to the east, the Golden Gate due west, and Marin County's flaxen hills north across the Bay.

Fred had always been distant and was more so that afternoon. We talked at the front door until he invited me in for a drink. Fred opened the refrigerator and asked me to help myself. I found a bottle of beer and poured him a glass of orange juice. I continued with small talk while we stood in the kitchen. Fred wasn't unpleasant; his expression was neutral, but he wasn't making it easy. I rambled on about Russia. Looking out a window at one of San Francisco's infrequent warm summer days, I suggested the patio behind the house. Fred agreed.

Fred was a blue-eyed blond, and about my height, just over six feet. The skin around Fred's neck and jaw was sagging. He had weary eyes and pallid coloring.

During an uncomfortable lull, I asked about Drew's gallery. Drew was an art dealer, and Fred managed the business. Fred perked up and told me about a recent showing. Fred turned glum, leaned back in the chair facing the sun, and closed his eyes. I got up to leave.

"Not a very good host these days, I'm afraid," he said. "As you suspect, I'm preoccupied."

"I'm sorry. I learned yesterday. And I barged in on you. Sorry about that too."

Fred opened his eyes. "I know you're concerned about Drew, but you'll have to ask him."

"I will."

Fred nodded. "May I tell you something? Drew mustn't know."

Seeing the anger in Fred's eyes, I said, "I'll save you the trouble. You don't like me, and I know why, but I don't think…" I didn't want to continue on that path, but there wasn't another to take. "Well, I admit that walking out on Drew without an explanation was kind of graceless, but that was years ago when we were youngsters."

"Kind of graceless?" Fred laughed. "Graceless, you say? Drew said you could be funny, but your comedic efforts aren't working today, certainly not with me."

"Look, I understand your feelings."

"I don't think you do," Fred said. "Drew has a thing for tall blonds. I mean, look at us; you're a larger-framed version of me. But, no, that's not it."

"I've got to get going."

Fred stood to face me. "Well, this tête-à-tête was your idea, wasn't it?"

"I'm not going to apologize to you for what went on between Drew and me years ago. Frankly, that's none of your business."

"Really? None of my business? But you see, it's definitely my business because I love Drew. And you, you tease him."

"No, I don't, not at all."

"At Drew's receptions, you were so vivacious, so charming. Underneath that stuffy exterior, you're most alluring, as far as Drew's concerned. Drew tries hiding it. But he can't, not from me."

"Fred, you've got it all wrong. I've never teased Drew."

"Go ahead, deny it, you shameless flirt." Fred sat down. "Well, that's off my chest." He clasped his hands behind his head. "I'm going to catch a few more rays. Please show yourself out."

I was at the garden gate when Fred called out, "Oh, one last thing: your forbearance, please." I went back. "I made this interlude unpleasant," he said. "Nevertheless, your coming around is more than some of my real *friends* can muster. My feelings about you notwithstanding, I'll edit out the acrimony when I tell Drew that you dropped by. He'll be pleased." Fred faced the sun.

CHAPTER 4

JUNE 1986

MOSCOW

Before I arrived, all of the Russian staff, except for one secretary, had resigned, so I contacted Boris Izmailov at the Soviet Foreign Trade Bank. Boris headed the North American desk and introduced me to his people, all of whom spoke excellent English. Boris and his senior management hosted a lunch; I explained my staffing problems and asked for their assistance. We sealed their assurances with vodka toasts.

After lunch Boris walked me to the elevators, and I asked, "Can we talk?" He nodded yes. "What happened to Ivan?"

"About six months after our encounter, he died: lung cancer. I went to the burial to make sure they nailed his coffin shut, with him in it." Stepping closer, Boris continued, "I didn't say a word to anyone about Ivan. Universal Bank will be the lead American bank for the pipeline project. So no problems from your end?"

"In my memorandum, I emphasized that you were forced into the situation, which had nothing to do with your bank. I also explained that Ivan was an alcoholic but had the power to force people to do his bidding. I sent the memo to Human Resources, where it was filed."

"Would anyone at Universal tell my bank what happened?"

"There's no reason to, and it might get in the way of the Sov-Gas financing. When I was applying for a Soviet visa and work permit, HR suggested that I attach an addendum explaining my grandfather. I did, and the work permit came back with a letter assuring me that my grandfather was not an issue."

"Children and grandchildren of the émigrés are coming back as businessmen; many speak old-fashioned Russian like yours." We laughed. "My bank will help. We'll keep in touch. I must repay you for helping me."

"Getting my office staffed will be more than enough."

Boris looked over his shoulder. "I would sell my soul to get out of here; it's collapsing."

Boris's colleagues sent over two retired women who spoke good English and a young man, Anatole Semenov, a recent university graduate. The Soviet bank would lend Anatole to us for as long as we needed him; the tradeoff was that Anatole would learn some American banking and improve his English while reporting our activities to his superiors, not that there was much to report. We were in a holding pattern, waiting for a permanent representative to be hired, and I spent most of my time working with Sov-Gas coordinating a proposed US Export-Import Bank component of the pipeline financing.

Early in September, I flew to San Francisco to interview a prospective Russian-speaking candidate, but my boss and I found the fellow unacceptable. The HR lady who had arranged the interview reminded me that I would stay in Moscow until a representative was found. A month later, HR, working through a headhunter, found a Russian speaker at a Canadian bank's London branch. I flew to London for an interview that went well and continued through dinner. Two weeks later, the candidate flew to San Francisco for more interviews. He accepted the position and returned to London to wind up his affairs and start moving his family while I prepared to leave.

Anatole invited me to my going-away supper on a Saturday evening. He suggested a hard-currency restaurant with good food and service and hinted that I might expense the meal.

My expense reports from Moscow were on the gray side of bank policy, such as the shopping list Boris Izmailov gave me before I went to London: Scotch whiskey, French perfume, American cigarettes, and pantyhose for his wife. The bank had rejected many of my claims, and there was a good chance I'd end up paying for my going-away party.

The party was inexpensive for seven of us: US$500 for Georgian champagne with Caspian caviar and blini, wild mushroom soup, shashlik, plum sambouk (a thick mousse), Armenian brandy, and good coffee. Throughout the meal, we fortified ourselves with toasts of potato vodka. Pacing the alcohol during Russian celebrations is tricky, but getting fairly drunk is almost expected. When the meal ended, all of us were singing, and the older secretary and her husband were sobbing—hallmarks of a successful Russian party. After brushing cheeks, I walked back to my hotel, hoping the frigid night would clear my head.

At that hour, most people on the streets were hurrying to get out of the cold; those who were too drunk to care might pass out and die from exposure. *Militsiya*, uniformed police, were busy picking them up and shooing home the drunks who could still walk. A tipsy Westerner was noticed but not bothered.

I had a two-room suite at a hotel catering to foreigners. When I entered my suite, the phone was ringing, a surprise since it hadn't worked for the past week. I answered, *"Zdrazdviytye, Alexander Andreivich."*

"Roman?" a faint, crackling voice asked over a bad line.

"Da?"

There was a burst of static followed by a pulsing buzz. I could barely hear an English-speaking male voice: "Alexander Romanovsky?"

"Who is this?"

"Drew, Drew Faircloth. I've been trying to get you for hours. What time is it there?" The buzzing stopped.

"Around midnight. Where are you?"

"Fiona's. She gave me this number. How are you?"

"Okay, and you?"

"You sound funny," Drew said, "or is it the phone line?"

"Just back from a party. I've been drinking." I found a pack of cigarettes in my coat pocket and lit one while Drew struggled to start a sentence.

"So, what's it like?" he asked.

"The old parts of Moscow are interesting. Last month, I took a long weekend and went up to Leningrad. I could have spent a week at the Hermitage; the collection is incredible."

"Your grandmother worked at the Hermitage after the Revolution, didn't she?"

"I'm sure this line is tapped. Drew, how's—"

"Oh dear, wasn't thinking," Drew interrupted. "Have you been in Russia all this time?"

"I had a meeting in San Francisco and flew right back. No time to call you, sorry."

"I see."

"How's Fred?"

"Died late yesterday afternoon."

"Drew, I'm so sorry. Before I left, I spent some time with Fred. I knew it was the last time I'd see him."

"I appreciate that. As it progresses, AIDS can be disagreeable, too much for some of our friends."

"How are you doing?"

"As best as I can, considering."

I said, "You two really cared for one another."

"Please stop."

I reached into the nearby cupboard for a Scotch bottle and a glass. "When is the funeral?"

"Fred downed a bottle of sleeping pills and slipped away. He was a Catholic, so I didn't bother asking for a funeral Mass."

I fumbled the phone, the Scotch bottle, and glass. "My God. AIDS is terrible, but suicide…suicide is…I…"

"I shouldn't have told you, like this, on the phone."

I managed to pour some Scotch into the glass and drank it. "The suicide's survivors never get it settled."

"Fred's death is quite settled. Fred's resting. Toward the end, that's all he wanted to do." Drew stifled a sob. "Tatiana's death haunts you… and me. But Tatiana's was different; Fred was desperately ill and had to escape."

My mother was ill and killed herself. But she was mentally ill; I assumed that was the difference Drew saw. "Will there be a service?"

"Yes, a memorial service."

"I'll be leaving here Wednesday and getting back to San Francisco next Thursday."

"I know, Fiona told me. I've scheduled the service for Friday afternoon. You'll be there?"

"Of course."

"Afterwards, we'll have supper?"

"Supper, that night?"

"I'm arranging my affairs and hope you'll assist."

"Sure."

"That summer was such a long time ago. We were boys, young boys."

"Drew, this call is costing you a fortune."

"It'll be a pleasant evening; I promise."

✳✳✳

That summer my mother told me to leave her. I implored her to explain, but she said, "Leave, I beg you." She turned her face to the wall and refused to answer me. "Alexander, I beg you, leave me."

I did and went to Drew. Around that time, the doctors told Fiona that my mother was self-destructive and should be institutionalized. Fiona asked for my advice. I was confused and couldn't think, didn't say. And my mother, well, she was Fiona's problem.

Drew and I were the same age and had known each other for years. His father lived in Texas, and he spent summers with Fiona. When Drew was fourteen, Fiona sent him to a New England boarding school without discussing the matter. Drew charmed his way through the interviews but couldn't charm Fiona out of her decision. For that Fiona would pay.

At fifteen, Drew was playing Fiona against his father; at eighteen, he was taking Fiona's money with a sneer. With exquisite sarcasm, Drew goaded Fiona into rages that left her speechless. Fiona retaliated by acceding to Drew's demands and replacing affection with frigid civility. Drew upped the stakes; Fiona withdrew ever further. Their hideous relationship was fascinating and repellent.

I couldn't imagine treating my mother that way. But when she sent me away, Drew was there and understood such things. He told me my elegance had captivated him; I loved Drew for loving me. We were vivid young men with a passion for the arts, not artists per se, but prophets of a refinement uncommon in America and virtually unknown in California.

Contemptuous of the philistines who would send us into the professions, we scorned American colleges as middle-class vocational schools for dreary types who would spend their jejune lives toiling in commerce. With my breeding and Drew's sophistication, the dreams we had fashioned were a far richer sustenance than any college could provide. As Drew put it, we had to "fly into the sun"—New York—where our talents would be appreciated and would flourish.

Fiona told me that she could not bear sequestering my mother in a mental hospital and requested my approval for twenty-four-hour homecare. Again, I had nothing to tell her. A few days later, Drew told Fiona that we were going to Santa Barbara to visit his friends from school. Fiona was consumed with my mother and agreed without a word.

Drew and I took all the Montrachet from Fiona's wine cellar and headed off for a week at the Sinclair summer home overlooking Lake Tahoe. Alone in the idyllic world we had fashioned, the languid summer days were spent embellishing our dreams; the evenings, we drank the wine and fascinated each other. Late one morning, Drew and I were in bed and heard a car approaching up the steep driveway. It was Fiona.

My mother had killed herself around dawn the day before, and Fiona had tracked us down. I don't remember the drive into Reno, the flight back to San Francisco, or the preparations for my mother's funeral, such as it was. A suicide, she was denied an Orthodox funeral, and Fiona arranged a service at a funeral home nearby.

Facing my mother's closed casket, Fiona, Drew, and I listened to Fiona's minister speak to us. I couldn't remember his sermon, or whatever it was. I do remember Shostakovich's haunting Opus 97 that Fiona had chosen. Mother was denied burial in consecrated ground next to my father, and Fiona gave her a secluded corner in the Sinclair family plot. Later Fiona would arrange for a granite Russian cross with my mother's name and dates in Cyrillic.

At the gravesite, the minister led us in prayers that I didn't hear. I do remember Fiona giving me a rose to place on the casket as it was lowered into the grave. I can't remember what went through my mind. Perhaps nothing at all, or too much to comprehend. I didn't cry.

I accepted that my mother was gone, and that was pretty much that. Drew convinced his father that art school in New York was a better idea than Princeton. Dazed and depressed, Fiona agreed before Drew could torment her. Knowing that Fiona was vulnerable, I told her that I was going with Drew, but she refused to allow it.

As much as I longed for Drew, Fiona intimidated me too much to argue. I spent the rest of that summer wandering around San Francisco, smoking cigarettes and sitting in movie theaters. In the evenings, Fiona retired early while I drank whiskey or wine in front of the television and slept late. She tried sitting me down to talk about my mother.

Fiona's guilt had numbed her into a stumbling incoherence, and I had nothing to say. Since we couldn't talk, Fiona sent me to a psychologist without consulting me. I convinced him that starting college that fall was unwise given my mother's suicide. Armed with his opinion, I tried persuading Fiona that I belonged in New York instead of a freshman dormitory. Fiona told me that I was going to college.

Early that September, she drove me to Palo Alto and left me at a Stanford freshman dorm. A week later, I hadn't attended a lecture or a class, and my faculty advisor called. The meeting was brief; I told him that I belonged in New York, where my talents would be appreciated—end of discussion. Fiona drove me to her home the next day.

CHAPTER 5

EARLY DECEMBER 1986

DENVER

Wednesday evening in New York after my flight from Moscow, I had a steak sandwich at the hotel bar and watched the television's weather reports. The weather lady said that the jet stream had plunged south, bringing storms down from Canada toward Colorado. My reserved flight to San Francisco changed planes in Denver. I called the airline and learned that all direct flights had been booked. Rerouting through the southwest had two options: standby connections through Dallas or Phoenix. I opted for Denver.

I left New York on a brisk autumn day. Around St. Louis, the upbeat pilot gave us the Denver weather reports: light snow, but the airport was open with all runways functioning. Somewhere over Kansas, the pilot reported that the snow had increased, but only one runway had been closed. As we descended over eastern Colorado, the pilot turned glum. "Folks, got some bad news, really bad. Denver is getting creamed, big time. Passengers with connecting flights, well, you'd better check with the airlines—not looking so hot." Touching down, the plane skidded. "Welcome to Denver's Stapleton Airport."

My plane was one of the last to land. My flight to San Francisco had been cancelled. The ticket counters were bedlam. Badgering the ticket agents was useless, hotels and motels in the Denver area were full, and there were no cabs anyway. Local television news crews had braved the weather and were filming the confusion and interviewing stranded travelers. My luggage had been checked through, and I would spend the night at the airport. I went to the newsstand, grabbed some magazines, bought a pack of cigarettes, and headed for the bar.

I managed to get a barstool and was thumbing through a magazine when the person next to me left. An irritated woman claimed the barstool and slammed her briefcase and carry-on between her stool and mine. Sitting down, she glared at my cigarette before making eye contact with the bartender. Late thirties or early forties, she was about six feet in her heels and wore the day's female power clothes: dark-blue suit and, a white silk blouse with a floppy red bow tie. Her dark hair was pulled back, accentuating her Mediterranean features, perhaps Italian or Jewish. She wore horn-rimmed glasses and looked as astringent as the martini she ordered.

Looking into her purse, she said, "Damn, it was just getting good."

"Misplaced something?" I asked.

"Left my book on the plane. And some guy in a blue suit and trench coat grabbed the last *New Yorker* before I got it."

I had taken off my trench coat and was wearing a blue suit. "Must have been me." I pushed *The New Yorker* over to her. "Borrow it or take it."

"I'll borrow it," she said. "Where were you going?"

"San Francisco."

"Me too. This is really too much. And the next flight is maybe sometime tomorrow morning. Three days in New York and now this. They aren't paying me enough for the hassle, they really aren't."

"Who isn't?"

"Growers and Ranchers Bank; I'm in their San Francisco office." Growers and Ranchers was a large Los Angeles-based bank.

"I work for Universal Bank." Universal was far larger than Growers and Ranchers, and San Francisco bankers thought Los Angeles bankers were polyester types more suited for the used-car lots.

"Really?" she said. "Quite a bank: arrogant, too big, and they've confused size with quality."

"You don't say." I turned away to look around; the bar had filled up with commiserating travelers. I planned to keep my barstool for as long as I could. I wanted a cigarette, but that would have annoyed her more than she already was.

She thumbed through *The New Yorker*, looking at the cartoons, then laughed out loud before going to the back of the magazine for the movie and book reviews. I sorted through my magazines and settled on *Gourmet*.

Later the bartender stood in front of us: more drinks or move for thirstier people. We ordered another round.

"My name is Helen Jacobs." She didn't offer her hand. I introduced myself, and she said, "Romanovsky. That's Polish, isn't it?" My name has a Polish ring to it; she said something in Polish.

"I don't speak Polish."

"What, embarrassed?"

"No, I…"

"You look familiar. We met before?"

"We could have." Banking was a small world, and San Francisco's was tiny; Universal's headquarters was four blocks from the Growers and Ranchers San Francisco head office.

"It will come to me," she threatened. "Whereabouts in Poland did your family come from?"

"I'm not Polish."

"Really? You look Polish; the blue eyes and straw-colored hair, I mean. So just what are you? Ukrainian? Russian?"

"Russian."

"Oh dear! Everyone knows that Russians are more anti-Semitic than Poles."

"Everybody knows that?"

"I've got it," she said with a sly smile. "Several years ago, you tried selling Growers and Ranchers a loan."

"Back then, I was in Universal's Syndication Department." When countries and large companies require loans that are beyond a single bank's capacity to make, bankers form multibank syndicates that accommodate those customers. Through their Syndication Departments, banks also manage their risk exposures by selling loans to one another. "We participated with Growers on several loans," I said, then mentioned the names of people I had worked with.

"Back then you were peddling crap from Bolivia to Thailand, and God knows where else. Talk about marginal deals. You were trying to convince Growers to buy into a Philippine deal—Bingo-Bango I?"

"It was Babuyan Copper Mines, Phase II, conceptually not a bad deal."

"We stayed clear, not a dime. What happened to Bongo-Bongo II?"

"There were problems around the second year. The loan was restructured. The original estimates were overly optimistic, and copper prices are quite volatile."

"So that was a good deal?"

"The loan was priced according to the discernible risk at the time. In the large sense, as you know, a good loan is one that gets paid. And since the rescheduling, Babuyan has been paying as agreed, I think."

With a theatrical head shake, she said, "In other words, you were peddling that junk, knowing that it was questionable." I lit a cigarette; she coughed and waved her hand at the smoke.

"The loan looked fine when I was shopping it around. And if bankers can't figure out a good loan from a bad one, they're in the wrong business, aren't they?"

"Who took most of that loan?"

"The big Texas banks—look how well they're doing." It was a banking joke; the big Texas banks were falling apart at the time. She didn't get it or didn't want to. "And what do you do for Growers?"

"I'm the Human Resources officer in charge of Northern California. I was being rotated through the International Department back then."

"Human Resources, that's rich."

"And you think HR is full of people who couldn't make it as real bankers? Or are you going to tell me that bankers make the money, and HR doesn't appreciate them, let alone reward them? Something like that?" She batted her eyes at me.

"Something like that," I said, "but you've covered it. HR? Isn't that a fancy name for Personnel Department? So let's be honest, Personnel has become a woman's domain—you know, more caring, more inclusive. All those soft, nonhierarchical traits women are supposed to bring to the table. Know what I think? I think that's a bunch of pop-psychology crap."

"Wait just a second," she said.

"No, you wait. You started this. What a lovely job you have, counting and sorting the people beans: black beans, brown beans, white beans, female beans. But when your bank gets tired of a particular bean, it's sent off to Personnel, and you fire them. No, sorry, *fire* is such a harsh, finite word. You probably say *deselect* or *concluding an employment experience.* I bet you're so empathetic that you give them a great big hug on the way out, or do you give them a hanky first?" I batted my eyes at her.

Helen put her elbow on the bar and leaned her head on her hand. "It amazes me how quickly I've come to dislike you."

Leaning my head on my hand, I said, "You know, Helen, I don't care." We stared into each other's eyes. "While we're at it, I'm not anti-Semitic—I resent the accusation."

Helen sat up. "Look, I'm sorry, that was—"

"I want my magazine back."

She pushed *The New Yorker* to me and turned away.

The bar was packed, and Helen joined a conversation with a group of people to her right that included a good-looking man who focused his attention on her. The bar's alcohol-charged atmosphere was like a Christmas party in overdrive. I went through *The New Yorker's* cartoons and found an article that looked promising but required too much concentration for a bar. I nursed another drink and flipped through my magazines. I was hungry and got ready to leave.

I was figuring the bartender's tip, when Helen turned and said, "Please wait."

"For another round of our contretemps?"

"Well, I'm tired of that. Actually, I want one of your cigarettes. The gin has wrecked my campaign to stop."

I handed her a cigarette, helped her light it, and said, "I'd quit smoking for years . . . wasn't even thinking about them anymore. Then a few months ago at a cocktail party, I bummed a Marlboro. That was the best tasting cigarette I've ever smoked. Of course, I was hooked again."

"I've quit twice, years at a time," Helen said. "Then something goes wrong, and bang, right back on them." She smiled and took a deep drag. "Are you Russian-Russian? I mean, you don't have an accent."

"My parents left after the Revolution. I was born in France; my parents moved to California when I was a boy."

"France to California? Why?"

"They were the two best surfers in France."

"Ah," she said, "deserved sarcasm."

"Actually, my father took a position at Cal-Berkeley; he was a mathematician," I said. "Why did you plunk yourself down and pick a fight with me?"

"This place is going nuts," she said with a hesitant smile. "The PA system hasn't stopped since I got off the plane. I walked into the bar and saw you leafing through a magazine, smoking a cigarette, oblivious to what's going on. I said to myself, This guy's gotta to get in touch with the rest of us."

"I was thinking about what I have to do in San Francisco."

"Look, I'm interrupting, and you've got other things on your mind."

"I'm tired of thinking of them. Let's start over?"

She extended her hand. "I'm Helen Jacobs."

"Alexander Romanovsky." We shook hands. "You and that fellow you were talking to seemed to be hitting it off."

She looked over her shoulder. "Mike's out checking flights. Mike lives in San Francisco. He's married and comes on very strong; I don't like that. He wants to have lunch. I don't go out with married men. I'm getting out before this turns uncomfortable…or ugly…or both."

"And I won't come on strong?"

"Women, at least this one, can sense that in a man. You're not that type. You're not married, are you?"

"No, and I'm not anti-Semitic either."

"And your best friends are Jewish?"

"Every single one of them; I think my tenants are. Roth, is that Jewish?"

"Can be," she said, putting her hand on my arm. "Ethnic slurs are nothing to horse around with. I'll tell you something else: socially I'm a passive-aggressive mess, sort of a Dr. Jekyll and Ms. Hyde. At work, I'm fine."

"Oh, I see."

"I'm sharing. Very California, isn't it?"

"I guess."

"But I don't suspect you do much of that, do you?"

"I'm not really a Californian."

"Maybe that's a good thing," she said. "Russians have always fascinated me."

"Why? They're wretched people living in a dreadful country with awful weather and terrible food."

"My mother's side of the family was terrified of Russians. They were from Lithuania, Vilnius, Wilno in Polish; it was part of Poland then. My mother and grandmother taught me Polish along with some Yiddish. What's the Russian word for elephant?"

"*Slon.*"

"Do you know that the word for elephant is the same in every Slavic language from Russian to Serbian?"

"I didn't. I wonder why?"

"Don't know. Just one of those things."

"Why the fascination with Russians?"

"Well, they were the bad guys," she said. "And the bad guys are more exciting. My grandmother said that all Russians were Cossacks at heart, capable of anything."

Pointing to my wrist, I said, "Not a drop of Cossack blood. Those guys are really anti-Semitic."

"Have you ever been there, Russia?"

"I was the acting Moscow representative for the past several months."

"Boy, that must have been something," she said. "It's like Russia has a Western veneer—the incredible music and the literature—but an Asian soul. What struck you the most?"

"The case can be made that Russians have been one of history's worst governed people. Power, always absolute, has come from the top, never from the bottom up like here or in England, or even France. Many wish that Stalin would return, and that's frightening."

"Draw me a sketch of the people."

"They're quite different. On the streets, in crowds, they come across like New Yorkers—indifferent, almost rude. Once you get to know them, they're most hospitable; their emotions are much closer to the surface than ours. Men and women cry easily."

"Why are they like that?"

"Well, they've had a lot to cry about. Now it's all falling apart; most Russians can't imagine it getting better."

"So you're fluent in Russian?"

"My first language. I've been trying to modernize it, but I'm sixty years out of date and sound like Bertie Wooster."

Mike returned. He gave Helen his best, but the conversation fizzled, and he stalked off. Helen watched him go with a forlorn expression.

I tapped her shoulder. "Why don't I buy you another drink?"

We spent a long time talking about banking and the coming mergers. Universal's CEO would retire early next year, and Helen briefed me on the rumors about his replacement. Nothing had changed much; the race was still between the bank's two vice chairmen. The conversation bounced from one topic to another. Somehow we got on to music; we both preferred classical.

Helen said, "The Russians are my favorite, Stravinsky in particular. His early music was so earthy, folk tales elegantly orchestrated. How about you?"

"I like Rachmaninov, especially his piano concerti. Music doesn't touch me like it does some people, I wish it did."

"Poor you," she said. "When I was in junior high, my father took me to see Aida…absolutely blew me away—passion, costumes, the music. Best of all, the females were big with large voices. I was a moose, even back then. I badgered my parents into voice lessons, but after a year, my teacher thought acting might be a better fit."

Striking rather than beautiful, Helen was tall, but hardly a moose. Her gestures were overdrawn, and she employed her pliable hands like the French and Italians. Light makeup and lipstick were the only compromises to her appearance. She wore glasses rather than contacts, a bump on her nose could have been removed, and there was a slight gap between her two front teeth.

"So you studied drama in college?" I asked.

"I went to Cal and majored in economics. Kind of practical, it suited Mom and gave me plenty of time for acting. I worked my way from Chekhov to Blanche Dubois." She grinned. "Put me in a slip, with a blonde wig and a glass of bourbon—instant Southern neurotic."

"Then what happened?"

"I wanted to go to acting school in New York but got talked out of it and got an MBA instead. My mother and my boyfriend argued for B-school. Daddy, God bless him, told me to go with my heart, my real passion." She shrugged her shoulders. "One of those things I wish I could take back. You know?"

"I do."

"Tell me."

"I started out with art history but ended up as an econ major like you. A victory of practicality over dreams, but sometimes I wonder."

"Who talked you out of it?" she asked.

"I did, all by myself. I had to learn something useful."

"Any resentment?"

"Oh, I don't know. Some, I guess. How about you?"

"I was Daddy's girl and should have listened, but…" Helen trailed off. "I can't blame Mom. She was born practical. But my boyfriend, Ed, him I resent. Ended up marrying him."

She tried catching the bartender's eye, then took a deep breath. "Shouldn't drink and think about Ed. So what do you say? Let's bust out of here." We left the bar and ate two stale turkey sandwiches from a vending machine and washed them down with warm Hawaiian Punch.

Helen asked, "Home for the holidays?"

"First I've got to go to a memorial service tomorrow."

"Oh, I'm sorry." She stood up. We had been on the same flight from New York and were on the same flight to San Francisco that might leave early the next morning. "We might as well go down to the gate."

CHAPTER 6

DECEMBER 1986

SAN FRANCISCO

On the flight home early that morning, Helen and I managed to sit next to each other. We slept for most of the trip and woke up as the plane descended over the Stanford campus before banking north for the final approach over the rain-swept bay. Helen's apartment was in Pacific Heights, up the hill from the Marina, where I lived. We shared a cab.

Settling into the back seat, Helen lit a cigarette I gave her. The driver tapped the No Smoking sign. She tossed out the cigarette and leaned her head against the window, gazing at the squalling rain. The driver turned on the radio to an oldies station playing "Last Kiss," a song from the '50s about a boy who crashed his father's car and killed his girlfriend. I sang along at the chorus:

Oh, where oh or where can my baby be?
The Lord took her away from me.

Helen perked up. "I don't know why I remember crap like this, but that's J. Frank Wilson and the Cavaliers. How did you learn the lyrics?"

"The song was popular when my mother and I watched *American Bandstand*. For a couple of weeks, we never missed it."

"You're the only person I know who watched *Bandstand* with his mother."

"Well, it didn't work. A few years after we arrived here, I was still trying to become an American teenager without much luck. When we got a television, my mother saw *Bandstand* one day and decided it was the answer to my problems. We missed one crucial thing: *Bandstand* was shot in Philadelphia, and California teenagers were a lot different. When I got that figured out, we stopped watching. But afterwards, when we heard music, like Mozart, my mother would ask me about it, and I was supposed to say, in Russian, 'Gee, Tatiana, I'd dance to it, but I wouldn't buy it.' Like some of the kids told Dick Clark when he asked them about new records."

Helen leaned back as we climbed the long hill by Candlestick Stadium. She seemed lost in herself and closed her eyes as the radio played an agonizing song about a teenager who had run away from home. The cab driver hunched over the wheel and cut off another driver who made a rude gesture. He snapped off the radio, and I listened to the wet cadence of the windshield wipers as we traversed the rolling hills of South San Francisco.

Driving into one of the world's most beautiful cities, I was uneasy. Coming into view, San Francisco was wary as well, biding its time behind the looming clouds and gray rain. Turning off the elevated freeway down onto the city's slick streets, the tires were sibilant on the pavement. I thought of the day before me.

Fred's memorial service worried me. Having been to only one other such service—my mother's, which I scarcely remembered at the time—I didn't know what to expect. All I had to do was sit through it, but I wondered if repressed memories of my mother's service might come flooding back. Annoyed with myself for fretting, I turned to Helen as she sat up and looked at the city with eyes flickering between resolute and morose. Feeling somewhat the same, I thought of asking what was troubling her but didn't.

As the cab climbed the hill to her apartment, Helen turned back toward downtown. "Funny, I grew up just miles from here, in Marin County, and went to Cal. Always lived in the Bay Area."

I thought she was talking to me. "We lived up in the hills behind the Cal campus."

She continued, "Every time I leave and come back here, I realize how much I've fallen apart. Worse, I'm still falling and don't know if I'll ever stop."

Approaching her apartment building, Helen emerged. "Sorry, feeling sorry for myself, been doing too much." Buttoning her coat, she said, "Well, nice spending last evening and part of this morning with you. Oh, and have a cool Yule."

"Cool Yule?"

"My ex-husband could do a perfect impersonation of Hugh Hefner. Hef, he's called, the *Playboy* guy. Hef says things like that." She laughed a little. "Sorry, rambling. My divorce is driving me crazy, literally. Actually, a judge helped me out with that."

"The final divorce decree?"

"The nice judge did that," she said. "The not-so-nice judge put me under a restraining order to stay away from Ed, my ex." She shuddered. "About six months ago, I attacked him in Golden Gate Park. Pretty serious, very complicated, and talk about embarrassing. But enough of that." She opened the door as the cab stopped in front of her building.

I asked the driver to pop the trunk, then got out. I grabbed Helen's luggage and carried it to the building's entrance. "I could have done that," she said, extending her hand. "Now you're wet." Helen left her hand in mine for a small eternity. "You're a nice man, Alexander Romanovsky, and I enjoyed meeting you. Hopefully we'll see each other again. Take care of yourself in the meantime."

"You too."

"Doing my damnedest," she said.

CHAPTER 7

DECEMBER 1986

SAN FRANCISCO

I took a cab to Fred's memorial service at a large funeral home out on California Street near Fiona's. Somber chamber music was playing when I arrived; an usher directed me to a pew's end seat. Looking around, I saw Fiona on the other side of the crowded, twilit room. I tried staring to get her attention, but she looked straight ahead as a man appeared at the podium and began *remembering* Fred with amusing anecdotes.

The *remembering* turned solemn with a poem by Anna Akhmatova, the Russian poetess. I had heard the poem before: it was about loved ones, their deaths, and ensuing emptiness. Translations seldom capture a poem's soul, and I repeated the first verse to myself in Russian. In its original the poem was more affecting, and the internal rhymes worked better. I was working on the second verse when the speaker returned to his seat.

I tried listening to the next speaker while looking around and recognized several of Drew's friends I'd met at his gallery receptions. In the front pew sat two men whose profiles resembled Fred's. The older man I decided was Fred's father, the younger his brother. More uncomfortable than grieved, they were witnessing the conclusion of Fred's journey when he stepped out of the closet in small-town Wisconsin and kept going until he reached San Francisco. Arriving in the late '70s, Fred was another fresh face in the sexual anarchy of the Castro's bars and bathhouses.

Before Fred, Drew had collected lovers and tried refashioning them into the men they were incapable of becoming. Most were tall, more than a few were blond; some lasted longer than others. All of them fled until Drew found Fred, who would not be made over; and, having given Drew his unconditional love, he could offer nothing more. With time, Drew returned Fred's love, and their bond provided Drew the stability that allowed his talents to flourish. I thought that Fred was somehow a surrogate for the parental affection Fiona had denied Drew.

Drew was approaching the lectern. Looking at my watch, the service had started a half hour ago, and I couldn't remember much of it. Drew spoke about death, its liberation for the ill, and the sorrow for the survivors. But it wasn't death he was addressing; it was suicide. I realized that I had avoided Fred's service as I had my mother's. Like my mother's, Fred's was a contrived ceremony memorializing self-destruction without benefit of church or clergy.

When the service ended, I stood up and saw Fiona leaving. The rain had let up, and Fiona was going down the front steps when I called to her.

"Alexander, you look terrible," she replied. "You're okay?"

"Jet lag and a night in the Denver airport," I said after we hugged. "Was my mother's service held here?"

"Yes, in one of the smaller chapels."

"I couldn't get out of there fast enough."

"Neither could I," Fiona said. "Sorry, I'm somewhat frantic. Drew's hosting a reception at home, and I have last-second things to do. We'll talk later. Oh, most of my family will be there. Nothing I can do about that."

"That's too bad."

"Isn't it though," Fiona said. "Do you want a ride?"

"Thanks, but I'm going to walk and try to clear my thoughts."

The mental picture most people have of the Golden Gate is looking west from downtown San Francisco through the bridge out to the

Pacific. Fiona's home was in the Sea Cliff neighborhood on the City's northwest side overlooking the Pacific Ocean, and the bridge was to the northeast and downtown San Francisco to the south. Sea Cliff was an eclectic collection of stately homes: French châteaus, Tuscan palaces, and '50s modern. The expensive neighborhood was one of San Francisco's foggiest, and the mist secluded the homes into individual manors or, in Fiona's case, a hacienda.

Zorro could have designed Fiona's California-Spanish home and commissioned Rob Roy to decorate it with paintings of Scotland. The collection's centerpiece, an original oil of a battle the Scots lost to the English over two hundred years ago, was displayed in the dining room. Drew called it "kilts and claymores"—the Scottish broadsword. The home and the paintings were a terrible mismatch, and I thought the collection had less to do with Fiona's Scottish heritage and more to do with Drew. Fiona appreciated good art, and Drew could have purchased paintings she would have enjoyed; instead, the dreary collection belittled Drew's talent and served as a testament to their relationship's desolation.

Everyone knew that Fiona and Drew didn't get along, but in public, they implemented a truce. At the reception, they would transform themselves into a sophisticated mother and son by virtue of Drew's captivating charm and Fiona's acting ability when her family was present. And that afternoon, Fiona's relatives would be out in full force; if Drew had AIDS, the implications for the Sinclair estate could be enormous.

The Sinclair fortune dated back to the Gold Rush when merchants like Leland Stanford made their initial capital by provisioning the miners and then went on to become tycoons. Three Sinclair brothers from Inverness started as teamsters and grocers. When the Gold Rush ended, the brothers and their descendants invested in California real estate. The extended Sinclair family was vast—direct descendants of the three brothers lived well; closer family had money for educations, distant relatives nothing. Fiona was the direct descendant of the oldest brother, Ian, and controlled the holding companies and trusts containing the fortune.

The crowd gathering at Fiona's grew to over a hundred and included

Drew's friends, the haut monde of San Francisco's gay community. I entered the cavernous living room when Robert de Montreville, one of Drew's friends, stumbled into me. "Long time, no see," he managed.

"Been in Moscow for several months on bank business."

"Russia: an enigma, inside a puzzle, inside a condom," Robert slurred. "Or a conundrum? Or something like that?"

"Something like that."

"Oh my good gracious," Robert said with a frown. "Have I offended the elegant Russian? What in the world got into me?"

"Sounds like a good deal of your inventory."

Robert called himself a wine merchant and owned three wine/liquor stores in San Francisco's upscale neighborhoods. He spoke Cajun and called it French; the *t* at the end of his first name was silent. I doubted if his original surname was the aristocratic-sounding de Montreville—not many of those types paddling around Louisiana's swamps.

Speaking with the precision of the very drunk, Robert said, "Needed lashings of hundred-proof fortitude to make it through this afternoon." He wobbled and didn't notice when I took his arm. "Need some advice, financial. Tomorrow might be better."

"I'm sure it will."

Robert was leaning against me. I leaned against him to hold us up. I stepped back and put my arm around his waist as he stumbled backward. We made it to the foyer, where I sat him down and went to call a cab. I returned to watch Robert's green Volvo station wagon lurch onto the street.

Behind me, Fred's father and brother were clinging together like the early Christians before the lions were turned loose. Drew's friends may have been too much. I extended my sympathies; they thanked me and said they were exhausted and would return to their motel by the airport. I told them that a cab was on the way; they waited outside even though it was sprinkling.

I joined the crowd around Drew, who was beguiling as ever. Friends and family jostled into his aura where the boring became clever, the unattractive appealing, and the dull unique. Drew broke free and took me aside. "You look dreadful."

"Tired, that's all. Spent the night in the Denver airport."

"Sounds uncomfortable," Drew said. "Still on for dinner this evening?" I nodded yes. "Let's say eightish, at that Italian place on the corner of Fillmore and Chestnut. Now go get yourself a drink."

"I was talking to Robert."

"Sad story. Robert has AIDS and is determined to drink his stores dry."

Another of Drew's friends wedged between us, and I went over to Fiona, who was talking to a nephew. I stood across from her when a sleek woman stood next to me and made eye contact with a well-tailored man standing to Fiona's left, facing me. The man looked familiar, and we smiled as he approached.

"Alex, how are you?" he asked, shaking my hand.

"All things considered, okay, I guess."

He slapped me on the back. "You don't remember me, do you?"

"It's on the tip of my memory."

"Townsend Morgan…people call me Townie, a cousin of Fiona's, a distant cousin and way out of the money. So compared to the rest of this family, I'm a pretty nice guy." He winked and made me laugh.

His unusual name brought it back. "Of course, you're a client of Drew's. You were at his receptions."

"Debra, the wife, was a client." He motioned to the attractive woman who had stood next to me and was talking to Fiona. "Look, I'd like a word with Fiona…and you too." Townie's wife called him over. "Gotta hop. Little woman beckons. Ah, I'll catch up after I've said hello to Fiona."

I caught Fiona's eye and motioned if she wanted a drink. She did, and I went to the bar and returned with a glass of wine, an austere California chardonnay in the French style, much like Fiona.

While Debra and Fiona discussed the opera season, Townie disengaged, guided me back to the bar, and asked, "I understand you're a banker. I've got a proposition for Fiona: market rates, fully collateralized. Kind of a no-brainer with a few bells and whistles to keep it interesting, you know?" He patted my shoulder.

"I'm sorry, but what's your line of business?"

"Construction…but branching out to real estate development."

Townie was a preppy in his fifties. He caught me looking at his tasseled cordovan loafers, and said, "Never one for bulldozing. Spend most of my time nailing the numbers and getting our projects in on time and on the money."

"So you're an engineer?"

"No, own the company, Morgan and Morgan. Been in the family for eons." Giving himself the once-over, he said, "Hey, now you've got me worried. I mean, you think I look like an engineering geek?" His deep infectious laugh made me laugh again.

"No, not at all. I meant an engineer by training."

"No, I went to school, back east."

"Oh."

"In Connecticut."

"Yale?" I asked and thought he was going to tell me about Yale, but he didn't. "Great school," I added. Townie stood a little straighter. "As for Fiona's business affairs, I've never had anything to do with them. Besides, I'm in international banking and don't know much about real estate."

Debra waved for Townie to rejoin her and Fiona. "Gotta scram," Townie said. "Nice seeing you again. Hey, let's get together. We'll do lunch, my club. Have your person phone mine and set something up, after the New Year."

"Sounds great," I said.

I went to the French doors leading to the covered patio at the rear of the house and turned to watch Drew's friends transform the occasion into a stylish cocktail party. It was wearing quite thin; a cigarette was irresistible. I eased open the doors, slipped outside, and was smoking behind a potted pine when I heard the doors open. Peeking around the tree, I saw Fiona.

A slim, attractive woman in her late fifties, Fiona took expensive care of herself. She was reserved and could be acerbic; if pushed, her volcanic temper erupted.

I flipped the cigarette away, stepped from behind the tree, and cleared my throat.

"Alexander, my God. What are you doing out here?"

"Getting some fresh air." We hugged.

She backed away. "Smoking again? That's the very worst thing you can do to yourself."

"I know. Everyone smokes in Russia. I bummed one at a cocktail party and was right back on them. I'll quit again, soon, promise. How are you holding up?"

"Well, how do you think?"

I stepped back and put my hands up.

"Sorry," she said, "but I so loathe my relatives; they're like wolves, packing together and tearing at me. And such ghoulish questions: 'Drew looks fine, doesn't he?' 'How's Drew feeling?' They want to know if Drew has AIDS, and I'll be damned if I'll tell them that he does."

"Oh dear, I thought so."

"Drew said that you and he are having dinner this evening."

"He wants to settle some issues between us."

"And those issues stem from that summer... that terrible, terrible summer when Tatiana..." Fiona went to the patio's edge and stared at the rain. "What are you going to do?"

"Play it by ear and see how it goes."

"I see," Fiona said, facing me.

"The service seemed like they were celebrating Fred's suicide." Pointing inside, I added, "And now Drew and his friends in fact are. It's macabre."

"I know, I know," Fiona said. "I knew it would upset you."

"Fiona, I'm concerned about you too."

"I know that too. Ridiculous as it may seem, for a while I thought Drew contracted AIDS to humiliate me one last time. But that was entirely self-centered, and I took your suggestion; Drew and I are going to the Tahoe house early next week to attempt a rapprochement. Drew will tell you this evening. I'll be quite busy getting Drew settled and arranging for his care." She came closer. "You're more than upset?"

"No, just tired."

"I hope that's all. I have a favor to ask."

A knock on the French doors interrupted Fiona. A lady leaned out. "Oh, Fiona, didn't mean to interrupt, but we have wonderful news: Jim Junior has been accepted early to Whitman College, up in

Washington…Walla Walla. Big Jim and I have to go over the financial arrangements with you. Anyway, we won't leave until we've talked." Big Jim waved to Fiona.

Fiona waved back. "Cousins from Sunnyvale. The trusts pay for their offspring's education." Her expression turned wistful. "Times like this, I think of Tatiana; she knew I had money and didn't care, unlike most everyone else in my life." Then she looked into the living room. "If I could walk away from that mob, I'd be a happy woman." Attempting a smile, she asked, "Do you remember how we met?"

"You took French lessons?" My mother had tutored Cal students in French and Russian.

"I didn't need French lessons," Fiona sputtered. She had been raised with a nanny from Brittany and spoke fluent French with a Breton accent.

"I was trying for some levity. We met at a hamburger joint around here."

"It was a Sunday," Fiona said. "Exhausted and miserable after one of these horrid family gatherings, I walked over to Nick's for a cup of coffee. I sat at the counter next to you and Tatiana. You both looked so European and had come from the Russian church a few blocks away. You ordered hamburgers and milkshakes in terrible English and went back to the imaginary house you and Tatiana were building in southern France: the garden, the design, colors—all of it."

"Back then, cheeseburgers and shakes made coming here almost bearable."

"While I was eavesdropping, I realized that the house was imaginary and said in French that the kitchen should have a view of the sea. You asked if I had more ideas, and the three of us sat there working on the house for the longest time. Time flew like it always did around Tatiana. We walked back here for tea, and I drove you home to Berkeley. Tatiana and I talked every day after that. She never asked for anything." Fiona dried her eyes. "It was my idea that she tutor French and Russian. I got her organized—not easy with her." She was about to cry.

"Fiona, that favor you asked?"

She took a deep breath. "Townie Morgan wants me to look at a deal. Actually, it's Chip's. Chip, his son, is floating around here somewhere.

Anyway, Townie's company has been around for ages, but I don't know anything about his business, or how he manages it. He banks at Universal; I'd like you to check around and see what you can find out."

"Of course, happy to do so."

Fiona winced when she heard the French doors open. Big Jim, his wife, and Jim Junior approached. "We'll keep in touch," Fiona said.

I took her arm. "I'd like to talk to you, away from these interruptions."

"Of course, of course, when I'm less frazzled, when I get back from Tahoe."

Big Jim guided Fiona into the living room with Jim Junior and wife following.

Fiona was right about my mother; she had never asked for Fiona's influence or money. Nor had I. However, when I graduated from college during Vietnam, my draft board wanted to see me; and Fiona told me to apply to a National Guard artillery unit in Oakland. Back then the Guard was a safe haven and impossible to get into, but the artillery unit took me. After the Guard, Fiona suggested that I send my resume to Universal Bank. The bank usually hired MBAs but made an exception in my case. When I became a bank officer, Fiona decided that my renting an apartment was a waste of money and loaned me the money to purchase a two-flat building in the Marina. Unlike her family, I never asked; then again, I never had to.

It was getting dark; the drizzle had turned to an earnest rain. I saw the lights of a freighter heading out of the Golden Gate. On the ship's bridge, two officers were looking through binoculars at their course; another two were at the charts that would guide them home. An officer turned south and pointed his binoculars in my direction. I waved and was surprised when he waved back.

No one noticed as I slipped out past Fiona and Big Jim's family, avoided the crowd around Drew, and found my raincoat and umbrella. I walked up to California Street and whistled down a cab.

CHAPTER 8

DECEMBER 1986

SAN FRANCISCO

The restaurant Drew suggested had developed a reliable clientele who appreciated its sturdy northern Italian cuisine. The décor was simple: wide-planked oak floors, stark white walls with framed black-and-white photos of Florence and rural Tuscany. The tablecloths were heavy cotton and whiter than the walls. I had eaten there and remembered the variety of tempting veal dishes. A Friday night, the restaurant was crowded. Drew stood up and waved from a secluded table in the back.

There was a lot of Fiona in Drew's features: the light-brown hair, the high forehead, the fine nose, the set of the mouth, and the large greenish eyes. Their countenances differed: Drew was sunny; Fiona was moody and a bit chilly. While Fiona was an attractive woman, Drew was so striking that men and women stared at him when we were young. Drew had changed from his suit and was wearing a blue blazer, gray slacks, a striped shirt, and a Charvet floral tie. His coloring was sallow, and his collar was loose. He stood up and hugged me.

We sat down, and Drew asked the waiter for drinks: a glass of white wine for me, mineral water for him. Drew leaned forward. "Thank you for coming. You're more relaxed without your banker's suit of armor." I had changed into a tweed jacket, shirt, and tie. "You look drawn. All the traveling? Or today's service?"

"Both. The service was difficult."

"The memories of Tatiana's funeral, of course," Drew said. "I wouldn't have blamed you if you hadn't come. But you did. I appreciate that, I do."

"That summer has been on my mind since our phone conversation. I'm sorry about the way I treated you. Everything was so confusing back then: you, the sex, my mother's mental state, her death. I couldn't handle it and crashed into something of a nervous breakdown. I am ashamed that I've taken so long to apologize. And there's one more thing I must say: Fred was in love with you, and you with him; you were kind to each other."

Drew put his napkin to his eyes. "Took me by surprise. You're usually more staid."

"I meant it."

"I know, and thank you," Drew said. The waiter returned with our drinks. We both ordered braised breast of veal. The waiter left, and Drew said. "Fiona told you that I have AIDS."

"Yes, what are you going to do?"

"I've finished my opened orders, and the business is on hold for the time being. I can't stay in my place, not after Fred; so I've moved back to Fiona's. Early next week, Fiona and I are going to the summer house at Tahoe. We'll try to reconcile, even at this late date."

"How long are you going to stay at Tahoe?"

"Oh, I'll die up there."

"Talk about sangfroid."

"How else to take it?" I started to speak, but Drew said, "Hear me out: you and Fiona are the most important people in what's left of my life, and I must say what has to be said and do what must be done."

"I have apologized."

"And I've accepted it. Nothing unpleasant this evening, I promise."

The wine steward approached. Drew glanced at the wine list and ordered a light Chianti. The steward suggested an expensive Barolo that would flatter our meals. Drew didn't agree; the steward tried again, and Drew insisted on the Chianti.

The steward smirked and left.

Watching him leave, Drew said, "That young man doesn't know

his trade. He's here to guide customers instead of selling them the top of the wine list. Wine has become like art: Salesmen bullying inexperienced customers into overpriced items they don't understand and won't appreciate."

The steward returned with the Chianti and poured Drew a tasting. Drew examined the wine from several angles, spun it around in the glass before tasting. "Tastes okay," he said, "but how does it sound?" He put the glass to his ear. Moving his shoulders, he said, "What a delightful tarantella." The steward stared across the room. Drew smiled. "Why don't you pour this vivacious little wine?"

The steward poured and stalked off. "For his effort, he lost his tip," Drew said. "Now, tell me about your dreadful flight." I was describing the evening in Denver, and Drew asked, "Who was this other person?"

"Another banker, Helen Jacobs, works for Growers and Ranchers."

"Marital status?"

"Recently and painfully divorced."

"And is Alexander Romanovsky, confident heterosexual, going to follow up?"

"Mordant observations don't make for the pleasant evening I was promised."

Drew arched his eyebrows. "Touchy, touchy. Going to call on the beguiling Ms. Jacobs?"

"I don't know."

"Didn't you tell me once that bankers are so boring that they're forced to talk to each other?"

"As a matter of fact, we did spend time talking about banking."

"Why not give her a call and continue the conversation?" Drew made a playful face. "Or drop by for a chat about foreclosures? That must turn on bankers?"

"Actually, that's one of the worst things that can happen to a loan." I laughed. "I'll give her a call."

Drew sipped the wine as the waiter served our meals. "Tell me about Russia," he said, looking at his plate with no interest.

I tasted the veal and said, "Well, the system is falling apart. Nothing works; corruption snares everyone."

I stopped and watched Drew roll a piece of bread into a small ball.

He put the bread down, looked at me, and blinked. He closed his eyes, then opened them. He seemed surprised to see me. "Sorry, I get distracted these days. Tell me more about Russia."

"Later," I said and got the conversation around to him. Drew always pretended to be astonished that millionaires ranging from Texas oil barons to Silicon Valley moguls paid him to buy *their* art with *their* money. His anecdotes were etched with acid diluted with self-deprecation. He was telling me about two Texans, Reba and Floyd, when I asked, "How many paintings did you sell them?"

"By the yard or in dollars?" Drew rolled his eyes. "Remember our plans, our dreams? As people get older, they become too self-conscious to wonder, too jaded to dream. That's a pity." He pushed his plate away. "I've compromised, boy, have I, and ended up fawning over the likes of Reba and Floyd. And you, you're a banker, of all things."

I shrugged.

"Say, speaking of my clients, what were you and Townie talking about?"

"He told me that he wanted to run a deal by Fiona. Townie lost interest when I told him I had nothing to do with her businesses."

"That's all?"

"No, after that, Fiona told me that Townie's son, Chip, was putting the deal together. She wants me to ask around at the bank about Townie and his company."

"Townie's quite something, isn't he?"

"You know, people who've gone to those schools—Harvard and Yale—always work it into conversations but never ask where you went to college."

"They're being polite and assume you'll reply with something like Panhandle A&M. Did Townie tell you that he went to Yale?"

"He did. Well, no, not exactly."

"You presumed Yale, like he hoped." Drew laughed. "Townie could convince a Yalie he went there. Not a bad guy; in a way, I feel sorry for him. Wife number two, the recently acquired, slim-hipped Debra, has Townie right where she wants him. I understand Debra wants Fiona to sponsor her into the Opera Alliance. Debra and Fiona, that'll be interesting."

"What's with Debra?"

"She's pushy," Drew said. "Pushy doesn't work with the Opera Alliance. Old money, and lots of it, does. Fiona setting Debra straight on that should be interesting. They're both quite volatile."

"Were Townie and Debra good clients?"

"Debra has a good eye and bought excellent pieces. Changing subjects…your job's going well after the Moscow assignment?"

"It's going okay. There will be a new CEO soon. That means a reorganization of some sort…probably major shifts in senior management with some bloodletting. But that won't impact me."

"Your time in Russia notwithstanding, same old thing, day in, day out?"

"Oh, in a way, sure. I've fallen into something of a routine."

"Spinning your wheels?" Drew asked.

"Sort of. That often happens in big organizations. After my last promotion, it'll be years until the next one or a new assignment."

Drew tented his fingers. "Maybe we can help each other. You know art and art history, and you're a natural at interior decorating. I want you to consider taking over my business and redirecting it to suit yourself. All I do is listen to people, shape their desires, inform and guide them. You'd love it."

"I'm thunderstruck…don't know what to say."

"Then let me do the talking," Drew said. "As it stands, one of Fiona's lawyers will liquidate my estate and the business when the time comes. Some of the funds will repay the loans I took from Fiona to start the business. I could have repaid her ages ago but didn't—just to annoy her. If you agree, I'll have my will reworked so you can take over the business and repay Fiona. Just be your charming self, and the business will remain quite profitable."

"I'm hardly charming."

"There may be charming bankers," Drew said, "but I doubt you're one of them. At the bank, I bet you're pretty stolid, but in my world, you effervesce. At my receptions, your enthusiasm was spontaneous, compelling. Why not do so for the rest of your life?"

"Why not?"

The waiter cleared our plates. We declined dessert, and Drew ordered a cognac for me and leaned back. "Sure, I make fun of my customers, some of whom think discrimination is a social problem afflicting black people. Others are vulgarity incarnate: a price I paid, the price you'll pay. But some people get it. Bringing them along is rewarding, and I'm not talking about the money. Many start loving art for art's sake."

"I'm too excited to think it through."

"Great to hear," Drew said. "Alexander, you don't like yourself; it's the residue of Tatiana's suicide. Self-hatred destroyed her, and"—he looked away—"you're doing penance for the suicide; wasting your God-given talent as a banker is wrong."

"I'm not doing penance. You don't understand. How could you?"

"But I do understand." Drew leaned closer. "Self-loathing, that's your problem. The older you get, the harder it will be to control. And I fear you might end up like, well, like Tatiana." Drew took my hands. "Sorry to get so personal, but it's true. You know that?"

"Oh, I don't know, there are times that, I wish… I pray… But, yes, from time to time the self-revulsion boils up."

"There's nothing you could have done to have prevented Tatiana's death. If you follow the path you were meant to take, I'm sure you'll start looking at yourself without the self-loathing. A fresh start; it's my gift to you." He squeezed my hands. "Say something."

"You told me this was going to be a pleasant evening."

"Take my offer, and you'll remember it as momentous."

"Don't you think I'm more stable than my mother?"

"You've got a lot of Tatiana in you: the physical resemblance, of course, her vulnerability, her passion for art." He shook his head. "Tatiana was amazing; there wasn't much she didn't know about paintings. Even with my lousy French, I could spend hours listening to her. That stopped when she got so confused and started going on about…" Drew shook his head.

"About what?"

"Crazy things." Drew frowned. "Bad word that. She kept going back to Paris and reliving the German occupation." Tapping his head, he added, "Memory is going, that's all I remember." Drew poured himself a glass of wine and drank it. "As for my business, I don't expect an immediate answer, but…"

"My mind's going a mile a minute."

"Excellent." He handed me a thin wrapped package.

It was a picture of Drew and me. He had taken the photo with a timed camera that summer at the Tahoe house. Tan and fit, we were facing the camera with our arms around each other's shoulders. I was wearing khakis, a white button-down shirt with the sleeves rolled up to the elbows, and penny loafers. He was barefooted in Bermuda shorts and a white polo shirt. Drew was smiling; my expression was neutral.

The waiter served my cognac, and Drew said, "I'll be damned, you're blushing. It's meant as a memento, not an embarrassment. Look at your eyes, what are they saying?"

"They're somewhat guarded."

"Your eyes were telling a story. Without Tatiana, you were lost and too terrified to admit it. Fred's eyes were the same when I met him—the initial attraction. With Fred I discovered something about myself: I'm a Samaritan. I rescued Fred. He was clinging to one man, then another."

"You want to rescue me from myself?"

"From where I'm afraid you may be headed." Drew's eyes were glistening, "I've said enough. It's been a taxing day for both of us; come on, walk me to my car."

We walked down the empty street without speaking. Next to his car, Drew took my shoulders. "Tell me one thing, please. You loved me when that picture was taken?" He put a finger to my lips. "No rationalizations, no time for that."

"I loved you."

"Did I use you?"

"I never thought so."

"I love you, Alexander, always have. But you've known that all along, right?"

"Yes, I have."

I thought he was going to kiss me, but we embraced. As the door opened, the car's interior light illuminated Drew—a man stepping from the shadows of a Rembrandt painting. But the fog-diffused light was more El Greco: a man approaching eternity. I watched as he drove toward the Bay and turned west into the fog.

I walked home and drank myself into a fitful sleep.

CHAPTER 9

SATURDAY, DECEMBER 6, 1986

SAN FRANCISCO

The Marina District is at the very north of San Francisco on the approach to the Golden Gate. As San Francisco neighborhoods went, it wasn't too foggy; and what fog there was usually cleared by the late morning only to return around sunset. The salt air was bracing, and one of the neighborhood's extras was falling asleep with the windows opened while listening to the doleful fog horns on the Bay.

A recent addition to the City, the Marina had been built on a landfill and was flat, unlike most of San Francisco. Many of the streets were broad, but parking was scarce, and there weren't many trees. The neighborhood had a small-town feel: Merchants often called their customers by name, residents patronized local restaurants and taverns, and I nodded to familiar-looking people.

I slept until noon and woke up with a throbbing hangover. The refrigerator was empty; I had to go shopping and phoned Sally Roth. The Roths had been my downstairs tenants for the past four years. Their household included Bert, Sally's husband, their twin daughters, and, Arnie, a black-and-tan dachshund devoted to the twins. Sally was a psychologist overwhelmed by recent motherhood; Bert was an advertising executive.

Three years earlier, after the twins were born, Sally decided that they needed a second car, and my car's repairs had reached the point of diminishing returns. The Roths and I bought a used Ford station wagon. I had first call during the weekends, Sally during the week. I was unloading the groceries when I saw Robert de Montreville approaching.

Robert said, "Didn't I make an appointment with you yesterday?"

"I'm surprised you remembered. You shouldn't have driven home."

"I know, I know. Thank God, I didn't find any dents this morning." We took the last of the groceries upstairs to my flat. Robert looked around. "Gosh, this is nice. One of my relatives might have decorated his Parisian townhouse like this. You see, the de Montrevilles are a cadet family from the old dukes of Anjou."

I clicked my heels and bowed.

"What did your family do in Russia?" he asked.

"My father's family were army people. Some hair of the dog?"

"That was a mighty big dog," Robert said, checking his watch. "Something light: gin on the rocks, Tanqueray if you've got it."

I showed him an unopened bottle. "The fridge is empty, but the liquor cabinet is full."

"Got your priorities right," Robert said. "Yesterday, I started pounding down the gin before that funeral, or memorial, or whatever they call those things." He gulped the gin and shivered. "When my turn comes, it's going to be cocktails, endless cocktails." He shook the ice cubes at me. "Join me? Your hangover looks as bad as mine."

I made him another drink and poured myself a beer that I pulled from a grocery bag. "Yesterday, you told me that you needed some financial advice?"

"I'm selling my stores to my employees."

"Taking your capital out with a leveraged buyout?" I swallowed a mouthful of beer and wasn't too sure if it would stay down.

"Right," he said. "Townie Morgan buys his booze from me. He's an affable guy, and we've always gabbed about this and that. I told him what I was doing with the stores and why. You see, I've got AIDS."

"I'm sorry, Robert. Drew told me. He has it too."

After an uneasy pause, Robert said, "You see, that's why I'm selling the stores. Make sense to you?"

"Yes. Do you have medical insurance?"

"I don't think it's going to cover all that I'm in for. A couple of days later, Chip, Townie's son, comes in and tells me about condos he's developing over in Marin County. Chip went on about working through him to avoid estate taxes and defer the medical expenses I'll be facing."

"Where will your estate go?"

"Chip asked me that too. When I told Chip that what's left of my estate would go to relatives, he lost interest. So I assume that Chip was hoping that my lover, if I had one, would get my estate. Tax shelters, I know something about those. But condo investments to avoid estate taxes and defer medical expenses? Doesn't that sound fishy to you?"

"I don't understand it, but I don't know much about real estate financing or estate planning. Anyway, why are you telling me this?"

"I like Fiona; she's been an excellent customer. But yesterday I was too loaded to talk to her. And I heard somewhere that Townie and Chip are Fiona's relatives, so I thought she'd want to know if they might be up to something. You know, Fiona puts a lot of stock in her…her…"

"Social standing?" I suggested.

"Right. A relative running a scam wouldn't look so hot if it hit the papers, would it?"

"Townie and Chip are distant relatives, but I'll certainly tell Fiona what you told me. Freshen your drink?" The beer was staying put and was addressing my parched mouth; the headache had settled behind my eyes.

"One for the gutter," he said, handing me his glass. "I was going to tell Drew, but I know Drew and Fiona don't along. Actually, you're Fiona's favorite son."

I topped up his drink and poured another beer. "When I was a boy, Fiona was a great help to my mother and me."

"That's what I heard." Robert made quick work of the drink and got up to leave.

I walked Robert to his car. Shaking hands good-bye, he said, *"Au revoir, mon ami. Et bonne chance."*

I answered with the typical reply. *"Vous aussi."*

"I ran out of luck when they told me I had AIDS."

"I'm sorry, Robert. Don't know what to say." We shook hands.

I looked up Morgan and Morgan Construction in the phone book and drove downtown to the address. Saturday afternoon, the building was closed, and I double-parked and looked through the glass doors at the office directory. Townsend C. F. Morgan was the president. Under the company's operating departments, I found "Fremont Developers, Chandler T. F. Morgan, Principal—Chip no doubt. Monday I would find out who handled the Morgan and Morgan account at the bank.

Chapter 10

Monday, December 8, 1986

San Francisco

Universal Bank's world headquarters, a sixty-storied whitish building designed to blend into San Francisco's overall Mediterranean ambiance, was surrounded by a plaza named after the bank's founder. The plaza looked down onto Montgomery Street, which ran through the center of the Financial District. In keeping with its stature, the Universal Building dominated San Francisco's skyline.

The International Department spread over four floors, and I worked in the European Division on the twentieth. The division included four sections based on Europe's principal language groups; I was the vice president in charge of Eastern Europe. There were eight of us in my group, and I reported to the Senior Vice President, European Division Executive. When I arrived that morning, he invited me for coffee and an update on the new Moscow representative.

As we were finishing, he told me that Human Resources had come up with a plan to use up my remaining vacation days. I went to HR and met with a pleasant woman who explained what they had in mind: as the year was winding down and business was slow, I would use as much of my accumulated vacation as possible before year end by coming into the office on an as-needed basis.

I spent the rest of the morning completing expense reports and catching up with the people in my group. I was invited to make a contribution for a birthday present and lunch for the German-Scandinavian Area Manager, Anton "Jesus" Kleist. The European Division was big on nicknames, and for a couple of days I was called Noodles until I pointed out the dish was Noodles Romanoff.

We went to a huge German restaurant at the edge of the Financial District; the seating was family style. Anton spoke to the waiters in German and explained the menu: sauerbraten was a specialty that most of us ordered with beer. Anton's present was a coffee-table book on North American birds, and he told us about his summer birding expedition to Alaska.

Several tables away, I saw Helen Jacobs and a group of men being seated. I thought she might recognize me as she looked around, but I was wearing a chalk-striped navy-blue suit and didn't stand out among the bankers and lawyers. I listened to Anton go on about birding, then looked at Helen, who was looking at me. She rolled her eyes and tilted her head like she was falling asleep. We looked at each other, smiling mostly until Helen was brought back into the conversation at her table. Leaving after lunch, I caught Helen's eye and motioned like I was phoning. She smiled.

Late that afternoon, I called the bank's Construction Lending Department, asked for the officer in charge of the Morgan and Morgan account, and was put through to James O'Meara, a vice president. I explained who I was and why I had called and offered to buy him a cup of coffee or a drink after work. He opted for coffee in a half hour, and we agreed to meet on the California Street entrance.

In his fifties, O'Meara was stocky with a truculent stride and a contagious smile. Shaking hands, he said, "I'm so coffeed out that I can hear my heart beating. Let's walk around the block. Now this friend of yours is *the* Fiona Sinclair? How do you know her?"

"Fiona and my mother were close. Fiona and Townie Morgan are distant relatives. Townie is offering Fiona a business deal of some kind, and she asked me to ask around the bank about him."

O'Meara whistled. "If Fiona Sinclair says jump, I jump—real high—and I dropped everything when you called. I didn't know Townie was a relative. Oh, one thing more: You're going to tell Fiona Sinclair what

I tell you?"

"Unless you object."

"No, not at all; I'll do her all the favors I can." O'Meara rubbed his hands together. "There was a problem with Townie at first. You see, I'm from a Pennsylvania coal town and worked my way through Villanova. So that Yale crap doesn't cut it with me. Well, I got that settled right away, and Townie and I get along okay. Did you go to Yale?"

"No. How does Townie manage his company? What do the books look like?"

"Townie does good work. His projects are sound and on schedule. The company looks pretty good on paper with a strong cash flow, okay liquidity for a construction company, and capitalized better than most. On the negative side, I think Townie has been paying himself way too much lately. Worse, he's branching out into real estate development. That bothers me—big time."

"Anything else bother you?"

"His son, Chip, scares me. That kid is bad news, really bad."

"Why?"

"Calls himself a real estate developer and rides Townie's coattails. I don't trust Chip…wouldn't do business with him if my bonus depended on it."

"Dishonest or dumb?" I asked.

"Slippery, thinks he's smart. There's something screwy about him. I've told Townie, but he shrugs it off. Well, that's it in a nutshell."

"Thanks for the time and candor," I said. "Let me know if I can return the favor."

"One more thing: you might tell Fiona Sinclair that doing business with Townie is one thing; she'll most likely get her money back, with interest. Chip is a punk who could end up in jail."

We shook hands. Through for the day, I walked down California Street.

***

I arrived at Growers and Rancher's San Francisco head office around 4:00 and went to the men's room to straighten my tie and comb my hair. My breast-pocket handkerchief was a little too high. I tucked it in, but that looked worse. I refolded the handkerchief and got it to where I liked it. Standing back from the mirror, I checked my teeth, polished my glasses, and headed off to Helen's office. The secretary interrupted her typing to greet me.

"I'm here to see Helen Jacobs. No appointment, just thought I would drop by."

"Let's see," she said. "Helen's on a call that's been going on for quite some time. Will you wait?"

"Sure."

"I didn't get your name." She took a notepad.

"Wilson, Frank Wilson." But Helen wouldn't put Frank Wilson together with J. Frank Wilson and the Cavaliers of the song "Last Kiss." I thought about saying I was J. Frank Wilson, but that was too obvious. I should have told the secretary about the joke I was playing. But I didn't. Instead I said, "My first name is Jerry. My father was Jerry too; it was confusing when people phoned. So for years I've used my middle name, Frank, but I'm going back to Jerry. I'm pretty sure that I introduced myself to Helen as Jerry." But Helen would never pick up on Jerry Wilson.

The secretary wadded up the note and started over.

"Look, I'm being a pain, but tell Helen my name is Frank Wilson."

With a withering smile, she said, "Got it."

I sat down and leafed through financial magazines on the side table. About ten minutes later, Helen appeared and collected her phone messages and spoke to the secretary, who pointed at me.

Helen turned. "Oh, hi there. The note says there's a Frank Wilson to see me." She checked the note again. "Did I miss something?"

"Frank Wilson…a joke…'Last Kiss.'"

"Oh, sure, got it. Afraid that I'm not in a funny mood right now."

"It wasn't that funny. I was in the neighborhood and thought I would drop in. But you're having a bad day."

"In the neighborhood?" she said. "Your office is what—three or four blocks from here. And what makes you think I'm having a bad day?"

"You more or less told me so. This was impulsive, and I'm going."

"Wait," Helen said.

The door opened when I reached for the knob and an important-looking man bumped into me, passed without an apology, and began talking to Helen. With hands on her hips, Helen motioned him into her office with an angry toss of the head. A major confrontation was about to detonate.

Talking in a snowbound airport didn't warrant dropping in—usually a bad idea. On the other hand, whatever was bothering Helen was no excuse for her brusqueness. Getting right down to it, I had made a fool of myself.

CHAPTER 11

TUESDAY, DECEMBER 9, 1986

SAN FRANCISCO

Philippa Tate-Palmer, my secretary and administrative assistant, had taken Monday as a personal day and was at her desk in front of my office when I arrived that morning. She put her hand over the phone. "Welcome back, stranger. This is rather important; I'll be in your office in a few minutes, okay?"

"Sure, take your time."

Philippa and I managed to get along well enough, but our relationship was uneven. Philippa had little to fear from me, while I was ambivalent about her. She was Andrew Neville's mistress, and Neville was one of two vice chairmen of Universal Bank. Although Philippa reported to me and I wrote her annual reviews, Andrew Neville was one of the most powerful men in the bank; I had no real authority over her. At first we tolerated each other, then later we became friendly but somewhat remote.

Philippa and I met four years earlier when Neville was the Senior Executive Vice President and Chief Credit Officer and I was an assistant vice president in the Syndicated Loan Department. Our group was up against a deadline that couldn't wait for the next General Loan Committee meeting. My boss was out that day with a lame excuse, something about his wife going into labor. I was the only other person in the department who knew the Babuyan Copper Mine loan well enough to take it to Neville for approval. Sitting across from Neville as he chaired Loan Committee meetings was tense; one-on-ones could be terrifying.

I arrived at Neville's office ten minutes before our meeting and introduced myself to Philippa, who was Neville's secretary at the time. Philippa was taking a tea break and motioned me to a chair, then returned to a crossword puzzle that she had clipped from the Sunday paper.

At the time, Philippa was in her early thirties and wore her auburn hair tied back with a grosgrain ribbon that accentuated her fine features, aquiline nose, and large blue eyes. She came across as aloof; it was her beauty coupled with a languid British accent and offhanded manner.

I was concentrating on my presentation when Philippa asked, "I say, don't mean to bother, but how are your zeds?"

I looked up. "I'm pretty good at crosswords. Got started when I was learning English."

"Well, aren't I a lucky girl," she said, tapping her teeth with a pencil. "Okay, four letters: his accusations saved Al from hell."

"Zola, Emile Zola, the French writer who wrote *J'Accuse!* and got Alfred Dreyfus released from Devil's Island. The Dreyfus Affair tore France apart around the turn of the century."

"I've heard something about that," Philippa said. "The last one: zed again, three letters. The middle one should be an *o*. Geraldine's king?"

"Zog, King of Albania. He was a regular on crosswords when I was a boy. I looked up King Zog; his wife, Geraldine, was from Hungary. But Geraldine doesn't sound very Hungarian, does it?" I was nervous and laughed.

"What's so funny?" It was Andrew Neville, who looked like an alpha-male timber wolf in a navy-blue suit.

Philippa smiled at Neville and said, "Does Geraldine sound Hungarian to you?"

Neville returned her smile and motioned me into his office. After grilling me for forty-five minutes, Neville signed the Babuyan deal and said that he trusted the loan would pay as agreed; I reassured him that it would. I said good-bye to Philippa and went back to Syndications for a celebratory lunch.

The next time I saw Philippa was a couple of years later when she replaced a woman who had retired as my secretary/assistant. I was never consulted about Philippa, never interviewed her, and never commented on how she had become my secretary.

Ten minutes later, Philippa came into my office, and we spent a half hour catching up. As the conversation was winding down, Philippa said, "By the way, that was Helen Jacobs on the phone, a rather pleasant conversation."

"Oh?"

"Helen extended her apology for yesterday afternoon. It seems you walked into an awkward situation."

"She was curt."

"Ergo her apology." Philippa paused. "Hmm, I understand you met at the Denver airport?"

"We were snowed in. What did you and Helen talk about?"

Philippa arched an eyebrow. "She's a clever woman and extracted rather a lot of information from me."

"Such as?"

"Am I detecting interest?" she asked with mirthful detachment.

"Just curious."

"Right, right," Philippa replied. "She was trying to find out if you were attached, seeing anyone. Now, how in the world would I know that?"

I replied with my blandest smile.

"Nevertheless, I took it upon myself to say that you were not." Philippa paused. "Shall we say your interest has wilted?"

"So it appears."

"No longer pertinent?" Philippa said, waving a slip of paper. "Helen's phone numbers: a direct line at her office and her home phone. Toss it?"

"Go ahead."

"The woman did apologize," Philippa said. "Egos do mend; albeit the male variety requires infinite time. I'll keep this on my desk next to the phone in the event yours recovers sooner than later."

"Helen said that my ego was damaged?"

"Probably irreparably." Philippa folded the slip of paper. "Although it's none of my business, I've become tangentially involved and have a suggestion: why not take a gentleman's approach and tell Helen that you have accepted her apology? After all, what harm could possibly come of that?"

My phone rang. It was business, and Philippa left.

***

On Tuesday morning, Fiona and Drew flew to Tahoe. She promised to call me once they arrived, but evening came, and she hadn't. About to leave the office for the day, I called Fiona's home and left a message, thinking she might check her answering machine. I was looking at the wet fog enshrouding the city when someone behind me cleared their throat. I jumped a little.

Philippa was standing in front of my desk. "Sorry, didn't mean to creep up. May I have a word? Most personal, I'd rather have this conversation out of the bank, at my flat, if you have the time and don't mind."

"Sure. After all this time together, I don't know where you live."

"Telegraph Hill. Let's take a cab."

Philippa's apartment was on the east side of the steep hill with a view of the Bay Bridge, Oakland, and Berkeley. As she took our coats to a closet, I went to the picture window. Under the bridge, a freighter headed east toward the Oakland docks and passed a container ship on its way out through the Golden Gate. The Bay was flat indigo; Oakland's smog was a caustic sepia.

"The Bay is in one of its off-putting moods this evening," Philippa said, joining me at the window. "You prefer Scotch and ice, don't you?"

While Philippa made the drinks, I looked around. The living room was done with pale gold walls and English prints of country scenes, horses, and old maps of the British Isles. On a side table was a collection of family photos, including several of a girlish Philippa in riding gear accepting prizes while horses looked over her shoulder. A framed wedding photo of a lovely bride who looked like Philippa and a hand-

72

some army officer in a full-dress uniform had to be her parents.

Philippa brought the drinks and motioned me to a wing chair.

"This is all quite lovely," I said.

"Too English, I think." She sat down in a matching wing chair facing me across a coffee table.

"It must remind you of home."

"A little bit of England," she said with a taut smile. "You told me once that you grew up over there?" Pointing toward Berkeley, she asked, "Ever go back?"

"I let those memories rest as they are."

Philippa took long sip of gin and bitters. "I invited you here because what I have to say is best said in private." She shifted in the chair. "I need some advice, some help actually. Bluntly put, I need some money and can't borrow it from the bank. The bank mustn't know."

"If it's within reason, borrow it from me."

"Really? No questions?"

"None."

Philippa put the back of her hand to her mouth. "I knew you would loan me the money. But I thought there would be questions." She looked away. "You know what I make; this flat and my salary don't tally, do they?"

"I can only guess what your rent is."

Philippa finished her drink and got up. I followed her into the kitchen while she poured herself more gin and didn't bother with the bitters. Then she said, "My elevated standard of living is thanks to a very important man at the bank." After downing most of the drink, she continued, "Well, aren't I terribly abstruse? You've known all along about Andrew Neville and me?"

I didn't answer.

"I'm about as mercenary as they come; you know that too, don't you?"

"I know no such thing. Look, you're upset."

The kitchen phone rang.

Philippa grabbed my arm. "Bloody thing." She backed away. "Please answer it."

I picked up the phone and said hello.

Andrew Neville asked, "Who is this?"

My career flashed in front of my eyes. "My name is Alexander Romanovsky."

"You're the fellow Philippa works with." He paused. "You brought me a loan to sign a few years ago, didn't you? A Philippine deal...copper mines, right?"

"That's right."

"Babuyan? Problems, weren't there?"

"Well yes, yes there were. Ah, actually, the loan had to rewritten and the term extended—a couple of years. Oh, and the rate was adjusted too. I mean, rather, I should say, the rate was significantly reduced for a couple of years, I'm afraid. On the other hand, I understand it's doing okay now."

"Let's hope so," Neville said. "Please put Philippa on the line."

"Ah, please wait a second."

Philippa shook her head no.

I said, "Sorry, Philippa is busy."

"Doing what?" he asked.

"Just busy."

After a long silence, Neville said, "Well, okay, I guess. Let me see if I've got this right: you and Philippa are having cocktails and discussing holiday plans, something like that?"

"Yes, something like that," I said. Philippa was biting her lip.

"I see. When Philippa isn't quite so busy, please let her know that I called. Also, I'd appreciate it if you'd remind her of the deadline she's under. Oh, one more thing, if you don't mind: Ask Philippa to call me with an update tomorrow morning, first thing. Got all of that?"

"Got it. Is that all?"

"For the time being, that should do it. Have a pleasant evening." He hung up.

I put the phone down. "He wants to remind you of a deadline and asked that you call him first thing tomorrow morning."

Philippa was about to cry. "If I'm not out of this flat by the weekend, Andrew said that he would have my possessions taken away. I can't let that happen to my family's things. I need the money for the movers and the deposit on a new flat I found yesterday." She twirled, ran to the front room, and collapsed on the sofa, sobbing.

The crying got worse as I stood next to the sofa, trying to think of something soothing to say. "This is rough going, I know."

She sat up and gulped several times. "I told Andrew that my leaving would have to be done gracefully since I don't have much money. Andrew promised me the money but changed his mind late this afternoon and told me that the only money he would give me was for a one-way, nonstop flight to London. I don't know why he's being so beastly." I gave her my handkerchief; she blotted her eyes. "I'm so, so all alone."

"Maybe you should stay at my place. There's a guest room, plenty of privacy, and you won't be so alone. Don't worry; I'm very polite."

"No, no, you've done enough."

"Where does it stand with the movers?"

"I've convinced them to come Thursday, but they won't commit unless they receive a deposit tomorrow. My new flat is being held until tomorrow." She wiped her eyes.

"We'll get all of this sorted out tomorrow morning," I said.

She choked back the sobs.

"What about reconsidering my offer?"

She shook her head no and began crying.

"I'm not leaving until I've finished my drink and you've calmed down. Do you want a drink? Or water?" She didn't answer. "Well, I'm going to get you a glass of water."

I went to the kitchen, finished my drink, and poured a much larger one. My hands were shaking, but I managed to light a cigarette and not gulp the drink. When I returned to the living room, Philippa was composing herself. "Don't bother with work tomorrow," I said. "I'll let them know you're not coming in."

Philippa agreed with a nod and drank the water.

"Philippa, I'll help you any way possible. I swear it." Her breathing relaxed. "When I leave, I want you to have a stiff drink and go to bed. A night's sleep might help. If you need anything—anything at all—call me. I'm the only A. A. Romanovsky in the phone book."

She nodded. "Now you're involved. Why are you doing this?"

"Let's talk about that tomorrow."

"Fine," Philippa said and leaned back with her eyes shut.

I left and waited until I heard her lock the door. Walking down Telegraph Hill, I couldn't find a cab, so I walked through North Beach and down Montgomery Street to the bank. I left a note at the receptionist's desk saying that Philippa wouldn't be in the next day and I'd be in after lunch. I checked my phone; Fiona hadn't called.

CHAPTER 12

DECEMBER 9, 1986

SAN FRANCISCO

I left the Universal building and walked across the plaza to California Street. Crossing the street, I saw an empty cable car at the Market Street intersection poised to start its climb over Nob Hill. Taking the cable car to Van Ness Avenue and walking home seemed like a good idea. I waited; my mind was racing.

The cable car hadn't moved; neither the brakeman nor the conductor was in sight. I thought of flagging down a cab, but there weren't many in the Financial District during the evening. A bite to eat was a possibility; a dark impersonal bar was even more appealing. I decided to walk over to the hotels around Union Square for a couple of drinks and maybe something to eat.

"Alexander?" A tall woman in a raincoat stood next to a Honda on the other side of California Street. Her voice was familiar. "You're standing in the street. Either come over here or get back on the sidewalk." As I approached her, I recognized her. It was Helen Jacobs. "I saw you standing there and drove around the block; you hadn't moved," she said. "You seem confused. Something's wrong?"

"I'm not thinking clearly."

"Maybe a cigarette would help." I handed her one and found my lighter. Helen steadied my shaking hand as I lit her cigarette. "Are you okay?"

"Stressed." I managed to light my cigarette.

"Care to tell me?"

"An associate of mine has a problem. You know, when relationships end, people often turn callous to people they once loved."

"Gosh, tell me about it," Helen said.

"Philippa told me that you called this morning. The apology was mine to make, not yours. Coming to your office unannounced was stupid, and I caught you at a bad time."

"It was a bad situation that got worse," she said. "On top of that, I'm kind of unpredictable these days. You're up to date of the scuttlebutt about the race for Universal's new CEO?"

"You seem to know more than I do."

Helen said, "Some people at Universal are getting out before the new broom sweeps through management. I've interviewed several of them. Apparently, Universal's board has made it known that, if Andrew Neville is to become the next CEO, he'll do so without his mistress, Philippa Tate-Palmer. I suspect that Neville wants that job more than anything and will sacrifice Philippa?"

"That's exactly what he's doing. Is there a Mrs. Neville?"

"There is, but something's wrong: illness, or the marriage doesn't work, or there's an arrangement. Anyway, I don't imagine that Philippa has many friends in San Francisco."

"Probably not. Philippa must have met Neville when he was running the bank's European operations from London."

"What's going to happen to her?"

"I don't know, but the heat really got turned up tonight."

"From what I've heard about Andrew Neville, if you've somehow aligned yourself with Philippa, you're either incredibly naïve or one of bravest men I've met."

"Naïve may be the adjective that fits."

"Philippa and I got to talking this morning; she thinks the world of you."

"Really?"

"Philippa said that you're a kind man. Not a good guy, or a great boss, but kind."

"We've worked together for years, but Philippa doesn't know me that well."

"Sounds like she does, but that's between you and her," Helen replied. "May I drive you some place? Have you eaten?"

"I'm not hungry."

"Drink?"

"Great idea, but I feel like drinking too much. And I've got a lot to do tomorrow."

"Come on, I'll drive you home."

In the car, I gave her directions and asked why she was working late.

She sighed. "My bank is reorganizing itself; the thirtysomethings have convinced senior management to sacrifice the generation in front of them on the altar of greater expectations. I'm in the middle of it." She downshifted to make a yellow light. "You know the old adage: if you can't trust your banker, then whom can you trust? Well, these days bankers don't trust the bankers they work with. Do you trust your boss?"

"No reason not to; we get along. I do good work, and he's too senior for me to be a threat. That works well enough."

"Would he stand up for you?" Helen asked.

"Getting down to it, I don't know. How about you and your boss?"

"Yesterday I dug my heels in and fought back over a good banker that management wanted to replace with a younger fellow, but I got overruled. So a guy in his midforties went down in flames; from his ashes will arise a shiny new face, as purposeful as a fox terrier with the ethics of a pit viper." She shook her head and said, "Boy, talk about getting into the holiday spirit."

We were heading into North Beach, the old Italian neighborhood that was going Chinese. Next to a bakery displaying Italian pastries, a Chinese butcher had hung smoked ducks in his window.

"Do you get gloomy around the holidays?" she asked.

"Sometimes. But for me, it's Easter."

"Russian Easter must be something." Helen brightened.

"When I was a boy in Paris, Easter services were incredible. The Orthodox church we went to was candlelit; the vestments were shimmering gold; the icons radiated an inner light. Funny, I can see it now."

"After the Easter service, the priest and the congregation processed around the church, didn't they?" Helen said.

"How do you know that?"

"I told you, Russia fascinates me, and I read a lot."

"You're right. After the third time around, the priest would proclaim: '*Christos voskres!*' Christ is risen. The procession replied, '*Voistinu voskres!*' Truly risen. Then it was to the food. Lent was serious back then; no meat or sweets. So the Easter meals were incredible: my mother prepared *kylebiaka*, an elaborate salmon dish in pastry. The sausages popped in my mouth; the tall Easter cake, *kulich*, was frosted like snow; and paskha resembled a kind of molded cheesecake. Oh, the colored eggs were like plump jewels."

"Enchanting," Helen said. "I've been in Protestant and Catholic churches but never an Orthodox one."

"Someone said that the difference between an Orthodox church and a Catholic church is about the same as between a Catholic church and a Baptist church."

"Are you very religious?"

"When I was a boy, I went through a religious phase. I was going to be a priest and later a metropolitan. Metropolitans are something like Catholic archbishops. Nowadays, I go irregularly. When I show up, parishioners and the priests ask: 'Been traveling? Feeling okay?' I wonder if they're nosy or concerned."

"I go through the same thing." She laughed and turned south, skirting the touristy Fisherman's Wharf and Ghirardelli Square. At the Marina Green, she pulled into the parking lot overlooking the Bay. The couple in the next car were making out. "Salt air clears the mind," she said. "Let's walk down to the Yacht Club and smoke your cigarettes. What was Christmas like?"

We got out of the car. "It's celebrated according to the Julian calendar, about two weeks later than the calendar we use. By the first week in January, the stores here had white sales; and my parents bought me linens, sheets, pillow cases, stuff like that."

"Makes sense, I guess."

"I was trying to be funny. I got the usual things."

She replied with a courteous smile as we walked along the sea wall toward the Yacht Club, listening to the water lapping against the moored boats below us. The fog had grown heavier, smudging Marin County's lights. Looking west, I saw only the Golden Gate's yellow and red lights. The fog horns were more despondent than usual. Nearing the Yacht Club, fragments of laughter from a holiday party mingled with the creaking hulls of the bobbing sailboats, their riggings playing off the water like saplings in a storm. The mood had changed; we were quiet.

Looking out to the Bay, Helen said, "A while ago, I went to see a shrink—you know, a psychologist. My moods were all over the place, sleep was erratic, I was obsessing about work…wasn't eating. The doctor said that I was recovering from a nervous breakdown, a walking breakdown—like walking pneumonia."

"Gosh, those are serious," I said. "Most people don't talk about them."

"I wonder why?"

"People see mental illness as weakness, or a character flaw. The victims are often ashamed of themselves."

Still gazing at the Bay, she said, "I've got a theory about nervous breakdowns: people who've been through one recognize people who've been through the same. Like nose jobs, not that I've had one." Helen faced me. "From what you just said, my intuition tells me that you've had a nervous breakdown."

"Well, I usually don't discuss that with people I'm getting to know. But I was eighteen and fell apart after my mother died; a psychologist suggested hospitalization."

"Were you?"

"No, I saw myself strapped down and receiving shock treatments. Talk about incentive; I made the proverbial glass go from half empty to half full in no time. Just curious, where are we going with this?"

"I'm not quite sure. You see, I have trouble with men, trusting them. I'm trying to take chances again, like I'm doing now."

"It seems to me that recovering is uneven, a work in continual process."

"You're still working on it," she said. "Is that what you're saying?"

"That's right. Profound things like death and, I guess, divorce get resolved only to a manageable level."

"So there's something unresolved?"

"There is. I rationalize and live with it as best I can. Maybe the lingering guilt is a reminder that I could have done better and should try harder going forward."

"So that gives you a certain nobility?" she asked.

"I'm not suggesting that."

"But you've turned yourself into a kind man. Helping Philippa… counseling me—but in fact pitying me." Helen looked shocked for an instant. "The phone numbers I gave Philippa, you threw them out, didn't you?"

"I will tomorrow. Look, it's been a long day. So thanks for the ride; I'm going to walk home. Oh, and one more thing…"

"Please don't leave me here feeling dreadful. I deserve it, but please don't."

"Helen, you can be delightful, but I don't know why I provoke your attacks—Denver, now this. But whatever it is, I'm not up to thinking about it tonight, or any other night. So good-bye." I started walking.

"Please stop, please," she said. "I'll drive you home, that's the least I can do." Helen started walking to her car, then turned. "Come on, this evening will end sooner; that's what you want." In the car, Helen said, "I've got to stop leading men on, like Mike, that guy in Denver. I didn't want to do that to you, but…" She started the car. "You see, my shrink thinks I'm acting out the rejection from my divorce."

"The guys you work with must think you're a lot of fun."

"At work I manage to put all of that aside."

"Can we get going?"

Helen headed out of the parking lot onto Marina Boulevard past the expensive homes facing the Bay. Some had decorated their front windows and lawns with elaborate yuletide displays: reindeer, snowmen, mangers, and angels. One picture window had a five-foot gold Buddha in lotus position wearing a Santa hat. Kind of funny, but not that evening. Drew and Fred had lived in one of those homes; their Christmas trees were understated perfection: clear Italian lights, silver bells, and red bows. As we passed Drew's, the picture window was dark. Drew had been on my mind since our dinner.

Helen was telling me how rejection could damage a person's iden- tity. I knew a lot about that. Before that summer, my mother had defined me: attractive, bright, and amusing. I was loved and complete. Then she sent me away. Without my mother's love, I was a blank can- vass. With Drew's encouragement, I began a self-portrait. The result- ing picture was more brilliant than I had imagined, and Drew fell in love with the alluring young man I had fashioned. Loved once again, I was complete. But after my mother's suicide, the canvas collapsed on itself. Drew urged me to paint another. But I couldn't, not for him.

Looking back at the dark window, I thought about my conversation with Fred; he was right after all. I knew that Drew had never stopped loving me and told him so after our dinner. Reentering Drew's life, I had become the nastiest sort of tease—out of reach but close enough to tempt. When Drew asked me if he had used me, I told him no. On its face, a truthful answer, but incomplete to the point of dishonesty; Drew never realized that I had been using him. Now he wanted to give me his life's work. Taking the gift garnered with such deceit was disgusting, but refusing would waste the time I had spent tempting Drew. I turned my attention to Helen.

Helen double-parked in front of my place and said, "So, you see, no more rejection, not for me. From now on, I'll have the upper hand and decide who walks and when. But when you get out of the car, I'll be left with my upper hand. Kind of ironic? Or neurotic?" With a sheep- ish smile, she extended her hand.

I handed her a cigarette.

She settled back and continued, "Consciously, I didn't want this to happen; subconsciously, it was probably inevitable. Under different, less neurotic, circumstances, this could have been a pleasant evening prompting more like it. I hope you understand."

Trying to light our cigarettes, my hand was shaking more than ever. "I do indeed." In Helen's conflicted state, what I was about to do was sinful. "Helen, we're a lot alike. We're manipulators. And let's be honest, when someone realizes they've been used, their expression is priceless. But you're new at this. Playing the coquette and teasing guys in bars? Come on."

Helen slid back against the door. "Don't make this worse than it already is."

"Some advice from an old pro: get into bed with them until they love you. Then end it, but not quite. It's all about control: too much and they walk; not enough and they're underfoot. You see, I've been at this since I was a boy."

"Really?" Her voice was flat. With only the dashboard lights, I couldn't read her expression.

"With some direction, you can become as nuanced as I am."

"You're mean."

"No, insightful is more like it," I said. "Seriously, I appreciated your scorned woman gambit; it was quite touching."

"You're spiteful."

"You're coy; I admire that."

"I don't like this."

"Gosh, in Denver, you didn't think I shared. Now you're uncomfortable with the honesty. And you call yourself a Californian?"

"This conversation is over," she hissed. "If you don't mind…"

"Being dismissed, am I?" I got out. Helen squealed the tires as I slammed the door. I couldn't remember being so angry and stood there until the cigarette burned my fingers.

CHAPTER 13

WEDNESDAY, DECEMBER 10, 1986

SAN FRANCISCO

Early that morning, I called Philippa—no answer, no answering machine. I dressed and tried again with the same result, then tried Philippa's work number and got the receptionist, who read back my message from the previous night. Figuring that Philippa was still at home, I went downstairs and asked Sally Roth for the station wagon. Telegraph Hill is steep with some of the worst parking in San Francisco. But on a work-day morning about a block from Philippa's, I found a legal space.

I rang the intercom—nothing. The building's main entrance was locked. I smoked a cigarette and paced about, looking helpless; a woman and her small white dog approached the front door. Helping her with the heavy door then stooping down to pet her dog, I explained that I was a new tenant and had left my keys upstairs. I looked respectable in a suit, her dog liked me, and she let me in.

There was no answer when I knocked at Philippa's, but I heard steps approaching. I put my ear to the door and called to Philippa. The steps stopped. I pounded on the door. The door opened on a sliding chain lock. Philippa's blue eyes were heavy and bleary. "Are you alone?" She sounded dopey.

"Yes. Are you?"

She nodded that she was.

"Then let me in, please."

"I've taken some pills and am going to sleep; come back later." Philippa was closing the door when her phone rang. I put my foot in the door. "Don't be brutish," she said. "I cannot receive anyone. Please leave."

"Out of the question."

The phone kept ringing. "I'm not letting you in."

"Then I'll kick in the door." We were face-to-face. I could smell gin on her breath. "Philippa, damn it, let me in."

"That bloody phone is driving me off the rails." She vanished.

I shouldered the door and broke the chain lock. Philippa was sitting on the sofa where I had left her last night. She hadn't changed clothes and was splotchy and puffy from a night of crying and gin. The phone had stopped ringing.

I took her by the shoulders. "What pills did you take? How many?"

"Valium, one, fifteen minutes ago."

"And washed it down with gin?"

Philippa tried fixing her hair. "No, water."

"Let me see the pill bottle."

"Steady, it's not what you're thinking. That's not to say it hadn't crossed my mind."

"Don't even joke about that."

She went to the bedroom and returned with a bottle that looked about full according to the prescription.

"Why's the phone driving you nuts?" I asked.

"Andrew's secretary calls here every fifteen minutes or so." She was about to cry. "Earlier this morning Andrew demanded, again, that I go back to London. I hung up. My God, he's treating me like a..." She choked on the indignity.

"Look, I'll take care of the phone while you shower, change, and pack a suitcase. You're not staying here—you shouldn't be alone."

"So you're storming in here and taking control of everything?"

"That's right."

"Thank God for that." Philippa went to the bedroom and shut the door.

I heard the shower running and went to the kitchen and found some tea. The water was coming to a boil when the phone rang; a female voice at the other end announced, "Andrew Neville calling for Philippa Tate-Palmer."

"Philippa is indisposed."

"Who's this?"

"Alexander Romanovsky. Who are you?"

With an exasperated sigh, she replied, "Andrew Neville's secretary."

"I spoke to Mr. Neville yesterday evening…"

She put me on hold, then came back on. "Mr. Neville will not discuss this with you. He wants you to put Philippa Tate-Palmer on the line, right now. Do you understand?"

"Look, Andrew Neville's secretary, Philippa Tate-Palmer is unavailable." Put on hold again, I worried that Neville would come on the line. Instead it was his secretary again. Before she started, I said, "Philippa will leave this apartment within an hour or so. Tomorrow, the movers will take her things. If Philippa wishes to speak with Mr. Neville, she'll contact him. Do you understand that?" She sputtered. "I'll take that as a yes." I was put on hold until the connection was broken.

Picturing Neville in a cab, I concluded that a scene at his mistress's apartment with me present was far too messy for a vice chairman of Universal Bank to risk. The hypocrisy was stunning: apparently it was acceptable under unofficial bank policy for a vice chairman to have his mistress on the payroll, but not the aspiring CEO. Or perhaps Universal's board was testing Neville's commitment. The chief executive officer would have to put the bank above everything: self, family, and surely his mistress.

Nevertheless, there was Neville's retribution to consider. While it was axiomatic that an officer at my level wouldn't survive a confrontation with a vice chairman, there were ethical considerations. If Neville engineered my firing for helping Philippa, he'd be on propriety's thinnest edge. And Philippa's and my personnel files limited Neville: I had given Philippa excellent performance reports, and my annual reviews were first-rate. Other than wait and see, I had no real options and tried convincing myself that Neville didn't either.

Hearing the shower stop, I took my time finishing the tea. Philippa came into the kitchen looking better; the previous evening had been scrubbed away, her hair was fixed, and the lipstick and light makeup were flattering. She was wearing gray slacks, a white shirt, and a black velvet blazer. "The last time I ran away, I was a school girl," she said.

"Don't look at it that way."

"You're right, I'm being thrown out."

"I didn't mean that. Pushed around is more like it."

"That's one way of looking at it, I suppose. In part I understand." Philippa looked away. "All of this drives me to tears, and I'm not that type of woman." She went to the windows and looked out toward the Bay Bridge. It was a fresh morning; last night's smog over Oakland had been replaced by a cloudless sky. "Why are you doing this?"

"We've worked together for a long time. We're friends."

"Friends? Come on, we tolerate each other."

"We're both private people," I said.

"I have a lot to be private about." She turned to face me.

"So do I. You would have helped me if I asked." A stupid statement I wished I hadn't made.

Philippa considered that. "You're wrong, dead wrong. In the first place, you would never come to me with your problems. But let's say you did. I'd have asked myself what was in it for me? If nothing, I wouldn't have lifted a finger. We know why, don't we? Because I'm mercenary." She turned back to the window.

I thought about telling her that mercenary women didn't spend the night crying when a relationship ended; they certainly weren't mortified when offered money to leave town. If I were to say such things, they would come later when Philippa could reassess herself from hindsight's mollifying perspective. "Philippa, let's go."

She studied the apartment. "So lovely up here watching the Bay's moods as clouds fractured the light and rearrange the colors. The colors, so mutable…the deepest blues, the palest mauve. And the morning and evening fogs were predictable, but not quite. When I wanted a foggy night, the fog stayed out, over the horizon. But that was such a long, long time ago." She turned and walked out the door.

I followed with her suitcase.

In the car, I asked when she had last eaten—tea and a sandwich for lunch yesterday. I was telling her about the breakfast we'd have when she said, "For God's sake, please, please tell me why you are doing this."

"Remember, you asked me for a loan and I agreed."

"Yes, yes, but why are you doing this?"

"You were polite when you didn't have to be."

"Meaning?" she asked.

"At work, you did what I asked without challenging me…or talking back…or making fun of me. If you had, I'd have had to take it."

"Because of Andrew?"

"That's right."

"I appreciate the frankness," she said, looking out the passenger window. "And now you're repaying me?"

"Somewhat," I said. "And I don't think you have a lot of friends to turn to."

"Other than Andrew, I don't have much of a life here," she replied. "At the bank, everyone kept their distance, much like you."

"You're twisting everything I say. What I'm trying to say is that my mother and I were in something of the same position after my father died when I was a boy. My mother's friend, Fiona Sinclair, saved us. Without Fiona, I can't imagine what would have happened to us."

Still looking out the window, Philippa said, "I've spoken to Fiona Sinclair when she's phoned you."

We pulled up to a red light by the park in front of Saints Peter and Paul Church. Elderly Italian men were playing bocci ball on the clay courts by the street. All of them were wearing black suits, white shirts, dark ties, and white socks. A man pitched a ball, and the others watched until there was a faint click of the ball hitting another. The man made a rude gesture and hissed something in Italian. Others sat on a bench, taking the sun and smoking thin dark cigars.

As we crossed the intersection, Philippa faced me and said, "Let's see if I have this right: since you can't repay Fiona Sinclair, you're helping me?"

"Better put, I appreciate your situation, having been there myself."

"A penniless foreigner?"

"Okay, we'll have it your way." We were going up the steep part of

Union Street on Russian Hill. "Look, beating yourself up and calling yourself names doesn't help. Why don't you do us favor and stop it?"

Philippa was looking north toward the Bay as we crested the hill. On that sparkling morning, the gusty wind had turned the Bay choppy. The running tide had layered the water: deep blue with green waves topped with white caps. North of Alcatraz, a ferry struggled through the heavy waves; effervescent billows of seawater gusted from its bow while clouds of bright seagulls wheeled over the stern. We watched.

"Stunning, isn't it?" Philippa said as we descended the hill. "My soul for a proper meal and a dreamless sleep. After that, Lord knows what's going to happen. I wonder what Andrew will do."

"Since you didn't knuckle under, he must be reconsidering his options. You have options too. If all of this went public, Universal's board wouldn't like that."

"No, couldn't do that. I do love Andrew, despite all of this. But less, far less." She shook her head. "Why, I don't know—when it's so bloody evident that he doesn't love me. Now I wonder if he ever did." She leaned back and closed her eyes.

At home, I put Philippa's suitcase in the guest room and went back to the living room. She was standing where I had left her. "This flat is magnificent," she said. "Did you decorate this?"

"An avocation," I said. "It started with some of the furniture my parents left. The dining table and chairs were handmade in France and are excellent. But over the years it's become cluttered."

Philippa walked around the living room. "Must look totally different at night."

"I was trying to capture the sunlight, so I tried repainting, then wallpaper. But facing north, the buildings on either side block most of the light. So I went with overhead recessed lighting that concentrates the light. At night, the conversational settings are delineated into pools of light. But the lighting's dated; I've got to think of something else."

"I think it's marvelous as is." Philippa said, looking toward the kitchen. "I'm not a very good cook."

"Why don't you unpack while I make omelets—onions, peppers, and cheese. Toast, marmalade…and I'll make proper tea. Then you'll take a long nap while I settle things with the movers and your new landlord."

She headed for the guest room and stopped by the side table to look at pictures of my parents, their families, and some of me growing up. "Some guests peer into medicine cabinets, others at the books, but I'm a moth to flame when it come to family pictures." She took the picture that Drew gave me at dinner. "A young you. And the other person?"

"Oh, that was a long time ago. The other person is Drew Faircloth."

"Must have been close back then," she said, putting the picture back. "Mind if we have some music? Something ethereal and French; Debussy's perfect for this flat."

I found a tape with *La Mer* while Philippa unpacked. I started sautéing the omelet fillings, beat the eggs, and brewed English breakfast tea steeped in a warmed pot. We sat on the living room sofa and ate the omelets over the coffee table. Over a last cup, Philippa said, "Russians are tea drinkers, aren't they?"

"They are. I prefer tea, but American tea is awful."

"Most Americans have never had a good cup of tea," she said. "They use tea bags, and the water's never hot enough." She dozed off for a moment. "Russians drink tea from glasses?"

"Men often do; women usually drink from cups."

Philippa put her cup and saucer on the coffee table and curled her legs under her. "Tell me a story, a Russian bedtime story."

"My mother used to tell me one about a princess and the Tartars— Mongols, they're called in English."

"Fine." Philippa closed her eyes. "Now what was the princess's name?"

"Tiffany."

Philippa opened her eyes. "Really, what was her name?"

"Tatiana. Tatiana's family lived on a huge estate in southern Russia when John the Dread—Ivan the Terrible—was czar. In those days, southern Russia was a frontier, kind of like Dodge City with Cossacks. And all kinds of people lived there: Russians, Ukrainians, Poles, Jews, Armenians. All of them were terrified of the Tartars. Tartars came from the east on their small horses and took captives back to their khanates by the Aral Sea. The captives were never seen again."

Philippa was drifting off.

I continued, "One day, Tatiana's brother went into the forest, looking for mushrooms and didn't return. Tatiana went to find him and heard galloping horses. Confused, she ran east—the wrong way—until she collapsed. She awoke, and a Tartar horseman stood over her."

Without opening her eyes, she said, "Wait, the Tartar's name was Todd."

"Actually, his name was Hankuu, which is Tartar for Todd. Well, Tatiana was taken back to Hankuu's and put to work on the palace he was building. Luckily, the Tartars had captured a big horse and put him to work too. Of course, the horse spoke Russian and befriended Tatiana. Finally, with a combination of Russian and equine bravery, Tatiana and the horse escaped and rode off across the steppes…And you've fallen asleep."

She seemed to be having a nightmare.

I shook her shoulder and said, "You need a good long nap." Then I led her to the guest room and pulled down the covers. "I'm going to get the cashier's checks for the movers and your new landlord. Then I'll be at the office for the afternoon. Call me if you need anything. This evening, we'll have a nice supper. Any favorites?"

I thought I heard her say, "Lamb chops and scalloped potatoes."

After clearing the dishes and loading the dishwasher, I knocked on her door. A muffled reply sounded like, "Come in."

Tiptoeing, I put an extra set of keys on the table next to the bed.

Philippa was nodding off and asked, "What happened to Tatiana?"

"She and the horse are just ahead of the Tartars. Are you going to be all right?"

"For the time being. Please finish the story and don't leave until I'm asleep."

I sat on the edge of the bed, and she held my hand. "The Tartars were gaining on them when Tatiana saw the spires and gold crosses of a Russian kremlin—"fortress" in English. The fortress gates swung open, and a prince and his men rode out and attacked the Tartars while Tatiana made it to safety. Later Tatiana marries the prince; Andre was his name, but his friends, the other princes, called him Buddy."

"What happened to Tatiana's brother? What was his name?"

"Alexander. No one knows; he vanished."

She was sleeping, so I put her hand on top of the bedspread and left.

***

Mellow Movers boasted the lowest rates in the Bay Area, and the Mellow vans were famous for their Woodstockian murals. Lance and Sundance and their kerchief-wearing black Labrador, Shunga-wen—Sioux for "beautiful dog"—were the team that would move Philippa. The mural on their van centered on Che Guevara and Allen Ginsberg smoking a hookah with Lawrence Welk looking on. Peeking from the hashish clouds coiling around the van were luminaries from the late '60s. I confused Big Brother and the Holding Company with The Jefferson Airplane. Jack Kerouac made sense, but Lawrence Welk didn't.

We were discussing the Welk juxtaposition when Lance took keen notice of my suit and asked what I did. I told him I was a banker at Universal Bank. Our budding bonhomie was replaced with business-like efficiency as Lance took my check and handed me a receipt.

Philippa's new apartment was in the Marina, on Buchanan Street, about a dozen blocks from mine. The landlady showed me the apartment, a cramped one-bedroom at the back of the building looking into a vent shaft. The thought of Philippa exchanging Telegraph Hill's panorama for that dingy apartment was disheartening. When the landlady asked how I knew Philippa, I told her that we worked together. She leered, took my check, and handed me a rental agreement for Philippa to sign.

***

Late the previous day, the Bulgarian Export Agency had sent a telex requesting pre-export financing of their next year's tobacco crop, a routine but sizable deal. The woman administering Bulgaria, Romania, and Yugoslavia had drafted a credit report for the General Loan Committee's approval. After some quick editing, we took the final package to my boss, who had to recommend the proposed credit facility before it was placed on the General Loan Committee's calendar for Friday morning. I wondered if fallout from Andrew Neville might have made it to his level; but, a cheerful man by nature, he complimented us on the presentation's quick turnaround.

Going home, I stopped at the Marina Safeway, the fashionable supermarket serving the Marina and Pacific Heights, for the evening's meal. The butchers were busy taking holiday orders. I took a number and saw Helen Jacobs waiting at the other end of the display cases by the poultry section. I needed string beans and salad greens, and the most direct way to the vegetables was past Helen. Helen was still waiting when the butcher handed me the lamb chops. I thought about apologizing to her when a shopping cart clipped my ankle. I got out of the way and looked for Helen, but she had gone.

CHAPTER 13

DECEMBER 10, 1986

SAN FRANCISCO

When I got home, Philippa was sitting on the sofa, reading a magazine. Although rested, she looked tense and told me that someone had left a message on the answering machine while she was sleeping. She hadn't played the message—thinking it could be personal. We listened; it was Fiona asking me to join her for cocktails the following evening when she returned from Lake Tahoe.

Looking relieved, Philippa stood up. "May I help with supper?"

"Sure," I said. "If you want a drink, there's an opened bottle of white in the fridge."

She poured two glasses of wine.

Explaining the dinner, I suggested, "Why don't you trim the string beans while I work on the potatoes?" I tried making small talk as we worked over the sink, but she wasn't tracking. "Philippa, I'm not about to ask or insinuate anything untoward from you. If you prefer, there's Fiona's home. You'd be alone, but I don't think that's the answer now."

"You're right. Sorry, I'm all sixes and sevens—"confused" in American," she said.

I prepared the scalloped potatoes while she trimmed the beans and picked over the lettuce and fresh greens. I whisked up a salad dressing and opened a bottle of Burgundy. There wasn't anything to do until the potatoes were done.

Leaning against the counter sipping her wine, Philippa said, "My emotions are a cauldron of humiliation and self-pity with a measure of trepidation and excruciating embarrassment. Being cast aside does that, I guess."

"I know what you mean. My mother was quite ill, and, for some reason I've never understood, she sent me away. All alone, I fell in love with Drew Faircloth, the fellow with me in that picture you looked at this morning."

"You're still in love with Drew?"

"I'm fond of Drew, but…my relationship with Drew changed all together, when I determined that I wasn't a homosexual. It's a bit complicated."

"Didn't mean to pry. From Fiona Sinclair's voice-mail, I assume that Drew is her son?"

"That's right. Fiona is taking care of Drew at the family summer home at Lake Tahoe, where that picture was taken. He's quite ill—AIDS."

"Sorry." Philippa grimaced. "Such a dreadful disease."

"Drew was an art dealer. He wants me to take over his business, but I don't know."

"Taking the offer would get you out of Andrew's way; men who get in his way don't last long." With a listless laugh, she added, "Neither do the women. But you're a brave man, Alexander."

I laughed.

"Seriously, most men in your position would have hung up the instant they heard Andrew's voice."

"Most men wouldn't have had another job offer."

"You weren't thinking about that last night when you agreed to lend me money…or brought me over here this morning…or decided to be the only American friend I have." Her voice quavered. "This afternoon, I discovered we have a lot in common. We're aristocrats; not many of us left."

"My family's titles became worthless after the Russian Revolution. My grandfather taught ballroom dancing to clumsy French teenagers, and my grandmother ended up as a nanny."

Philippa said, "I read somewhere that a Romanov grand duke sold champagne in Florida."

"That was Grand Duke Demitri, one of the men who killed Rasputin."

And a Russian general sold newspapers at a Paris train station. Of the Russians who fled the Revolution, those from the professions and trades adjusted and often prospered in their adopted countries. Those at the top of the old order had elaborate pedigrees but few marketable talents. Many became destitute. Some had fled to China, where the term white girl in a brothel meant a Russian, some probably from the old aristocracy.

"There's a wonderful picture of Comte—Count—Adrian Romanovsky and his family, dated May 1914. He was your paternal grandfather?"

"That's right. That picture has always fascinated me."

"In photographs back then, the people seem like mannequins, but in that photo, they're alive and engaged. Your grandfather is gazing at his wife with the deepest affection. The oldest son may have teased his sister, the exquisite young woman who's laughing next to him. The middle son is trying to look older; the youngest son looks amused. They were a proud, happy family. What happened to them?"

"Adrian Romanovsky and my father—the youngest boy—were the only two who survived the Revolution and the Civil War."

"Those lovely people..." Philippa shuddered. "I'm not sure if I should ask about your mother's family?"

"After the Civil War, the Reds enlisted my maternal grandmother to catalogue and appraise paintings they'd confiscated. A few years later, she and her two children were allowed to leave and made it to Paris. The three of them were all that was left of a large and ancient family."

"How old?"

"Their surname was Trepoff, one of the original boyars going back over thirty generations—about the tenth century. Before the Revolution, my mother's family would have had reservations about her marrying into the Romanovsky family, whose title went back only to Catherine the Great during the late seventeen hundreds."

"Do you ever wonder what your life might have been like if none of that had happened?"

"When that picture of Drew and me was taken, I was quite the aristocrat tossing around terms like *breeding* and *pedigree*. Trying to emulate Drew, I mistook sarcasm for wit and grace for fashion. I was a dreadful young man."

"We all go through difficult phases." Her eyes were tearing. "My mother died giving birth to me; Daddy died just before I met Andrew. My father would have been mortified if he saw me like this."

The timer for the potatoes went off.

"Philippa, how do you like your lamb?" I asked.

During dinner, Philippa told me about growing up: her family, the schools she attended. Phillipa's father was the youngest son of a marquis; her mother was from the English landed gentry. Much of Philippa's self-esteem and dignity were based upon her aristocratic lineage—my mother had done the same.

In California, my mother was a foreigner who spoke broken English with a thick Russian accent. Americans thought she was just another exotic refugee who'd washed ashore, but she paid them no mind. However, around the Russians at church, she was imperious—"those people," she'd remind me with a dismissive wave. The Russians called her Princess behind her back, but she cared less. She was splendid, like the French aristocrats sneering at the cheering masses from the tumbrels taking them to the guillotine.

Lingering over coffee, Philippa told me about her father. "My father's families have served in the army since Cromwell. My father was a lieutenant colonel—Horse Guards, Blues, and Royals."

"Oh," I said, "Adrian Romanovsky was a colonel in the Preobrazhensky Life Guards, one of the original guard regiments Peter the Great founded."

Philippa went to the living room and returned with two pictures. Coming around beside me, she said, "This picture was taken in England in August 1940. Who are those men?"

"Frenchmen who fled to England when France fell. My father wasn't a French citizen, but the French army needed mathematicians for their codes and drafted him." I pointed to my father standing in a group of men. "He spent the war in England deciphering German military codes."

"Must have been one of the code breakers at Bletchley Park; they shortened the war considerably." She studied the picture. "Handsome man, looks exhausted and somewhat wary." She handed me the other picture, "This one? The writing's Russian."

"My mother's writing. It's my mother and father's engagement party. Behind them are Adrian Romanovsky, my maternal grandmother, Olga, and her son, Alexander Trepoff. Life was improving for my parents: my father's work had become recognized; my mother worked for an important Parisian art gallery. That might have been the last time the five of them were together before the Germans invaded France."

"Your mother's family has a strong resemblance: tall, fair, weak eyes behind glasses," Philippa said. "Longish noses and straight lips. Your grandfather was a dancing instructor?"

"Yes, and I was told he was quite graceful. Like many of the old aristocrats, he grew up speaking better French than Russian."

"Some dancing instructor," Philippa said. "He went from a smart officer to a dangerous man, didn't he?"

"He was very dangerous; as they said back then, a man who'd lost his soul and had nothing more to lose. He headed a White association that kept the Civil War going in the streets of Paris. Whites and Reds were kidnapping and killing each other until the French authorities stopped it. After that, the association lost its purpose; and the older men told tales about a Russia that ceased to exist to younger men, like my uncle."

"What became of them?"

I stood up. "I'm going to have a cognac. How about you?"

Philippa looked uneasy. "Small whiskey, no ice."

Bringing the drinks back to the table, I said, "They returned to Russia with the Germans during the war. During my first trip to Moscow, I learned that the Reds hanged Adrian Romanovsky as a war criminal. Alexander Trepoff vanished."

"Like your mother's fairy tale that you told me."

"Kind of," I said. "But knowing that blood relatives had joined the

Germans still bothers me."

"If people I loved—my family—were murdered, I would have joined anyone and taken my revenge any way I could," Philippa said.

"I only know pieces of their stories. One day my mother took off without me." Philippa's eyes widened. "Mother and I could go to imaginary places. However, Mother suffered from depression and sometimes traveled without me. She referred to the episodes as the Russian wolves. One time when she came back, I asked why she didn't take me to look for her brother in Russia. She burst into tears and told me that Russia was no place for boys. Later I asked her to tell me all about her brother. She promised to but never did."

"Do many people know about your relatives?"

"Fiona does. I chanced that you'd understand. You do, and I appreciate that."

Philippa finished her whiskey. "Thank you for everything, Alexander, especially your trust."

CHAPTER 15

FRIDAY, DECEMBER 12, 1986

SAN FRANCISCO

Friday morning I presented the Bulgarian export financing to Universal's General Loan Committee that Andrew Neville chaired. As one of the bankers presenting a loan for consideration, I sat at the end of the long conference table facing Neville and met his hazel eyes a couple of times, only to find elaborate blandness. The deal was approved after a few questions from other committee members. Treated like the other bankers that morning, once again I tried convincing myself that Neville wouldn't bother with me.

When I returned home early that afternoon, Drew called me from Tahoe and said, "I've been thinking a lot about you and my business. Art collectors often decorate their homes around their collections, and many asked me to suggest innovative decorators who appreciate art. With you, it could be one-stop shopping. And here's another idea—"

"Drew, I don't deserve this, not after the way I've treated you." I didn't let Drew interrupt. "Teasing you for all these years precludes taking your offer with anything approaching good faith. I'm sorry, but there it is."

Drew was quiet before saying, "Teased? Me? Afraid not. Your last conversation with Fred was something of a mystery, but I suspect it was unpleasant with Fred venting some spleen. From his comments, and now yours, your teasing me was part of it?" I didn't answer. "Okay, I'll set you straight. Fred thought I carried a torch for you. I tried telling him that he had mistaken a torch for longing to dream again as you and I had that summer. As far as your teasing me, you wouldn't do that, would you?"

"Not consciously, but maybe subconsciously."

"I'm the judge of that, and you weren't," Drew said.

"Look, everything is a little confused right now. Let's talk about this later."

"As you know, I don't have much later left. Have you talked to Fiona about this?"

"No, not at all."

"Why?"

"Well, she's been with you since I got back from Moscow."

"Sure, of course, sure. Short-term memory is shot." Drew sighed. "She left this morning for San Francisco."

"And there are some bank politics that complicate things."

"Screw the bank's politics and get out. While you're at it, start getting out from under Fiona's thumb."

"I'm not under her thumb."

"Oh, I see," Drew chortled. "Speaking of Fiona, she's in a dither about Christmas and is determined to spend it with me."

"Your reconciliation is working?"

"There've been some rough patches, but, yes—for the most part." Drew hurried on. "Look, I'm going to have my accountant walk you through the gallery's books. You and he speak the same financial patois. The sooner we can put this together, the better."

"You told me that the loans you took from Fiona are unpaid."

"Good Lord," Drew exclaimed, "Fiona will extend, or whatever bankers call stretching out a loan. When we've buttoned up this deal, just tell her what you need; she won't refuse you anything. Alexander, you know that my love for you is unconditional and unequivocal, right?"

"I do. I love you, but the love is lopsided."

"Life isn't always fair," Drew replied. "Don't do this for me, even a little; do it for yourself—a lot. Start dreaming again; your new dreams will come to fruition."

"I'll talk to you soon."

I met Drew's accountant at his office late that afternoon. Drew asked him to be candid, and he estimated the business could break even if I maintained a third of Drew's clients; with half, I could make a decent living. We didn't go into my standard of living, but my salary the previous year was about half of what Drew had paid himself. Fiona's loans were unpaid, but the interest was current; the accountant estimated that the loans could be retired in three or four years if they were extended.

I knew I could make Drew's business work but was unsure how to approach Fiona.

***

I arrived at Fiona's early that evening. The phone rang when she opened the door, and she hurried to answer it. She took the call and sat at her desk in the study, taking notes. I kept out of earshot by the French doors, looking at the fog gusting through the Golden Gate. Fiona put her hand over the phone and asked for a drink. She usually drank wine but wanted Scotch. Pouring the drink, I was close enough to hear, and Fiona swung the swivel chair with her back to me. I put the drink on her desk and went outside for a cigarette.

When I returned, Fiona was resting her chin in her hands. Wearing a blue suit, a canary-yellow silk blouse, and pumps, she looked weary and motioned me to the chair in front of the desk. "Sorry," she said, "the call was important. How've you been?"

"Fine, looks like you've had a busy day?"

"Very." Fiona finished her drink and was studying the empty glass. "How's work?"

"Just got a large Bulgarian deal approved; it's been a good year for my group. We came in over budgeted loans and profits."

She removed a lipstick smudge from the glass and held it up to the light. "When are they going to promote you?"

"Oh, that's way down the road," I said as she took off her reading glasses and pinched the bridge of her nose. "Something bothering you?"

"My asinine life." Fiona massaged her temples. "It's my family and their hoops. I'm so tired of jumping through them. I dream of going away, far away, and staying there."

"Say, I checked around with Jim O'Meara in Construction Lending. You know O'Meara; he thinks Townie is okay, but he's worried about Chip getting into Townie's business. O'Meara thinks Chip's slippery and has a screw loose. I talked to Robert de Montreville—"

"None of that matters. Thanks for going out of your way, but I've made up my mind."

"Meaning?"

"Meaning, it's none of your business." I stepped back as Fiona went to the side table for another drink. Without asking, she poured one for me.

"I've upset you?" I asked.

"It's been a long day. Edgy…preoccupied. Hoping the Scotch might be settling." She sat down behind the desk.

"You asked me to check around about Townie, remember?"

Pressing her hands on the desk, she stood up. "I want to make myself perfectly clear: I don't want your help or your meddling. Do you understand?"

"Has something happened to my English?" I asked with a heavy French accent. "I am—how you say—a puzzle? Or are you puzzling me? Perhaps Madam could speak slow and clear. Another mistake, it's slowly and clearly."

"Such cheap sarcasm." Fiona raised her voice. "Making a fool of me? Me, me of all people? Well, I'm not having it."

We stared at each other as I stepped back. "Okay, sorry. You've done so much for me, and I wanted to start balancing the books between us."

Fiona stamped her foot. "It's come down to accounting? You're insulting me."

I went to the French doors and pretended to study the garden until I heard Fiona sit down. I let her sit there for a time before I said, "How's Drew doing?"

"As you know, he's dying." In a less hostile tone, she added, "That awful disease is attacking his mind. Sometimes Drew is lucid, other times quite forgetful, a few times he makes no sense at all." She paused. "Alexander, please look at me when we're talking." She was trying to smile when I turned to face her. "If you wish, come up to Tahoe for Christmas, but—"

"It would be better if you and Drew spent that time together."

Fiona said, "Sorry, but you're on your own this year."

"I'll manage."

"I'm sure you shall," she said. "After Christmas, I'll have no time until the first of the year—family business in LA. So let's exchange presents on Epiphany, like you did in France."

"That's fine. I've got plenty of vacation time to use up before the end of the year, so I'll come up to Tahoe after Christmas and stay with Drew while you're busy."

"Just what I was going to suggest. Drew will be pleased."

"Fiona, I would never intentionally upset you."

"I know. Sorry, but I'm just about to snap."

"Well, I've made a stressful day even more so," I said. "So I'll get going. Maybe we could get together tomorrow? Lunch…or something like that?" I started to leave.

"No, no, don't leave." Fiona came around the desk, then looked at her drink. "Good Lord, I've been making short work of these. You know that I have a vile temper."

"And for the most part, I've managed to stay out of its way."

"I was looking forward to this evening but may have torn it," Fiona said, looking at me from the side of her eyes. "You seemed distracted. Something, someone on your mind? Helen Jacobs perhaps? Drew told me that you're quite taken with her."

I laughed. "Helen Jacobs is the most neurotic person I've met in a long time. And she's a tease."

"She teased you?"

"In a manner of speaking. We met at the Denver airport during that storm and talked, that's all. Then I ran into her downtown one evening, and she gave me a ride home. All of a sudden, we were arguing."

Fiona arched an eyebrow. "About what?"

"We were talking about banking. She works for Growers and Ranchers. Then somehow she got to her divorce. She's not getting over it." I shrugged. "None of that matters since I'll never see her again."

"But she's about your age?"

"Come on, I don't care about that. I've told you so countless times."

"I know, but still."

"Fiona, I've been faithful to you. You know that?"

"I do. But I worry. Not too much, but enough."

"And so do I."

"Don't be fatuous."

"Fatuous? You're awfully easy on the eyes. And your legs are to die for." She laughed out loud. "Fiona, you're a trim little package and know how to use it."

She blushed.

I put my arm around her and drew her closer. "When I was in basic training, our drill sergeant shared with us his idea of a perfect woman: a swinging broad who owned a liquor store. Then he asked me what I thought."

"Why you?"

"Several reasons. I was one of the few guys who'd gone to college, a fancy one at that. And somehow it got out that I had taken art courses, which meant light in the combat boots, which meant I got picked on. Anyway, I told him that my girlfriend had a great wine cellar."

"Girlfriend." Fiona giggled. "What did the sergeant say?"

"Called me a bleeping wiseass and made me do fifty push-ups. Back then I could do them by the hundreds."

"You really called me your girlfriend?"

"My only girlfriend. The armed forces community has less flattering terms for women in general, sexy ones in particular." I nuzzled her ear. "Ah, I'll tell you some of those, starting alphabetically or in order of obscenity."

"Girlfriend." Fiona kissed me.

"Fiona, making love with you has been on my mind since I left for Moscow. And I was thinking that we might get to that sooner than later. Then maybe a late supper?"

Fiona sighed. "The last time we were together was when you flew in from Moscow to interview someone. That was all rather hurried; I believe such encounters are called quickies."

"We haven't really talked since I got back from Moscow. So let's have supper. I want to tell you about Russia and hear what you were up to."

Fiona smiled. "Perfect."

"There's a small French restaurant in my neighborhood. I've talked to the owner; he's from Languedoc and cooks with the seasons. About now it's probably duck with glazed turnips or rabbit in mustard sauce. The wine list is limited but good. But getting back to our last time together, I don't remember it being that rushed."

"The sex wasn't, but everything else was," she said. "That motel by the airport…the sheets were still warm." She paused. "I'll get my things."

Fiona packed an overnight bag when she came to my flat, thinking that coming and going in different clothes would deceive her neighbors; but it was so foggy in Sea Cliff that distinguishing people, let alone their clothes, was difficult.

***

After leaving college, I moved back to Fiona's. When she asked why I hadn't attended classes, I told her that college bored me and refused to discuss it further. That I was living off of Fiona's generosity and had wasted her money didn't concern me.

When Fiona asked about my plans for the future, I said that I was going to be an artist, perhaps an impresario of some kind, or an interior designer. That was it, nothing definite, just inchoate musings. I tried New York again, but she refused to listen. With nothing more to say, I went back to drinking myself to sleep and sleeping late. A few days later, Fiona announced that I was going back to the psychologist, but twice a week instead of once.

It could have been seven days a week for all I cared. The psychologist wanted to talk about my mother's death, but I sidestepped his questions and taunted him. After several meetings, the psychologist concluded that I had refused to accept the suicide emotionally; I told him that he didn't know what he was talking about.

Composing himself, the psychologist declared that I was clinically depressed and required help he couldn't provide. He would urge Fiona that hospitalization might provide the intense treatment I required. I didn't know what intense meant but assumed shock therapy; having electricity pulsed through my brain was out of the question. I had to go to New York.

Since Drew got everything he wanted from Fiona, with forethought, so could I. I cobbled together a three-point plan. First, the psychologist was a complete waste of my time and Fiona's money, and I would not see him again. Secondly, I loved Drew and was leaving for New York. Thirdly, if she refused, I'd hitchhike; should something happen to me, she'd have to live with the guilt. Drew's confrontations were far more ingenious, but I was desperate.

When I brought up the psychologist, Fiona said that she wasn't going to make the same mistake with me as she had with my mother. Mistake? I wanted an explanation. Instead, Fiona said that she was committing me to a mental hospital. I demanded the details of her mistake. Fiona was evasive; I kept pressing her.

She sat me down and explained that early one morning the nurse discovered that my mother, who appeared to be sleeping, had slashed her wrists under the covers. Doctors had told Fiona that my mother was self-destructive and should be committed. Fiona refused; the guilt was crushing. As Fiona sat next to me, she took my hands and pleaded for my understanding.

Taking Fiona's confession as vulnerability, I stood up and told her that she might work out her guilt with the psychologist I was no longer using. Trying to stand up, Fiona staggered, steadied herself on the sofa, and sat down. She went quiet. I knew from watching Drew that her silence meant submission. I was about to proceed when Fiona stood up and came toward me with measured steps and clenched fists. I backed away and went to my second point—New York and Drew.

Who would pay for art school? I would use my inheritance—there had to be something left. No, my mother's care had used it all; I was penniless. Backing away from her, I said that money didn't matter; I would wash dishes if that's what it took. Fiona sneered. I told her I'd hitchhike. She reminded me that she was my legal guardian and would call the police if I did.

Stalking me, she asked about the draft. Simple: the army didn't take homosexuals. Backing me into a corner, she asked about my education. I told her that American universities, catering as they did to the middle classes, had nothing to teach me about the aesthetic lives Drew and I would lead. Fiona went chalk-white and stared with unblinking eyes. I tried slipping away.

Fiona grabbed my shirt, pushed me against the wall, and slapped me, again and again. My glasses disappeared; tears burned. Then Fiona twisted my collar. I deserved the beating for having forsaken my mother and didn't resist; my submissiveness enraged her even more. Everything spilled out in torrential Russian: why had my mother sent me away and left me? Fiona thought I was swearing and closed her fists.

I tried English; the words wouldn't come. But there was French. Sobbing, I asked Fiona why my mother had sent me away, why she stopped loving me. I was alone, and alone I was nothing and about to go mad as my mother. Fiona switched gears to translate.

I was crying, my nose was bleeding, and my shirt was torn. She stepped back. Hitting Fiona was out of the question. So I kissed her; it was a physical attack. To defend herself, Fiona held me close.

We kissed again. She stroked the back of my head and buried her face into my shoulder. Fiona stood between me and insanity; that realization was as sudden as it was complete. The sex that followed was clumsy on my part and deliberate on Fiona's. Later Fiona decided that I had seduced her, but I hadn't seduced anyone and wasn't about to start with my mother's best friend. Fiona was approaching forty, and I was eighteen.

For several months Fiona wouldn't let me out of her sight, which was fine with me. I told Fiona that I was terrified that she would leave me if we were discovered. Fiona promised never to leave me. Fiona and I realized that to endure my mother's suicide, we would do so together. Fiona's decision to care for my mother at home was an act of compassion that set the stage for the suicide I had done nothing to stop.

Our guilt bound us. There was no room for Drew.

CHAPTER 16

SATURDAY, DECEMBER 13, 1986

SAN FRANCISCO

Saturday morning, I was aware of Fiona leaving and coming back to bed before the reading lamp on her side went on. Fiona was sitting back against the pillows, reading through papers.

"Good morning." She leaned over to kiss me, then gasped when I ran my hand up her thigh. "You like sex in the morning, but I've got too much on my mind for that. I was wondering if you would help me with this deal of Chip's."

I found my glasses. "Let's see, sex or Chip's deal? I vote for sex."

She wiggled away. "About my tantrum last evening," she began, looking over her reading glasses, "I was angry with myself, not you, and the position I've gotten myself into. You may not have been paying attention when I told you that last night."

"I was absorbed with the beautiful woman in bed with me."

"You flatter me so." She handed me the papers. "Here's the deal: the title report, the appraisal, financial statements, and the rest of the usual. There's a description of the new round of financing they want me to provide. I want your help, sincerely." She got out of bed and stepped out of her nightgown.

"Fiona, get back here, right now."

"I'm going to shower and get dressed. I'll have coffee and toast, if you don't mind?"

Fiona took forever in the shower, and I stayed in bed, going over the proposal. When I heard her turning off the water, I got into a bathrobe and went to the kitchen, started the coffee, and was sitting at the table when Fiona came in.

Always understated perfection, she wore a dark-gray wool skirt with a white blouse embroidered in cornflower blue under a blue blazer. "So what do you think?" she asked.

"You look great."

She waived that aside.

I took her toast out of the toaster and filled her cup. "Have you shown this to your lawyers?"

"No, I hate it when they smirk at me with their meters running." She sat down and nibbled the toast.

"Chip wants you to take a second mortgage. You know how seconds work?"

Fiona's eyes narrowed.

"Temper, temper. Of course, you do. At the bank, we talk ourselves through new deals to make sure that we're all on the same page. Why don't we?"

"Fine." Her smile was as dry as her toast.

"Okay, Chip and a group of investors own the property outright, and a small bank in Marin County is financing the condos he's building; however, two problems: the financial statements indicate that Chip is running out of money, and worse, the condos aren't completed. Chip's banker must be worried sleepless and doesn't want to lend another penny. So the banker and Chip need someone to come up with the money to finish the project, right?"

"And that's Aunt Fiona of the deep pockets. Chip calls me Auntie Fee."

"Don't know much about real estate lending," I said, "but I do know that a partially completed real estate project that's run out of money terrifies lenders. I suspect that Chip's banker hopes that Auntie Fee will take a second mortgage behind his first."

"Thereby putting the banker back into the driver's seat," Fiona said, rolling her eyes. "Then the banker could threaten Chip with bankruptcy, putting Auntie Fee behind the proverbial eight ball, forcing her to take him out."

For a second mortgage to become the first, the second pays the first mortgage and hopes to recoup his money—a difficult situation, since uncompleted building projects facing possible bankruptcy most often don't repay even the first mortgage.

"Backing into the numbers," I said, "it looks like Chip needs about a half million to complete the project, or does he want more?"

"A two-step proposal." Fiona pushed the toast aside. "Five hundred thousand dollars to complete the condos, with an additional two hundred thousand available should more be required—odds and ends, he calls it. The term is eighteen months that gives Chip time to complete and sell condos."

"Once Chip has you behind the eight ball, he'll keep you there."

Fiona tapped the coffee cup. "So?"

"You haven't told Chip to take a hike, so there must be other considerations?"

"That's right." Fiona went to the sink, tossed the toast into the garbage disposal, followed by the coffee, and looked out of the kitchen window.

"You're being forced into this?" I stood next to her and couldn't tell if she was frightened, angry, or both.

"That's right. Townie and his wife, Debra, know about us. So does Chip."

"My God, how did they find out?"

"We haven't been as clever as we've thought. Your confirmed bachelorhood has become shopworn,"

"You're sure they know?"

"Positive," Fiona said. "Before this, they kept their distance. I kind of liked Townie and put up with Debra."

"When did all this start?"

"The day after Fred Imhoff's service, Townie dropped by for cocktails. He got right to the point and told me that he knows about us and suggested that I sponsor Debra into the Opera Alliance. I thought that was all he wanted."

"But?"

"Townie was testing the waters. Early this week, Chip and Townie flew up to Tahoe with this deal and told me that they wanted it done before the end of the year. I more or less acquiesced, with the condition that Townie, Chip, and Debra must keep quiet about us, and—"

"Oh my God! Was Drew there?"

Fiona arched an eyebrow. "I met Townie and Chip at a restaurant at State Line, miles from the Tahoe house. Townie phoned last evening when you arrived to go over the final details and set up today's meeting. I hope this stupid deal ensures that Drew never learns about us. So, my dear, time to pay the proverbial piper?"

"Prolong the negotiations. Ask for Townie's personal guarantee, his company's guarantee. Ask...I can draw up a list of conditions that will slow the deal down and give us time to think."

"In the meantime, perhaps Drew will die, and this won't matter as much?" Fiona said.

"I didn't mean it that way."

"But I've thought about it that way," she said.

"I've always wondered what I—we, I mean—would do if Drew found out."

Fiona shook her head. "Good Lord, you were just a boy when you and I started. Maybe this shakedown is the price of our relationship or a down payment."

"Down payment? I've always thought our love is priceless."

"Priceless—that's one way to put it." Fiona backed away from me. "If I can keep it only to money, I'll be lucky."

"You regret our being together, for all these years?"

"Don't you?"

"I regret this, what Townie is doing. But not you and me."

Fiona looked at her hands. "What a foolish old woman I am."

"You're leaving me, aren't you?"

"I'm considerably older and certainly will at some point. What will you do then? I worry about that. Tatiana couldn't bear being alone; you can't either."

"This is only making matters worse," I said. "When's your meeting with Townie and Chip?"

"A tour of the project late this morning," she replied, looking at her watch. "After that I fly up to Tahoe."

"Do you want me to go with you? Or drive you to the airport?"

"No, I don't," Fiona said. "I want you to have nothing whatsoever to do with Townie and Chip."

"Shouldn't be too hard since I've never met Chip and have seen Townie only a few times."

Fiona frowned. "I'll take a cab to the airport."

"I must do something, something to help you and Drew."

"Oh, you will, you most certainly will. You and I are going to keep Drew to ourselves. I'm determined that he'll die without knowing about us. Imagine his chagrin: his mother taking away the love of his life."

"Do we have to go through all of that?"

"Let's be honest. I did take you away from Drew. That Drew and I are reconciling is quite amazing." Fiona paused, as if considering that. "It's not amazing; it's a testimony to my deceit—our deceit, I should say."

"Stop it. You didn't take me away from Drew. That was my decision; so was staying."

"And where would you have gone? If you had gone to New York, eventually Drew would have tired of you. All alone, you'd have fallen in love with the first man you met, then another, and another. You're far too delicate to have survived that." She turned away.

"Well, are you leaving for your meeting with Townie?" I asked, embarrassed.

"I don't know where you parked my car last night."

After dressing, I got Fiona's car that I had parked a block away after dropping her at my place. I put her bag in the trunk and opened the driver's door. With the door between us, Fiona said, "This interlude has ended much like it started, hasn't it?"

"I guess so."

Fiona sighed. "I'm so angry—furious—that Townie, that perfect swine, is doing this to me...when I'm so vulnerable, when Drew's so ill."

"Call me when you get to Tahoe. I'll do whatever you wish."

"Whatever happens, Alexander, I'm very proud of the way you've turned out," she said.

"You had everything to do with that." Fiona was getting into her car. "Fiona, please, don't leave me this way."

"Alexander, this so dismaying." I thought she was going to cry or fly into a rage. Instead, she said, "Kiss me good-bye."

With the car door between us, the perfunctory kiss was awkward. Watching Fiona drive away, I felt as if I had been dropped off for my first day of school. Then I felt a tap on the shoulder.

"You need a proper breakfast," Philippa said. "Came to return the keys you lent me," she added, jingling them. "Breakfast?"

"Sounds great," I said, and we started walking.

"My goodness, we're dressed almost alike," Philippa said. She wore a gray hacking jacket, jodhpur-cut cavalry-twill slacks, and a trench coat; I was in a gray tweed jacket, khakis, and a trench coat. "That attractive woman you just kissed was, I've deduced, Fiona Sinclair?"

"A correct deduction."

"Oh, I don't wish to meddle," Philippa said, taking my arm as we turned a corner. "My place is so terribly dreary, and I'm hoping that you might have some ideas to brighten it up."

"I'd love to."

"You're distracted?"

"Got a lot on my mind."

The whole dreadful mess was my fault: I came into Fiona's life with my mother, then I fell in love with Drew, only to take his mother after mine had killed herself. Without me, Fiona might have remarried an adult instead of spending the last twenty years looking over her shoulder while raising me. And then there was Drew; if not for me, Fiona might have allotted him some measure of affection and remedied their alienation. And during all that time, what had I done? Nothing, not a thing. Had I been forced to make my own decisions, I might have gone to art school and found a livelihood that suited me better than banking; or I might have become a failed artist. All conjecture, since I hadn't the courage to be alone.

Philippa and I were looking at the menu in the front window of a restaurant specializing in breakfast, and she said, "At home we call these big breakfasts fry-ups; they can include kidneys, kippers, and a splendid variety of bacon." She laughed. "You continental types don't go for big breakfasts, do you?"

"After eggs, meat, and potatoes in the morning, I want to go back to bed."

Philippa smiled. "You prefer croissants and milky coffee, like you had in France?"

"I should have stayed there."

"I've been thinking of home too." She grew reflective as we entered the crowded restaurant. "I'll be going home at some point, but not this way, not discarded."

We found an empty table next to the front window. The waiter came over with coffee and menus. Philippa ordered two eggs with ham and hash browns; I asked for a soft-boiled egg and toast. She continued, "There's nothing holding me here, and you're my only friend."

"I'm flattered."

"Something bothering you?"

"Fiona."

"I also deduced that might be the case."

"Fiona has a great deal of money. She also has a greedy family. It's a lousy situation. I've got this awful feeling that she's leaving me."

"That is serious," Philippa said. "I'm guessing, but you and Fiona have been involved for a long time, right?"

"Fiona and I became, well, 'involved' twenty years ago. We were alone in that dreary house of hers, both depressed after my mother's suicide."

"Suicide," Philippa blurted. She put her hand over her mouth, then lowered her voice. "How dreadful."

"Terrible times. My mother was ill. Actually, she was insane. Fiona tried caring for my mother. I was scared and ran off. The ensuing guilt was devastating."

"You ran away?" Philippa made a doubtful face. "You told me that your mother pushed you away."

"Once pushed, I ran."

Our breakfasts were served. I pushed mine aside after a few bites. Philippa made quick work of hers and asked, "You were about eighteen, starting university?"

I described being asked to leave Stanford and said, "About six months later, I apologized to my academic advisor and gave him a letter from a psychologist describing the progress I'd made since the suicide. I was readmitted." I handed the waiter a credit card.

Philippa asked, "So during university you were never far from Fiona?"

"I spent most weekends in San Francisco. Other than the National Guard, my time in Moscow was the longest Fiona and I have been apart."

She leaned forward. "I do know something about messy situations. Do you have friends to turn to in times like this?"

"Oh, I know lots of people. But friend friends, not really, other than Fiona. And you."

With an encouraging smile she said, "While this sounds terribly un-British, talking about it may help. It'll go no further."

"The problem is that I've become a parasite like Fiona's relatives; they're so venal, so awful. A distant cousin is forcing Fiona into a lousy real estate deal because he found out about us." I added the tip and signed the receipt.

"How perfectly dreadful," Philippa replied. "Let's walk up to the shops on Union Street for some window shopping that may inspire a few ideas for my flat." As we walked, she continued, "Look, I'm not one to eavesdrop, but when Fiona calls you at the office, she introduces herself as Mrs. Sinclair. So I assumed she was a family friend or a friend-friend, not a…" Philippa paused. "Looking back, I should have figured it out. You seem happy to take her calls and smile when you're talking. As far as her relatives, to hell with them, really."

"But you see, when I ran away, I ran to Drew."

"Drew, I hadn't thought of him."

I stopped walking. "Drew was attending art school in New York; I was supposed to join him. Instead I fell in love with Fiona. Picture explaining to Drew that I'd left him for his mother? We didn't speak until Drew invited me to a showing at his gallery a few years ago."

Philippa started and stopped. "Given Drew's illness, might it be reasonable to assume that he'll never know about you and Fiona?"

"So I'm waiting around for Drew to die so I can take over his business. Nice isn't it? This is so convoluted and money driven that it makes me sick. And Fiona is sick of it too. Long story short: Fiona and I betrayed Drew, and Drew still loves me."

"Drew can't determine whom his mother loves, or you either. You were much younger, but an adult nonetheless when you and Fiona fell in love."

"We were depressed."

"And turned to each other for comfort—mental, emotional, and physical," Philippa said. "The point is, you're not a homosexual; and, if Drew loved you for all these years, that's his doing, not yours, isn't it?"

"I loved going to his gallery showings and enjoyed them—perhaps too much."

"Of course, you did," she said. "You'd love that life. Look at your place, an elegant Parisian flat. I'm not saying that you're not suited for banking, but I do think you'd make a far better interior designer."

"Here I am thinking about myself when Fiona is getting blackmailed. If her family finds out, they'll demand even more from her. And her society friends, I don't know how they'll take it."

Philippa made a puzzled face. "As for her society friends, you and Fiona have stayed together while many of them may have been traipsing through the divorce courts. As for Fiona's family, she should tell them to buzz off. And bloody well *stay* buzzed off."

"They've got Fiona cornered."

"Because she's honorable and bound by familial obligations?"

"That's right, but there're other things that could be embarrassing. The difference in our ages."

"For what it's worth, I'm fifteen years younger than Andrew and didn't have a problem with that. You're what—about twenty years younger than Fiona?"

"It's different for males, the other way around."

Philippa shook her head. "My father was one of the best men God ever created, so it only stands to reason that I'd try to find an approximation. If it's something of the same with you and Fiona, so what?"

"And there's Fiona's money."

"And?" Philippa asked. "It looks to me like you support yourself?"

"I do, but Fiona financed the flats I own. To take over Drew's business, I'd need Fiona's cooperation to rewrite loans she made to Drew. So I'm pretty much like the rest of her family."

"The mortgage on your flats, it's at market rates?" Philippa asked. "And the loans for Drew's business would be a reasonable business deal, standard terms, conditions and all that bumpf?"

"That's right. But there are other considerations, too."

"Nevertheless, they're two business deals," Philippa said. "So what's wrong with that?"

"It's not that easy. Fiona paid for my college; it was expensive."

"People in love do things for each other, don't they?" she asked with bubbling exasperation.

"Maybe the past twenty years of dealing with me is catching up with Fiona."

"You're going through a rough time, that's all. Your mother and Fiona were close. If you don't mind, tell me why."

"They spoke French because Mother's English was so bad. Mother had this incredible imagination; she could take Fiona away from her family."

"You told me that you and your mother did that too."

"That's right. I hated it here; Mother was my escape, my refuge."

"Fiona wanted out and probably still does," Philippa said. "You and Fiona should go to France and get out of this meddling, middle-classed Yankee respectability. You're above that. After all, you're an aristocrat; so do what you please and to hell with the rest of them."

"That might have worked a hundred years ago in Russia."

"Here's what I think: your mother—I don't know her name."

"Tatiana."

"Of course, the princess in the fairy tale. Tatiana bound the three of you in her fantastic French-speaking world that ended with her suicide."

"And I was a mother's boy without a mother. So I found Fiona."

"Tatiana and you lived in a secluded world. The only person allowed in was Fiona, and I suspect that she was happy to be included. With Tatiana gone, that left you and Fiona. Sexual proclivities notwithstanding, Drew never had a chance." She shook my shoulders.

"Tatiana brought you and Fiona together. Why not accept that?" Stepping back, she said, "Some of the advice you gave me: stop calling yourself names." She then took my arm. "Come on."

We walked up the hill in silence. I glanced back at the Bay; dark clouds had turned it pelican gray. "Maybe it's my mood," I said, "but all hell's about to break loose at the bank, I can feel it."

"So do I," Philippa said and looked at her watch. "Somewhat early, but we must brace ourselves for whatever's coming. A bottle of champagne might put all of this in better perspective."

"I love champagne."

CHAPTER 17

CHRISTMAS EVE 1986

SAN FRANCISCO

All hell did break loose, but the timing was a surprise. I had returned from errands midmorning and found a message on my answering machine from Adam Demowski, Universal's Senior Vice President–Human Resources, setting an appointment for 3:30 that afternoon and requesting that I confirm with his secretary.

I recognized Demowski's name from the bank's organization charts, but knew nothing about him. However, for a man on my level, meeting with the executive in charge of Personnel meant one of two things: a phenomenal promotion or termination. Having no doubt it was the latter, I changed into my favorite navy-blue suit. My shoes were shined, the fresh shirt was snowy white, and the dark-maroon tie was held in place with a collar pin. I buttoned my vest, put on my jacket, grabbed my trench coat, and headed out to find a cab.

I calmed down enough to realize that, if nothing else, I had to keep my wits and couldn't allow myself to be stampeded. A simple tactic that I hoped would maintain my dignity and stand up to the forthcoming reality.

Five minutes before our appointment, I walked into Demowski's office on the twelfth floor. His assistant directed me to a conference room down the hall. The room was functional: straight-backed chairs around an oval table, overhead florescent lighting, and windows looking into a building across the street. Right on time, Demowski entered. In his early sixties, he was a regal man with blondish hair going gray, deep-set blue eyes, and translucent skin. After a perfunctory handshake, we sat down facing each other across the table.

"Romanovsky, interesting name; sounds Polish," Demowski said.

"Maybe it was a long time ago. Real Russian names, they say, end with *n*'s or *v*'s."

"Where was your family from?"

"My father's family came from Pskov, near the Baltic."

"That's old Russia, isn't it?"

"Real Russia, my father used to say." Detecting a faint accent, I asked, "Where are you from?"

"Oh, the same part of the world. I grew up in Warsaw." He attempted to smile. "Poles and Russians have never gotten along, have they?"

"From the history I've read, Russia has always been an aggressive neighbor."

"So are the Germans. Unfortunately, God placed Poland between them. Obviously, we're not here to discuss that." He managed a wintery smile.

"Obviously," I replied. "This must be important, given the short notice on Christmas Eve."

Folding his hands on my personnel file, he said, "An embarrassing issue has arisen requiring an immediate resolution, regardless of seasonal festivities."

"What in the world are you talking about?"

Demowski took a report from my file. "Your time in Moscow has come to my attention. This bank cannot, and will not, be associated with any improprieties in a country as sensitive as the Soviet Union; you were explicitly told that before you took the assignment." He paused. "I've had your expense reports audited."

"Why?"

"Your expense reports have linked you to black marketeering."

"Really? I explained virtually every penny—kopeck—that I attempted to expense."

He studied one of my expense reports. "You went to London on business and returned with typical black-market frippery: American cigarettes, Scotch whiskey, and lingerie for a fellow at the Foreign Trade Bank—what's his name?"

"Boris Izmailov. He asked me to buy that stuff. It wasn't lingerie; it was a couple of dozen pantyhose for his wife. And I detailed the gifts on the expense report you're holding and noted that Izmailov helped me staff our office. When I arrived, all but one of the Russian staff had quit, remember? The gifts were a thank-you to repay a big favor." Demowski blinked at me. "And what are we talking about, a couple of hundred dollars? Oh, that expense report was rejected, in total, and I ended up paying for everything."

"You can prove that Izmailov didn't pay you rubles for that merchandise?"

"Boris offered me rubles, but I refused. Why don't you confirm that with him?"

"Boris Izmailov? The same man who assisted blackmailing you during your first assignment to the Soviet Union?" Demowski arched an eyebrow. "I'm afraid that man has no credibility, none whatsoever. Back to my original question, can you prove you weren't paid rubles?"

"Of course not. You know I can't. I mean, if I were paid, it would've been cash. I'm an officer of this bank with a sizeable lending limit; my word must mean something."

"Since you can't prove that Izmailov did not pay you rubles, the transaction could be construed as black-market and a flagrant violation of Soviet foreign exchange regulations, correct?"

"Everyone in Russia brings those things back from the West."

"And doing so flaunts not only the Soviet law's spirit but its letter as well."

"You can't be serious."

"Serious?" Demowski replied. "Be assured I'm most serious. Now tell me: what is your relationship with Fiona Sinclair?"

"Fiona?" I stammered. "That's none of your business."

"I'm afraid it is." He leafed through my file. "Fiona Sinclair does a great deal of business with this bank, doesn't she?"

"I suspect she does. I don't know the details."

"Is that right?" Demowski said with a doubtful scowl. "As you know, Mrs. Sinclair was instrumental in getting your first job with us. So Mrs. Sinclair must be a close friend?"

"She is."

He went back to my file. "Born in Paris, White Russian émigré parents, and a naturalized American citizen. Your father was a mathematician, a rather famous one in those rarefied circles. Russians have a talent for mathematics, don't they?"

"They seem to," I said. "So you've done a complete background check on me? When?"

"We're entitled to run such checks," he said. "And how did you come to know Fiona Sinclair?"

"My mother and Fiona were close friends."

"I see," Demowski said, turning the pages of my personnel file. "There's a note here that your mother, ah, she..."

"What does my mother have to do with this?"

"Nothing, nothing at all." Demowski was going through my file. "Ah, a memo you wrote over a year ago detailed a problem with the Soviet authorities, more precisely, a high-ranking policeman. Your uncle and grandfather, according to this memo, were Nazi collaborators." He looked up with wide eyes.

"What is in that file about my mother?"

He shrugged.

"I want to know what that says."

"Nothing germane to this conversation," he said, placing my memo in front of him. "Back to your grandfather and uncle?"

I focused on his question. "I didn't say they were Nazi collaborators. I said they worked for the Germans; there's a considerable difference."

"You don't say?" Demowski tilted his head back. "I don't see it that way. Anyone who lived under German occupation doesn't either. By definition, a citizen of an occupied country working for the Germans was a collaborator. Even though I've had firsthand experience with the Nazis, perhaps I've missed something?"

"My relatives were czarist Russian citizens, not Soviet citizens. Communists, as you must know, had been killing people like my relatives since the Revolution. So I see those family members as anti-Communist, not anti-Russian. That's the difference."

"And that sounds like a meticulous rationalization."

"You brought me here to talk about my relatives?" I asked.

"No, I thought it peculiar that any person would make such an admission."

"Wait a minute, when I wrote that memo, I was following bank policy to its letter and spirit. I was the target of an attempted blackmail, and you—of all people—must know that it's bank policy to report such incidents in detail."

"Indeed I do, but still…" He pursed his lips in disgust. "I don't imagine your parents shared that information with US Immigration?"

"You'll have to ask them."

"They died before you joined the bank."

"You brought up my mother. Why?"

Drumming his fingers on the table, Demowski said, "If it were up to me, I would terminate you outright. But there's Fiona Sinclair to consider. How would she react to a press release saying that you've been placed on indefinite leave while the bank, suspecting that you violated Soviet foreign exchange regulations, conducts a full audit of your dealings in Moscow?"

"Fiona would believe me."

"Nevertheless, such publicity would render you unemployable."

"Sure, after the bank called me a scam artist."

Demowski settled back in his chair. "But in deference to Fiona Sinclair, we have come up with an amicable resolution: you'll resign today, salary and benefits for six months. That's the best we can do under these circumstances."

I took out a cigarette and tapped it down on the table. I ignored the No Smoking sign that Demowski pointed to. He got up and found a saucer in a side cabinet that he placed in front of me. I knew that most negotiations have fallback positions and hoped that Demowski's did. Grinding the cigarette out in the saucer, I looked him in the eyes. "No dice."

"You must be joking." Demowski pushed his chair back. "Perhaps you need time to think this over." He stood up. "I'll leave while you reconsider."

"No, we're going to finish this right now. That file of mine is full of excellent performance reports. I've worked here for fifteen years and want one month per year."

"Twelve months, no more."

"Done," I said.

Demowski sat down and handed me a folder containing a one-sentence letter. "You'll sign this letter of resignation." I signed four copies and kept one. "The termination agreement has to be amended to one year." He picked up the phone to call his secretary. When he finished, he continued, "You'll hand over the keys to your office and desk; your personal possessions will be boxed and sent to your home. When we've finished, my assistant will escort you from the building. No scenes, none of that."

I pushed the keys across the table.

Demowski seemed relieved. "I'm still curious: Your relatives, to put it your way, working with the Germans—doesn't that bother you?"

"It does. They led awful lives; I pity them. I'm curious too. You made an implied threat: if I didn't cooperate, you'd inform the US Immigration and Naturalization Services that two of my relatives were, to put it your way, Nazi collaborators. My naturalization forms could be checked for false or misleading statements that I might have made, right?" Demowski folded his hands. "While we're at it, my mother's suicide troubles me far more than my relatives do."

He peered out the window until his assistant came in with the termination agreement. She stood behind Demowski's chair as I read the agreement: the bank would limit its comments to the dates of my employment and state that I had resigned for personal reasons. I was obligated to notify Demowski if I became employed during the term of the agreement; if so, my salary and benefits would end upon the date of my new employment. I kept one of the four copies that Demowski and I signed.

We stood up, and Demowski started to extend his right hand but dropped it to his side. "Well, good luck wherever you land."

"I'm still curious, Mr. Demowski. How do you feel about this, this hatchet job of yours? Exhuming my relatives and trumping up these charges for Andrew Neville's retribution." Demowski turned his back to me. "Cat got your tongue?" He went to the window.

His assistant took my elbow.

I brushed her hand away. "Oh, I've got it: you're just obeying orders from above, a mere cog in the machinery?" That was the standard German excuse for atrocities during World War II. Aimed at a Pole who had endured the German occupation, it was the meanest thing I could think of.

Demowski spun around. "I don't have to take that, not from you."

"But, Mr. Demowski, it fits. Something to reflect upon during Christmas Mass?" I thought he might hit me and hoped he would.

His assistant grabbed my elbow and led me out of the room. We stepped into an elevator with several people, including the man from the European Division in charge of Spain and Portugal. We had been friendly, but he avoided my eyes and left as soon as the door opened. It seemed obvious that my termination had been announced. In the entrance lobby, the assistant motioned me to the revolving doors onto the plaza. Outside, I turned back and saw her pointing me out to the security guards.

***

The wind had picked up. Rain clouds were coming in from the north, and cabs would be scarce. I put on my trench coat and walked down California Street to a large hotel's cabstand with one cab and a sleeping driver. Across Market Street, I saw a promising bar with the drink I needed.

The restaurant catered to the lunch crowd; its hardwood and brass bar looked onto the street. Except for the bartender huddling with a couple at the end of the bar, the place was empty. The woman was telling an elaborate joke about a Spanish matador who got lost in San Francisco and wandered into a gay bar. The music, something by Stravinsky, was cheerful—like children waiting for Christmas Day. I didn't care for Stravinsky but remembered that Helen Jacobs did. She seemed like a long time ago.

The bartender interrupted the joke and approached. The Stravinsky was from his ballet about a puppet that came to life only to be betrayed. *"Petrushka?"* I said, pointing to the sound system behind the bar.

"Never heard of that one," the bartender said. "We've got Stoly, a couple from Poland I can't pronounce, and domestic vodka."

I asked for Scotch. The music turned ominous. "Odd music for Christmas Eve, isn't it?"

"I'll put on the Crosby tape."

Bing began singing "Christmas in Killarney." Stravinsky to Crosby; Russia to Ireland; the slanting rain against the windows; the bartender and the couple laughing at the matador joke—it was agreeably surreal. Other than the Christmas Eve party with my downstairs neighbors, I had no plans for the rest of the day or the holiday itself. The bar Scotch tasted medicinal.

Fifteen years at Universal Bank had been wasted for the most part, and I was left with a collection of gray and navy-blue suits. People I knew at the bank would avoid me like the man in the elevator; that's the way it went when big banks got rid of people. So many things to think about, so much time.

I lit the last cigarette in my pack and considered upgrading the Scotch and drinking until I fell off the barstool. Putting that thought on hold, Philippa came to mind. She was all alone; maybe I was too. Fiona might have left me. Then there was Drew. He would be happy that I had to take his offer; the problems started wrapping themselves around each other. Without Fiona's assistance, I couldn't take Drew's business; then I'd be unemployed and alone. I downed the Scotch.

I watched the rain while Bing sang about Christmas in Hawaii. When the couple left, the bartender pointed to my glass. I asked for a neat Johnny Black. Pouring the drink, the bartender started on the matador joke, but I told him that I had just been fired. The bartender poured more Scotch and said, "On Christmas Eve? Pal, you're drinking on the house."

The Black Label tasted better, but I was out of cigarettes. A cost-benefit dilemma: buy an expensive pack at the bar or wait until I got home where I had a carton. Besides, there was plenty of Scotch at home, and falling off the barstool was less appealing than falling into bed. I downed the drink in two gulps, bought a pack of cigarettes, and tipped the bartender. Bing was singing "O Come, All Ye Faithful" in Latin when I left.

CHAPTER 18

CHRISTMAS EVE 1986

SAN FRANCISCO

My downstairs neighbors, Bert and Sally Roth, had their traditional Christmas Eve open-house they called "Too Late Now." Most of their friends lived in Marin County, and stopping by the Marina for a quick drink was convenient. The parties had become more elaborate: instead of a glass of wine and a handful of nuts, the Roths were having the parties catered.

Their front door was opened. Philippa was standing inside talking to a man and a woman. All three had British accents. I tapped Philippa's shoulder.

"Oh, thank God, there you are," she said. "I came looking for you, and Sally Roth invited me in. How are you doing?"

"Not so hot." I waved to Sally across the packed room. Philippa introduced me to the British couple; the man worked for the same ad agency as Bert Roth and had been transferred from the London office.

We chatted until Philippa led me to the foyer outside the front door and said, "I thought this might be coming, but honestly, Christmas Eve? There was an announcement this afternoon that you had resigned. No reason, no details. This is my fault. I didn't expect such calculated cruelty from Andrew."

"I didn't either, but I was fooling myself. But let's talk about this later. What are your plans for Christmas?"

"That nice couple I introduced you to invited me over for Christmas dinner. There will be a mob of us, all Brits away from home—should be a jolly old time."

"Gosh, I was thinking…"

Helen Jacobs dashed in from the rain, carrying a gift-wrapped package.

"Hi," I said. "You know the Roths?"

"No, I wanted to drop off this present."

I introduced Helen to Philippa.

She said, "We've spoken on the telephone."

"We have," Helen said, stepping towards me. "You look like those people on the side of a road after bad car wrecks. Maybe you should sit down?"

"Had a terrible afternoon, but I'm okay. Please stay, I've got to talk to you. Oh, I heard some Stravinsky a while ago and thought of you."

"I'm flattered, I think."

Sally Roth tapped my shoulder. I introduced Helen to Sally, who insisted she have a drink. I saw a waiter working through the crowd with a tray of wine and edged toward him. When I returned, Sally had left and Helen and Philippa were talking; Philippa excused herself and returned to her British friends. I gave Helen a glass of wine.

Helen said, "Philippa told me you were fired this afternoon."

"It's a long story."

"From what Philippa said, it's very short."

"Short and brutal," I said. "Look, I've got to explain myself and that night in your car. I was way, way out of line. I was angry and frightened about several things, but that doesn't excuse my behavior."

"Thank you. I appreciate that," Helen said.

I had left my raincoat in the foyer, and Helen was still wearing hers with the present under her arm and a glass of wine in her hand. I said, "The catering is excellent." A tray went by, and I handed her a stick of chicken saté. "Last year, they had small lamb chops, medium rare, fantastic. Keep an eye out for those."

Helen started on the saté and pointed. "Lamb chops behind you." I took two. After we ate them, Helen handed me the present. "I bought it the weekend after Denver from a charming Russian lady at a small shop on Clement Street. She wrote the card in Russian. Please read it."

I read it aloud in Russian, then translated: *Sasha, Have a wonderful Christmas and accept my wishes for a Happy New Year, Helen.* "When I was a boy, I was called Sasha; it's the diminutive of Alexander; later, I became Sandro. Helen is Elena in Russian. Shortened, it's Lena."

"Elena. That's pretty," Helen said. "Given your situation, wishing you a merry Christmas might be inappropriate?"

"Not at all, your present is a wonderful counterpoint to an awful day. Going to eat and run?"

"Oh, I have another party to go to," she said without much enthusiasm. "But not before making my apology."

"The present is more than enough."

"I thought you'd be out teasing someone, leading them on. After all, people are more vulnerable around the holidays."

"I give it a break around Christmas. What with all the shopping and parties, I can't concentrate."

"That's encouraging," Helen said. I helped with her raincoat and unwrapped the present, a Russian lacquered box about the size of a paperback book. The tops are often painted with scenes from Russian folklore and history.

"Beautiful," I said. "Alexander Nevsky and the Battle of the Ice, in the thirteenth century, I think. The Russians won that one. Nevsky's on the big white horse; the men with the black crosses on their tunics are Teutonic Knights—Prussians. They fell through the ice on Lake Peipus, near Pskov where my father's family came from."

"I thought of an icon, but they looked cheap and mass produced. The Russian lady told me about the *krasny ugol.* You know about those?"

"*Krasny ugol* means "beautiful corner," where the icons are kept in a home."

"After that night in my car, I wanted to return the box, but the Russian lady had been so sweet that I couldn't. Then I thought the present might facilitate what I must say. First, I'm ashamed that I got you to open up about your mother's death when you were trying to be helpful. I thought, consciously thought, that you were one of the few reasonable men I've met since my divorce. But there was a problem: I don't deserve to be happy." Helen tapped her head. "Up here I know that's wrong. Emotionally that's another matter. Lastly, my psychologist and I decided that I had to apologize to you in person."

"Like you, I'm often too hard on myself."

"Okay, both of our apologies accepted." Helen looked at her watch. "I should get going. You must have things to do this evening: hanging stockings, mistletoe and eggnog."

"Other than drinking too much, no plans," I said. "Why not come up to my place for another glass of wine?" Her smile was an agreement of sorts. "Better yet, dinner. I made boeuf bourguignon this morning; it's upstairs mellowing. What do you say?"

"Then I should phone to let him know I won't be coming."

Upstairs at my flat, Helen asked for a bourbon and ice and looked around. "What, no Christmas tree?"

"Very few people in France had them when I was a boy. Here, my parents didn't bother, and I never got around to buying all the tree stuff." Pointing to the phone, I said, "I'll be in the kitchen."

Helen's call took about five minutes. She came into the kitchen. "Well, that's that. Dave, a lawyer at my bank, was hosting the party. We've gone out; it's always the same. We tell each other how miserable we are since our divorces. Dave and I have to get our respective acts together, and we've got to do so separately." Helen shrugged. "Do you mind telling me about your firing?"

"The real story is Andrew Neville had me fired for helping Philippa. The official story was concocted about my black marketeering when I brought back gifts from London for a Russian banker who had helped staff the Moscow office. It's impossible to prove that the Russian didn't pay me in rubles. Details?"

"No. I've met Demowski and thought he was a class act; surprised he'd do something like that." She sipped the bourbon. "I've heard that most of the senior and executive vice presidents at Universal have chosen sides between Neville and the other contender."

"My boss put his chips on Neville and washed his hands of me. I liked him, it's disappointing."

"What'll happen to the executives who've bet their careers on the wrong man?"

"I suppose they'll get canned or transferred to Bakersfield."

"Neville will do anything to get what he wants," Helen said. "Which brings us to Philippa?"

"Neville wants her to go back to England. Maybe that's not such a bad idea."

There was a knock at the door. "Speaking of the devil?" Helen asked.

I opened the door. Philippa was weaving a bit and said, "My goodness, I was talking to Sally Roth and noticed that the room had slipped its moorings. I've really been swilling down the wine and need to talk to you while I still can." She came in and saw Helen. "I'm interrupting, sorry." Philippa turned to leave.

Helen said, "No, come in. We were talking about Alexander's firing."

Philippa came in and sat on the end of the sofa opposite Helen at other end. Speaking to Helen, she said, "I don't know how much you know about all of this. I mean Alexander getting sacked—fired. This is all about Andrew Neville and me. Andrew paid for my old flat and then threw me out. Alexander lent me money for the movers and my new flat. And he stopped me from diving into a gin bottle."

"What are you going to do?" Helen asked.

"I don't know. I'm rather frightened."

"Do not, under any circumstances, allow Andrew Neville to intimidate you," Helen said. "Firing Alexander was telling you that he'll make it unbearable for you, as he wishes, when he wishes. He wants you to go home; are you?"

"Not now, but later." Philippa's voice caught. "It's all quite muddled."

"That's because you're too frightened to think clearly. So get out of the bank as soon as you can."

"Easy for you to say," Philippa said.

"You don't know me," Helen said, leaning to take Philippa's hand. "But I can assure you that I know about fleeing an unbearable situation."

"I haven't the money to walk out."

"I'm sure you're a good executive secretary," Helen said. "See me after the first of the year, and I'll get you something at my bank. Maybe a temp spot, but something. That's a promise. Money won't be great, but your self-respect means more."

Philippa agreed with a nod. Helen finished her bourbon. Philippa took Helen's glass, went to the liquor cabinet, and asked, "You're doing this because of Alexander?"

"Not the case," Helen said. "Neville's bending you to his will. When you go home, do it on your terms." Philippa gave Helen a fresh drink and burst into tears. Helen motioned for me to leave.

I went to the kitchen and stirred the beef, added wine, and chopped the parsley. Looking outside, it was darker than a commissar's heart, as my mother used to say. About a half hour later, Helen called me. She and Philippa were sitting on the sofa.

Philippa said, "Sorry, I'm not the crying type, but lately..."

"I think Philippa should spend the night in your guest room," Helen said.

"My new place is dismal, a nun's cell," Philippa added.

"That's fine. Sleep in one of my shirts," I said. "The day after Christmas, I'm going up to Lake Tahoe to be with Drew. So why don't you stay here while I'm up there? I'll tell Sally Roth and have her leave a set of keys for you."

"That's wonderful," Philippa gushed. "And how is Drew doing?"

"Not so well." I turned to Helen. "An old friend, Drew Faircloth, has AIDS and is staying at the family summer home at Lake Tahoe." To Philippa, I added, "You should eat."

"Feasted unwisely." She stood up. "And I'm too tipsy to be good company. Thank you both."

Helen stood up. "Come on, Philippa, we'll get you squared away."

CHAPTER 19

CHRISTMAS EVE 1986

SAN FRANCISCO

Helen returned to the kitchen and said, "Philippa needed a woman-to-woman talk, even if the other woman was a relative stranger. You know, all feelings, emotions, uncomfortable things for men." I started to speak; she put up her hands. "Come on, guys have a hard time dealing with crying women."

"Is she going to be okay?"

"I hope so. I told her what happened to me: crying jags, anger, depression. Little by little, it gets resolved, one way or the other."

"Oh?"

She blushed. "I told Philippa that since I couldn't come to terms with my divorce, a judge forced me to. When I learned that Ed, my ex, and his new girlfriend were seen rollerblading in Golden Gate Park around the Japanese tea garden, I went out there and waited. They pirouetted by in matching polyurethane shorts, tank tops, and crash helmets. Ed wouldn't have been caught dead looking like that when we were married. I lost it and grabbed a rock and caught Ed in the back of his head just below the helmet. Six stitches."

"Really?"

"Yup," she said. "Ed's girlfriend in hysterics, cops, sirens, ambulance, flashing lights. Thank God, Ed didn't press charges, but he did get a restraining order. Talk about embarrassing: going to court, the judge lecturing me about self-control. But, in retrospect, it was for the best; I gave up and went to a psychologist." She asked, "Is your father still alive?"

"No, he died before my mother."

"Sorry, sorry." She looked around the living room. "This place belongs in Paris." Pointing to the kitchen, she said, "Smells French and probably will taste that way. Ever go back?"

"After a business trip, I went back to our old neighborhood. Some minor changes: the butcher's son took over from his father; the baker's widow and her son ran the bakery. The French don't move around much."

"Did they remember you and your parents?"

"We were the Russians who went to America—California, no less."

"Did you miss France? Did your parents?"

"I had a terrible time adjusting here. My parents spent their lives on the periphery as émigrés and were used to it. My father spoke good English, but my mother's English was terrible and limited her friendships to French and Russian speakers. I, on the other hand, was desperate to fit in."

Helen cocked her head. "Do you feel at home now?"

"I do. My English doesn't have an accent; my mannerisms and most attitudes have become Americanized. And I dress like an American banker."

"Dressing like a banker is superficial," she said, missing my attempted humor. "What I meant is that seeing this place and knowing you briefly, I think your interests are elsewhere. You don't belong in a bank any more than I do."

I checked my watch. "A couple of hours ago, I was thrown out of one of the world's largest."

Helen went over to my family photos and picked one up of me and a group of men in uniform standing in front of a howitzer. "You were in the army?"

"National Guard, an artillery unit. If the Oregon Guard had invaded, we'd have blown them to pieces before they got to Chico." I was trying too hard.

Helen laughed a little before putting the picture back and glancing at the others. "Philippa told me that you might take over Drew Faircloth's business. Compelling, given today's events? Do you mind telling me about it?"

Helen followed me back to the kitchen as I explained Drew's business and our plans to change its direction. Finishing, I said, "I've had a sit-down with the accountant; the numbers look okay, and I'm pretty sure I could make a go of it. And you're right; hopefully I'm more suited for that life. I better be."

"Trying to sound enthused?"

"I'll be enthused once I get into it."

"I'm sure you will," Helen said with smile. "Hate to admit it, but I read the society section of the paper first. Drew Faircloth was quite the man about town: scion to the Sinclair fortune, fashionable art dealer, and one of the most prominent gay men in San Francisco. You're going up to Tahoe to be with him. So you and Drew are close?"

"We were very close, but that was a very long time ago."

"Did you love Drew a very long time ago? Still do?"

"After my mother died, I fell in love with Drew. Then he went to art school in New York, and I stayed here. And well, one evening, my sexual compass got reset. I treated him badly when I ended the relationship."

"Oh dear, pretty sensitive stuff."

"Look," I said, "when I was telling you about leading people on, I was thinking about Drew. We get along now. I envied the life he led and loved going to his gallery receptions. Then when I got back from Moscow, Drew told me he was dying and offered me his business. In your car, I convinced myself that I had been leading him on."

Helen looked out the kitchen window.

"Too much sharing?"

"No, thinking of how you described yourself in my car: using people and all of that. You could have made short work of Philippa, but you haven't." With a cautious smile, she asked, "Why does Drew want to give you his business?"

"He thinks I'd enjoy it."

Helen was quiet for a moment. "If someone had teased me, or

treated me badly, I'd be inclined to get even instead of giving them my life's work. For a gift of that magnitude, I'd have to love that person. Same for Drew?"

"Yes, but it's lopsided."

"It seems to me that love is measured out so that only the most fortunate receive to the extent that they give." Helen paused. "Philippa intuitively came to you for help. Why?"

"Frankly, she's got nowhere else to go."

"Lucky for her," she said. "Philippa told me about your working arrangement."

"There was some underlying tension, but it wasn't that bad."

"Call it what you will," Helen said, "but for years, Philippa held all the cards, yet you didn't hesitate to lend her money and look after her. Not to flatter myself, but in Denver, I had you pegged as a decent guy. I'm glad I came over here and tested my initial assumption." She gave me a spectacular smile.

During dinner, we stumbled into politics. Philosophically we had little in common; and since we didn't know the level of each other's convictions, continuing was risky. Helen changed the subject. "With the coming mergers, Growers and Ranchers won't survive. A money-center bank will buy it, and staff positions like mine will go first. Maybe that will be for the best. I should have gone with my heart years ago."

"Acting in New York?"

"Right," she said. "Now that part of my life is limited to the opera and volunteer work I do for the Opera Alliance." Dinner was finished, and Helen refilled her glass with Burgundy and lit one of my cigarettes. "Speaking of opera, you must know Drew Faircloth's mother, Fiona Sinclair?"

"Fiona and my mother were close."

"Your mother was in Fiona Sinclair's crowd?"

"No, not at all. My mother hated opera and barely spoke English, but Fiona speaks French. I don't think a day went by when they didn't phone or see each other. Fiona was kind to my mother and me after my father died. I escort Fiona to the opera to repay her."

"I heard some resignation in your voice; you don't care for opera?"

"I've really tried. I kind of like Rossini but can't stand Wagner. Years ago, I went to an Opera Alliance presentation on Wagnerian opera; it didn't help."

"Wagner is so German." Helen made a sour face. "A few years ago, Fiona Sinclair hosted a lovely supper at her home for Opera Alliance volunteers, followed by a discussion of baroque opera. Not your cup of cappuccino, is it?" We laughed. "She comes across as…oh, what's the word I'm looking for?"

"*Haughty* might be one of them," I said. "*Guarded* is another. It's her family; they're awful. As a result, Fiona is standoffish until she gets people figured out."

"She trusted your mother?"

"More than anyone. Mother didn't want anything from Fiona."

Helen finished her cigarette and got up to clear the table.

"Plenty of time for that," I said. "Do you do anything for Christmas?"

"These days everyone dumps on Christmas, but I've always liked it." She sat down. "When my father was alive, we had Christmas: exchanged presents, ate roast beef—all of that. Daddy said it was a public holiday, and we weren't going exclude ourselves. After he died, our Christmases stopped, and my mother and her sister started taking cruises. What do you usually do?"

"Oh, it's been Christmas dinner at Fiona's since I was a boy, but this year she's looking after Drew. You were close to your father?"

"Yes," she said with a sad smile. "Daddy was a lawyer, a big firm downtown. He was a better father than a husband. Daddy was curious and engaging; Mom was cornered and distrusted Gentiles. Sometimes when we were out, Mom would look around and tell me that we were the only Jews there."

"Does that bother you?"

"Oh, not really. Of course, there were annoying things: the names kids called each other, later college sororities. When I make someone mad, I'm a Jewish bitch instead of just a bitch. Once I asked Daddy how to tell if people were anti-Semitic; he told me that's a sense I'd develop." She misted up. "Daddy and I, we were explorers."

She leaned back in her chair. "We went to a rodeo at the Cow Palace, one of strangest things I've ever seen. We drove up Napa to learn about wine making. Best of all, he introduced me to the opera." She stood up. "Holidays and the memories do come flooding back."

We cleared the table and loaded the dishwasher. We were sitting on opposite ends of the sofa. She asked, "Why did you go into banking?"

"I wanted to learn how money worked. And I've learned that lending money is fifty percent analyzing financial statements; the rest is common sense. Banking was a mistake, but a comfortable one."

She closed her eyes. "My God, so simple, so complicated. I should have listened more to myself and made the hard decisions about career and marriage." She sighed. "If I don't stop, I'm going to start feeling sorry for myself."

The conversation got going like the evening we spent in Denver. Subjects folded into one another with effortless associations. We were talking about the theater, and Helen thought I might have a unique take on Chekhov; but the only insights I had were from a Russian literature course I took in college. We moved on. She asked about learning English.

"Compared to Russian, English is very streamlined," I said. "People learning Russian always screw up the cases, the declensions. English doesn't bother with that, or gender; and it uses possessives unlike Russian and French. English pronunciation is fairly easy except for the exploding *th* sound, which, I think, is unique to English. If I'm tired or have been drinking too much, *th*'s start sounding like *z*'s and *that* becomes *zat*."

"Your English had a French or a Russian accent?"

"We had Russian accents."

The conversation got around to movies; we both thought French movies were the best, those of François Truffaut the very best. I knew it was getting late; Helen checked her watch and said, "Four thirty, how did that happen?" She stood up and stretched. "This was fun. I don't feel tired but must be."

Walking Helen to her car, I said, "Thanks for staying. Without you, my thoughts would have sloshed into darker territory—not good on Christmas Eve."

"My pleasure," Helen said. "Look, if you're not doing anything, later on today, people in my building are having an open house and supper party. My place at six, jacket and tie; what do you say?"

"I'd love to."

She unlocked the car door and stood to one side. Shaking hands would have been awkward; kissing more so. The polite hug was brief. We waved good-bye.

Philippa was waiting for me. "I was up and heard you and Helen talking. Nice woman, isn't she?"

"We spent the evening talking, that's all."

"It's none of my business. Would you mind walking me home?"

Dejected and hung over, Philippa walked with her hands in her coat pockets. I put my arm around her shoulders; she put her arm around my waist.

CHAPTER 20

THURSDAY, CHRISTMAS DAY 1986

SAN FRANCISCO

I got out of bed Christmas afternoon and played the two messages on the answering machine. Fiona had called from Tahoe to wish me a merry Christmas and to tell me that she was leaving for Los Angeles after an early supper with Drew. She sounded okay but didn't say when she would return to San Francisco. Drew had called later to say that he was looking forward to my visit and asked for my travel plans.

I phoned and told Drew I would leave the next morning and expected to arrive that afternoon. Drew was jovial and said that he was enjoying his time with Fiona. When Drew asked about my plans for the rest of the day, I told him that banking friends had invited me to a dinner party. We wished each other a merry Christmas.

I dressed in a blue blazer, gray slacks, and a green-and-red tie. When I arrived at Helen's, the doorman pointed to the elevators and said that she lived in 5-B and was expecting me. Helen was wearing a long emerald skirt and a crimson-red silk blouse, with her hair loosely tied at the back.

After a polite hug, she put my coat in the hall closet. "More minimalist than your place," she said, pointing at the uninteresting modern furniture. Framed opera posters, some quite old, brightened her living room. "With your new business, maybe I could ask for some help. Drink? Glass of wine?"

I followed Helen to the well-used kitchen.

"About tonight…" Helen handed me a wine bottle and corkscrew. "Sy and Greta Frank are hosting the party; they're up on ten. Greta is one of the kindest women I've known, she's a mother-earth type. And Sy, well, he's an architect and a little flamboyant with more than a few pretensions—overbearing actually. I think you'll enjoy most of their friends; but there's this fellow, Julian, from Sy's firm. I'm pretty sure he'll be there. Last week Sy and Greta had me over for dinner. Kind of a blind date with Julian. He's…well, you'll see."

I had pulled the cork and poured the wine, a fresh California chardonnay. "Maybe you should be going with Julian?"

"If you hadn't agreed to come, I wouldn't have gone because of Julian." She didn't elaborate.

We went to the picture window looking south over San Francisco. Low clouds had gathered behind Twin Peaks and were billowing down onto the City.

"San Francisco never fails: always dramatic…and just a little temperamental," she said with a wonderful smile. "When it's foggy or raining, this place gets dark; but the view more than offsets the gloom." We finished our wine. "Well, off we go."

Greta, a large woman in her early sixties bejeweled in silver and turquoise, rushed to hug Helen when we came in. Greta called for Sy, who looked like a taller, more intense Leonard Bernstein. Sy hugged Helen. Julian arrived, hugged Helen, and put his hands on her shoulders. Helen introduced me to Julian, who replied with a sparkle of flawless teeth and continued staring into Helen's eyes.

Julian was a cute guy dressed in a flared tweed jacket with suede elbow patches, stonewashed jeans, and expensive Italian loafers. An ottoman silk tie was loosely knotted beneath the unbuttoned collar of his tapered shirt. About six feet, slim and coltish, Julian tossed back his thick chestnut hair so that it cascaded over his large brown eyes.

I made small talk with Greta and Sy until they greeted more guests. The living room was carpeted with tasteful orientals, the furniture was eclectic but held together, and the expensive art was showy. Julian's hands were still on Helen's shoulders when I joined the gathering.

Helen stepped away from Julian and asked me for a bourbon; Julian opted for Perrier.

I returned with Helen's drink and mine, and we formed a rough triangle. Realizing I hadn't brought his drink, Julian frowned, tossed his hair, returned his hands to Helen's shoulders, and urged her backwards. As they danced past me, I tapped Julian's shoulder.

"Who does your hair?" I asked him. Helen stood next to me. "I've always wanted my hair to cascade like yours and have tried everything: hundred-dollar haircuts, styling gels, riding around in convertibles with the top down. Nothing worked. Nevertheless, I developed a theory…"

"You're a comedian, or something?" Julian rolled his shoulders at me.

"Gosh, I don't think so. Back to my theory: most guys who use blow-dryers on their hair wear bikini underwear." Julian looked down at himself. "I knew it. I knew it the second I laid eyes on you."

Julian pushed his hair way back and looked at Helen. "What's with this guy?"

"Julian, Helen's with me. So why don't you keep your hands off her and find someone else to fascinate."

Helen said, "I don't like being touched unless—"

Julian interrupted, "Maybe that's why your marriage failed."

I put my glass down. "You better apologize."

"Get real."

"Are you going to apologize?" People were turning to watch us.

"Hardly," he said with a truculent hair toss.

In a loud whisper, Helen said, "Stop it, you two."

Julian grinned. "Better listen to your date."

He stepped around me. I grabbed his left hand and twisted it. "Your apology?"

He mumbled what might have been an apology, wrenched free, and stalked away. The people around us tried restarting their conversations. Helen was difficult to read.

I said, "Sorry, these are your friends. You're angry?"

"No, kind of flattered." Helen giggled. "Two men almost fighting over me—wow, that's a first."

"Should I leave? Should we?"

"No, Julian was rude and deserved it. You really would have hit him?"

"Wouldn't have happened. Julian's too cute to let anyone hit him."

"How do you feel?"

"Like a million bucks; it's the adrenaline."

"You do that a lot? Threaten other men, get into fights?"

"No. As a boy, I got pushed around, cried easily, and ran home to my mother. Which only made things worse."

"At dinner with Julian, I didn't lead him on," Helen said.

"Lead Julian on? How in the world would you, or any other woman go about that? Julian assumes women are as infatuated with him as he is. Besides, Julian is cuter than you."

Her eyes narrowed. "You don't think I'm cute?"

"No. You're stunning and exotic. I thought so when we met in Denver." Eyes glistening, she looked away. "And you're very kind. Philippa appreciates your help and so do I. Helen, you're a lovely woman going through a rough time; but you'll get through it."

She blinked her eyes clear. "I'm touched."

"You deserve it."

"I'm honestly trying to get that through my head." She raised her glass, "Merry Christmas, Sandro."

"Merry Christmas, Elena."

When we arrived, there must have been sixty people, but the crowd had thinned to about thirty when the buffet supper was served: fine china, real silver, heavy napkins, a standing prime rib roast, a moist turkey, an array of trimmings and vegetables with an impressive selection of California wines. People sat in informal groups. The meal ended and a loose crescent began forming in front of Sy. Sy sat in a low chair with his back to the large picture window, San Francisco's panorama flattered his strong features.

During the expectant hush, Helen whispered, "Sy fashions himself an intellectual. He chooses the subject and holds court."

"Like a college seminar?"

"To Sy's thinking, it's a salon, like they had in Paris a hundred years ago; and Sy wears the blue stockings." Helen patted my hand and winked.

Helen and I sat toward the back of the assembling group as Sy shaped the evening's deliberation: government's role in the arts. Sy suggested that Americans might emulate the European paradigm whereby the common man uplifts himself by virtue of his taxes that support the arts. A guest countered that the government shouldn't make artistic decisions. Others contended that, left on their own, the arts would flounder under the more common appeal of sports. Sy conducted the discussion, emphasizing some points, muting others until the under-lying argument became circular: government or the market as arbiter. The party began breaking up around midnight.

Helen invited me back to her apartment for a brandy. Once inside, she said, "With a bit more effort, Sy could have been really affected."

Helen went to get the drinks while I looked at the view from the front windows. She returned, and the telephone rang. Her eyes wid-ened. "Got to be bad news at this hour." She answered, then put her hand over the receiver. "It's for you. Who knows you're here?"

"No one."

"You're being followed. This must have something to do with Andrew Neville. Oh dear, I hope Philippa's okay. Do you know where she is?"

"She went to a Christmas dinner party with some British friends." I took the phone. "Who's this?"

A male voice replied, "Alexander Romanovsky, Fiona Sinclair's friend?"

"Yes, who's this?"

"You've got a meeting tomorrow; the details are on your answering machine."

"Who is this?"

"That doesn't matter. Your meeting's important; Fiona Sinclair would agree."

"Fiona?"

The man hung up.

Helen said, "Fiona?"

"You're right; someone is following me."

"Whoever it is knows my name and phone number." Helen shud-dered. "Ah, back to Fiona Sinclair; she's having you followed?"

"She'd never do anything like that."

"I don't like this, not at all. What's going on between you and Fiona Sinclair?" I didn't answer. "You're not just friends, are you? No, you're involved with her, I mean, really involved. You're lovers, aren't you?"

"Well, that's all ending; it's complicated."

"Ending? How long has it been going on?"

"Oh, a long time."

She put her hand to her mouth. "Of course, I see. It wasn't just you who treated Drew badly. No, you and Fiona did that?" I was too embarrassed to answer. "And Fiona reset your sexual compass?"

"That's none of your business," I said.

"Well, pardon me for prying," she said. "Thinking about it, last night I did most of the talking. Sure, you talked about learning English but deflected most everything about yourself while prodding me to go on about my divorce, being Jewish, my parents. You slipped away from personal matters to hide your relationship with Fiona?"

"I…I…I guess so."

"Guess so?" Helen put her hand up. "Do you and the oh-so-very-proper Fiona Sinclair have one of those arrangements? What do they call those? Open marriages? But then again, you're not married."

"No, it's not like that, not at all."

"Then why didn't you tell me?"

"Because you would have gone away. I didn't want that to happen. To be honest, I was falling in love with you."

"Falling in love? When did that happen?"

"Last night, talking. I didn't want that to end."

"You're right, something did happen last night," Helen said. "I thought we were connecting. But silly, silly me, I was the fallback girl when Fiona leaves you. And why do you think she's leaving? Gosh, let me guess." She cocked her head. "A question of honesty?"

"No, stop, please. I'm not making sense."

"No, you're making plenty of sense." Her face hardened. "You know what they say about the men in San Francisco: They're either married or gay. And it looks like you're—" She stopped.

"Go ahead, say it." She shook her head no. "Come on, you were going to tell me that I'm a little of both?"

"May I have a cigarette?" I handed her a pack and a plastic lighter. She got the cigarette lit. "I will not resort to name calling. However, you should leave. Oh, and don't forget your coat."

"Yes. I'm sorry about all of this. You deserve better."

"Got that right."

Outside, I looked back toward Helen's as she came to the window, opened the window, and turned off the lights. I watched until she flicked the glowing ember to the street, where it bounced in a shower of sparks and died.

At home there was one message on my answering machine from Townie Morgan asking me to meet him in his office around eleven the next morning. The message was received just after I had arrived at Helen's.

CHAPTER 21

FRIDAY, DECEMBER 26, 1986

SAN FRANCISCO

The embarrassment at Helen's would have made for a difficult night's sleep; Townie's message made it impossible. I kept asking myself why Townie wanted to see me after Fiona had decided to invest in Chip's deal.

Too anxious to be exhausted, I drank coffee while considering my options. Townie's man had phoned Helen's, which meant he had figured out who Helen was. I didn't want to explain Helen to Fiona, not that there was much to explain. However, I had to tell Fiona that I was going to meet with Townie. I was about to phone the hotel in Los Angeles where Fiona was staying when my phone rang.

"I wanted this so much," Fiona said with a plaintive gasp. "Drew and I were getting along so well. Now I'm afraid it's ruined, all ruined. After agreeing to everything, Chip didn't keep his end of the bargain."

"What do you mean?"

Fiona took a deep breath. "Chip told a cousin down here that you and I are having an affair. Now everyone in the family knows; shortly so will everyone in San Francisco. And I'll become a grotesque caricature: an old woman keeping a younger man. How in the world do I explain you and me? No one could understand us."

"Where's your deal with Chip?"

"Signed, but no money. Alexander, please tell me what to do."

"Townie wants to see me in his office today. About this, I'm sure. Don't release a dime until you hear from me, okay?"

"Okay." Her voice was small.

"When are you coming back to San Francisco? I miss you."

"No idea, less inclination. I want to get on a plane that's going far, far away." She blew her nose. "When you're talking to Townie, I beseech you to keep Drew in mind. Drew mustn't know about us, he mustn't. The money is secondary. Good God, the money doesn't matter. Tell Townie and Chip to take as much as they wish." She was hyperventilating.

"Fiona, calm down. Drew doesn't know; hopefully we can keep it that way. There's still time; maybe I can fix this. Anyway, I'll call you after I've seen Townie."

"You'll see Drew later today?"

"That's the plan, but it depends on what Townie has to say, doesn't it?" She groaned.

"Fiona, we're going to get through this, I promise. But no matter what happens, you know that I love you?"

She started crying. "I'll wait to hear from you."

I took a cab to the car rental agency. Arranging a long-term contract took time; around 10:30 a.m. I drove a blue Buick to Townie's offices and found a parking place a couple of blocks away. At an office supply store on Market Street, I bought a small Dictaphone like I had used at work. I loaded the tape, recorded my name, the date, and the time, and played it back before dropping the recorder into my jacket pocket.

Townie's office was on the southeastern side of Market Street, the major diagonal street slanting across San Francisco. "South of the Slot," old-timers called the area. Before the mushrooming gentrification, the neighborhood was warehouses and small factories with an evening population of winos and night watchmen. The Morgan and Morgan Building had been restored: the exterior was cleaned to highlight the bas-relief adornments, the windows were modernized, and art deco lighting brought the exterior theme inside.

A pretty receptionist with tired eyes escorted me to Townie's office.

Approaching the door, I heard two men arguing. The receptionist looked uneasy and knocked; I pressed the Dictaphone's record button.

Townie had spent a lot of money on his clothing with flattering results: a tailored navy-blue suit, a blue shirt with white collar and cuffs, simple gold cufflinks, and a yellow tie. He was sleekly barbered with the faint smell of citrus. Except for his hungover eyes, Townie was a picture of the prosperous executive.

Townie came around his desk and took my hand with both of his. "Alex, great to see you again." We could have been meeting in one of San Francisco's better clubs. Guiding me to a younger version of himself slouched in a chair, Townie said, "My son, Chip." Chip didn't get up or extend his hand.

A more powerful version of Townie, Chip was in his late twenties and was more hungover than his father. Dressed in a blue Brooks Brothers suit, pink shirt, green suspenders, and a green-striped tie, Chip's preppy look was not a popular San Francisco fashion statement. If Debra was Townie's second wife, Chip's mother had been the first.

Townie said, "Afraid you walked into a family spat. Gotta watch it with the Ol' Chipper—one tough cookie, varsity wrestling."

Chip rolled his eyes. "Townie, always the wiseass; it's so tiresome."

"Varsity wrestling?" I asked Chip. "You went to Yale like your father?"

Townie's smile collapsed. Chip's expression went from a sulk to contempt. "Neither Townie nor I could get into Yale. Both of us went to Trinity College; it's in Connecticut."

"Oh, a Catholic school?"

"Not hardly." Townie reconstructed his smile. "Trinity is Episcopalian."

"Episcopalian, Catholic: aren't they six of one, half dozen of the other?"

"Not by a long shot," Townie replied with a contrived chuckle.

I turned to Chip. "So Trinity is one of those small New England colleges?"

Glaring at Townie, Chip said, "That's right."

"Like Williams and Amherst—choosy, very good? Isn't Bowdoin another one of those?"

"Yeah, sure," Chip mumbled.

"The only thing is..." I waited to get Chip's complete attention. "The only thing is, I've never heard of Trinity College."

Chip laughed out loud at Townie, who looked embarrassed. Going behind his desk, Townie motioned me to a chair in front of the desk. I pointed to a cut-crystal ashtray on Townie's desk. "Mind if I smoke?"

"Sure," Townie said, pushing the ashtray toward me. "I quit about six months ago but still sneak one every once in a while." He looked like he wanted a cigarette, and I gave him one. "Drink?" he asked.

I had to think: a drink might calm me down, but my stomach was empty and I wanted to keep a clear head. Townie went over to a cabinet that opened to an elaborate wet bar, made two potent Bloody Marys, and handed one to Chip. Back behind his desk, Townie said, "I guess you're wondering why we're meeting like this?"

"I'm also wondering about the person you have following me," I said. Chip studied his burnished loafers while Townie stirred his drink. "So, I guess, we're not discussing that?"

Townie shrugged.

"Let's see if I've got this right: you forced Fiona into Chip's real estate deal, and Fiona agreed in return for you two keeping quiet about the two of us. But Chip couldn't keep his mouth shut, so the original deal has to be restructured?"

"Something like that," Townie said. "But not restructured. We want you to tell Fiona to release the funds immediately."

"I don't tell Fiona much of anything, especially when it comes to business. What makes you think I can persuade her?"

"You damned well better," Chip interjected.

"Townie, you've got plenty of money; so why blackmail Fiona?"

Chip answered, "Because my deal is so smarmy that Townie couldn't stomach it. Besides, Auntie Fee spills more than I'm asking for. But you know that."

"Now that you've mentioned it," I replied, "one of Drew's friends thinks you're working a scam involving AIDS victims and estate taxes, or something like that. He didn't know the details, but it sounds like tax evasion, illegal conveyance, or maybe bankruptcy fraud?"

Chip replied with a crooked smile.

"Okay," I continued, "let's say the partner with AIDS buys one of your condos and puts it in his lover's name through a trust, or an elaborate gifting program, or something like that. What happens when the fellow with AIDS runs out of money for medical expenses? When he dies?"

Chip flushed. "You must have been talking to Robert de Montreville?"

"If your deal didn't pass the smell test with Robert, just imagine an IRS auditor or district attorney sniffing around."

"Robert doesn't know what he's talking about," Chip snarled.

"There's that to consider." I turned to Townie. "How long have you had me followed? Was Fiona followed too?"

Chip and Townie spoke at the same time, but Townie prevailed. "Just you, not Fiona. You're more predictable—job and everything. Chip started having you followed after the memorial service for Drew's lover."

Townie had told Fiona the day after Fred Imhoff's service that he knew about us. "Why did your detective start following me then?"

Chip tried answering, but Townie talked over him. "We used him to verify what I already knew about you and Fiona. For the longest time, I thought you were a confirmed bachelor, a light-in-the-loafers type who was simply fascinated with period-piece furniture." Townie had lisped his observation. "Hell, I was so sure that you were gay that I was surprised—actually surprised—to find out that you and Fiona were…were…what's the word I'm looking for?"

"Getting it on," Chip clarified. "You and Drew were lovers too. You did Drew, then Auntie Fee. That's really sick."

"Shut up, Chip," Townie said. "You've already screwed this up." To me, he said, "We want you to get Fiona on board with this deal even though Chip—"

"Why should I do that?" I asked.

"Otherwise, we show Auntie Fee these." Chip handed me photos of me coming and going to and from my flat with Fiona, Philippa, and Helen.

I glanced at the photos. "Didn't Fiona admit that you had her cornered when she agreed to your deal?"

Chip said, "I wanted to make sure you were on board."

But when Fiona acquiesced to their deal, my being on board didn't matter. Townie had said that I was followed to verify what he knew about Fiona and me; a second later, that he was surprised to find out that I wasn't gay.

I said to Chip, "Nothing here. Nothing I can't explain."

"Really?" Chip rolled his eyes. "You spent a night with your secretary. Then another with her and Helen Jacobs—kind of kinky."

"Fiona and I trust each other."

Chip tapped the photos. "I don't think Auntie Fee's trust would stand up to these."

"If I'm to advise Fiona to do the deal," I said, "I'd like to tell her that I've seen it."

"Standard real estate deal," Chip said.

"No, it's not."

"Chip, get him a copy," Townie said. "Fiona has a copy anyway." Chip left. Finishing his drink, he added, "Chip's a handful, always been difficult."

"Is Chip angry that you divorced his mother? Or something else?"

Townie started to the bar. "Chip's always been his mother's boy. Way too close, same temperament, same obstinacy." Pointing to the bottles, he asked, "Reconsider?"

"Sure, neat Scotch. I'm still curious, how did you find out about Fiona and me? We thought we were circumspect."

"A couple of things didn't make sense."

"Such as?"

"Just things," he said, handing me a Waterford tumbler with a generous measure of Scotch. "I do know that Fiona doesn't want Drew to find out."

"How do you know that Drew doesn't know already?"

Everything revolved around Drew's not knowing, and Townie hadn't answered my question. I tried sipping the drink but downed most of it. I lit a cigarette and offered Townie one. He lit up and leaned back in his chair. We sort of smiled at each other. I finished the drink, "There's something wrong with Chip; I've asked around, and people think he's a hopeless screwup. All he had to do was keep his mouth shut; instead he deliberately ruined a done deal. Why?"

Chip returned with documentation that answered my question. The original deal was for eighteen months; the new deal was a three-year bullet loan—the entire principal payable at maturity. The amount had been increased from seven hundred thousand dollars to a million; and Fiona's loan was subordinated, meaning that she would be repaid after the project's other lenders. Worse, there was no second mortgage; Fiona would have no collateral.

"This is outrageous," I said.

Chip smirked.

I said to Townie, "Fiona doesn't have much choice, does she?"

"Better put, you and she don't have a choice," Chip replied.

Once again to Townie, I said, "Drew must never know about Fiona and me. You've got to promise me that…and Chip too."

"Yeah, sure," Chip snorted.

"What's that mean?"

Beaming at Townie, Chip said, "Hell, Drew told Townie and me about you and Auntie Fee and how we could force her into this deal. Oh, one more sleazy detail: Fiona will be sponsoring Debra—Townie's trophy wife—into the Opera Alliance. Right, Townie?"

"Chip, why…why?" Townie said, putting his hands to his temples.

"For the same reason Drew told us about Auntie Fee." Chip made a pensive face. "What's the word I'm looking for? Hatred? Revenge? Come on, Townie, help me out."

The private eye's photos and their timing made sense. Even though Fiona admitted our relationship, they wanted to document what Drew had told them. So Drew must have known about Fiona and me at our supper: the reminiscing, the introspection, the gift of his business followed by blackmailing us.

I stood up. The Dictaphone buzzed that the tape had ended; I turned it off and went for the door.

Chip spun me around. "Give me that." He grabbed my jacket lapel and pressed his thumb into my shoulder. I tried shaking loose; Chip pressed harder. "Give me that." He pinned me against the door and reached for my pocket.

I pushed Chip's elbow up; he stumbled into me and got an arm around my neck. As I shook myself free, my glasses disappeared. Chip forearmed me; my head bounced off the door—black for an instant, then stars. I turned to open the door. Chip spun me around. I didn't see the punch and doubled over, trying to breathe. Chip straightened me up and punched my nose.

I was on the floor in front of Townie's desk, retching whiskey and blood. Chip hoisted me to my feet. I pulled away and stumbled against the desk, facing Townie. I was tearing and couldn't hear Townie yelling. My right hand bumped the crystal ashtray that I grabbed. Chip pulled me; I went with it and swung the ashtray at him. Chip fell backward to the floor. I leaned against the desk—more stars and flashing lights. Townie was on the phone. The receptionist rushed in; Townie bent over Chip. The receptionist seemed to be yelling into the phone.

I caught my breath, found my glasses, and went to the windows to look at my reflection: eyes blackening, nose bleeding. My handkerchief turned sodden. My hands were steady enough to light a cigarette that tasted coppery from the blood. I sat down. Everything in slow motion; my peripheral vision was narrowing. Two men picked up Chip and left with Townie and the receptionist. I fainted.

The cigarette smoldering on the rug woke me. I stumbled to Townie's phone and asked an operator to connect me to my doctor's office. I put Chip's pictures in my inside jacket pocket. My shirt and tie were bloody; the shoulder of my suit had popped. I gave the doctor's receptionist my name and told her I was injured and was coming to the office. I looked up; Townie approached.

"Stay away."

"Chip's jaw is broken; I'm calling the cops."

"Go ahead. Here's the phone."

"On second thought, no." Townie poured a glass of water at the wet bar.

I washed my mouth out and spit blood back into the glass.

"Now what?" he asked.

"Well, the deal is off, that's for sure. Townie, if you, Chip, or Debra ever write, phone, approach, or communicate in any way whatsoever with Fiona, Drew, or me, I'll file battery charges against Chip. Then Fiona and I will file blackmail charges against you and Chip. This tape probably won't be allowed in court, but Fiona and I will make a public statement and dare you to file slander charges. That's all I can think of right now. Understood?"

"Yes, completely."

I started toward the door. "One more thing: I don't want to be followed. I don't want Fiona followed either."

"I understand. Where are you going?"

"To my doctor's."

"Where?"

"Union Square."

"You're not going to make it." Townie took my arm. I pushed him away. "You shouldn't drive; I will," he said. "Now settle down and put your arm over my shoulders."

We made it out the building and were going to my rented car. "What happens if a cop sees us?"

"That would complicate matters," Townie said. We hurried. I gave Townie the keys.

In the car, I asked, "Shouldn't you be looking after Chip?"

"The guys who took Chip to the hospital will say that he fell down the stairs. Maybe that'll work. Anyway, Chip's on his own. Tried bringing him into the business, but he's determined to ruin me with his stupid deals. So he'll be going back to Los Angeles and his mother." At the Union Square Garage, Townie asked, "You're not going to report this to the police?"

"No. But you're paying my medical bills and replacing this suit."

"Fine. Don't worry about anything legal from our end. That's a promise."

"Townie, it's clear that you can't control Chip. What if he decides to report it?"

"I'll testify against him on the assault charges you'll bring. A father testifying against his son—Chip wouldn't stand a chance." Townie pulled into a parking space; my nose started bleeding again. Townie gave me his handkerchief. He started to get out but stopped. "Oh, and tell Fiona I'm sorry."

"Tell Fiona that you're sorry? Chip's in the hospital, my nose is probably broken, and 'sorry' is all you can manage?"

"Later, after Drew has gone, I'll apologize to Fiona, in person. If she wants to slap my face, I'll stand there until she's finished. To answer your earlier question, Chip adores his mother and hates me for the divorce. Chip's deals were tearing me up, financially and emotionally. Debra put her foot down."

"That's when you decided to force Fiona into Chip's deal?"

"Yes," Townie said. "When you had dinner with Drew after that memorial service, you told him there was a deal I wanted Fiona to look at. The next morning Drew came over and told Chip and me how we could force Fiona into it." Townie walked me to my doctor's building.

At the entrance, I asked, "Did Drew say why?"

"He said that he wanted to help you but didn't elaborate. While not to mitigate what I've done, keep in mind what you and Fiona did to Drew."

"I don't want Fiona ever to know what Drew did to her. It would serve neither of them well."

"It would serve none of us well."

CHAPTER 22

DECEMBER 26, 1986

DR. STERNBERG'S OFFICE

SAN FRANCISCO

Dr. Richard Sternberg, a general practitioner, had become my doctor when Fiona took my mother and me into her home. A staid man with a light German accent, he was polite; but I always sensed that he didn't care for me.

Dr. Sternberg and I arrived at his office within minutes of each other. He sat me down on the stainless-steel table and prodded my nose. "The fracture is clean and simple," he said. "I'll set it, but you should see a specialist. Any other injuries?" I pointed to my stomach and took off my shirt. "Beginning to bruise, fist sized. The proverbial other guy?"

"Long story. I was attacked, but I'm not filing a police report. The other party won't either, I'm sure. Do you have to report this to anyone, the authorities? It would be embarrassing."

"Your consideration is appreciated," he said before turning away to load a syringe. "I'm going to numb the area around your nose." Over his shoulder, he said, "I've known you since you were a boy, and I've known Fiona since I was a boy. I'm most discreet. So, what happened?"

"The other guy has circulated information that is harmful to a person I know well. Love, I should say."

Dr. Sternberg approached. "Stretch out and try to get comfortable; this may sting." I closed my eyes as he concentrated on the injections. Finished, he backed away. "Fiona is the person you love?"

"Fiona must have told you?" Dr. Sternberg didn't say. "Told you about our relationship?"

Dr. Sternberg nodded and began collecting the instruments he would use. The procedure didn't take long. The bone-on-bone grinding was sickening; wondering how much Fiona had told him was distracting. Taping my nose, Dr. Sternberg said, "Tell me: what does Fiona know about this?"

"Not the altercation, but most everything that led up to it. I'll call her when I get home and sort everything out."

"Stay on your back," Dr. Sternberg said, taking off his rubber gloves. "To be candid, when your relationship started, I told Fiona that it would eventually come to this: embarrassment at best, humiliation and blackmail at worst. A woman of her standing taking up with a boy half her age was asking for trouble, especially from that family of hers. But there were overriding considerations. You weren't dealing well with your mother's suicide. Back then, you were a…"

"A nitwit, a selfish, self-possessed nitwit."

"Put another way," he said, "you were unstable. Fiona and I were quite worried."

"As unstable as my mother?"

"You and your mother were quite close."

"Too close, don't you think?" I sat up and was dizzy.

"Easy, easy. Get the blood circulating. Breathe through your mouth and put your head down."

"Too close?"

"I'm a physician, not a psychologist. I do wonder, however, without Fiona, what would have become of you."

"I've thought a lot about that and don't know."

"You were clinging to Drew. Drew was a manipulative young man, far worldlier than you. He would have tired of you, as he did with most of the men in his life. Alone you'd have gone from bad relationships to worse, searching for your mother's affection. You were lucky that Fiona prevented that."

"So, you and Fiona are that close, close enough that she tells you everything?"

"Fiona trusts me implicitly," he said. "Fiona's father, Mr. Duncan Sinclair, hired my father when we arrived here from Prussia. My father managed the Sinclair's agricultural properties. Mr. Sinclair lent me the money for college and medical school. And I paid back every dime, with interest."

"I didn't know that. What was Fiona like as a girl, a young woman?"

"Happy, fun to be around, impetuous, rash. That family of hers changed everything, made her cautious, distrustful. People think she's cold, but she's one of the kindest people I've known."

"Fiona was happy around my mother, wasn't she?"

With a broad smile I had never seen, Dr. Sternberg said, "Around your mother, Fiona was her old self." Leaning against a small sink, he added, "Tatiana was very Russian, extravagant and passionate. Fiona said that Tatiana knew everything about paintings. There wasn't much middle ground with Tatiana; paintings were either fantastic or trash. Her enthusiasm captured Fiona; their chattering away in French took Fiona away from her family responsibilities." He handed me my shirt and threw the tie in the disposal. "How are you feeling?"

"Okay, I guess."

"We'll get something for the pain," he said, checking my nose. "A wonderful woman, Tatiana; it's a shame what she endured." Dr. Sternberg was getting a little misty and wiped his eyes. "Fiona trusted your mother and has always trusted me; nowadays, it's you and me. Fiona's relatives are at the bottom of all this, aren't they? The details, please."

After my explanation, Dr. Sternberg asked, "Between the two of us, do you think Drew knows about you and Fiona?" He watched my eyes.

"Drew knows, but Fiona doesn't know that he does."

"What are you going to do?"

"I'm going to keep Fiona from ever knowing."

"You must, you really must," Dr. Sternberg said. "We share the same concern for Fiona, don't we?"

"We do," I said. "While this may be none of my business, are you

Fiona's doctor?"

"No, too close. I fell in love with Fiona when I was a young man, but my love was not returned in the manner I had wished. Most men would have walked away, but I settled for her friendship."

"I didn't know that."

"You're all grown up now." He shook my shoulder. "Fiona binds us."

In his car, I said, "Back to my mother, she was very haughty—imperious, I should say—around other Russians. She considered herself above them. Before the Revolution, she was above almost every Russian in terms of social rank."

"She knew that life briefly as a young girl before it ended forever," Dr. Sternberg said. "On the other hand, perhaps the old title was part of her identity—a touchstone, so to speak—that allowed her to weather the chaos that swept through her life. That's what Fiona thinks; so do I." He turned his attention to a stalled bus in front of us. We were trapped until a driver let us into the next lane. Then he added, "When Tatiana became ill, you turned yourself into quite the aristocrat. What prompted that?"

"Like I said, I was a nitwit."

"Too easy. Come on, think about it."

"I was terrified. Mother had told me that we were special; we were aristocrats. It was the only thing we had."

"Like mother, like son? When their worlds fall apart, people start grasping: possessions, other people, inert memories, unattainable hopes. Alexander Herzen, a Russian émigré, wrote something like that over a hundred years ago."

We pulled into a drug store's parking lot. I fell asleep as soon as Dr. Sternberg got out. I woke up when he pulled up in front of my flat. He gave me a bottle of pills and asked, "How are you doing?"

"Tired. I didn't sleep last night. I've got to call Fiona, then Drew."

"We're comrades, Alexander?"

"We are. Thank you, Doctor."

***

Fiona picked up on the first ring. "Everything is okay. Your deal with

Chip is cancelled, for good. Chip hired a detective; that's how they found out about us."

"Why did they hire a detective in the first place?"

"Townie said they did it on a hunch: how we're always together, how we looked at each other—you know, two people in love."

"When did they hire the detective?"

"Oh, a long time ago. They must have been planning for ages."

"I see," Fiona said. "You sound stuffy."

"Well, Chip lost his temper, and we got into a shoving match. After the scuffle, Townie agreed to leave us alone. He assured me that neither he nor Chip will ever contact Drew. So, you see, everything is going to be fine."

"God in heaven," she said. "You're really okay?"

"I'm fine. I've got to phone Drew."

"Thank God Drew doesn't know."

"Got to hop," I said. "I'll keep in touch."

My nose had started to throb. I took a couple of painkillers and called Drew. The nurse said Drew was sleeping.

Minutes later, Drew came to the phone, sounding groggy. "Where are you?"

"San Francisco. Drew, what's going on?"

"Terrible nightmares, afraid to go to sleep. But if I don't sleep, I start hallucinating. Don't know which is worse."

"Oh dear, I'm sorry. I meant what are you up to?"

"Up to?" Drew replied. "I'm waiting for you to take over my business."

"I've just had a very unpleasant meeting with Townie and Chip."

"Oh," Drew said. "You sound funny, like you've been crying."

"Chip and I got into a fight, a bad one."

"Alexander, I want you up here right now," he said. Then he talked to someone before the phone went silent. He came back on. "Nurse Ratchet doesn't want me getting upset." I heard more talking at Drew's end, then, "I've forgotten where I was."

"Please tell me what's going on?"

"The old noggin is falling apart," he said. "Getting loopy. The doctors suspect cerebral lesions." Drew turned cheerful. "Now when are you getting up here?"

"I need some rest. Maybe I'll drive up tomorrow, or the next day. I'll let you know."

"Oh, that's right, Chip and you got into a fight. Why?"

"Because Townie and Chip blackmailed Fiona. Anyway, it's all sorted out. We'll talk about this when I see you."

"How could they have blackmailed Fiona?" Drew persisted.

"Because you told Townie and Chip that Fiona and I have been lovers for years."

After a long pause, he said, "Don't you see what I'm doing? I'm helping you, like I helped Fred."

"Helped Fred?"

"He was suffering. I didn't stop Fred, that's what I meant. You didn't see him at the end; if you had, you'd have done the same."

"If you want me to come up there and help you commit suicide, or stand by while you do it, that's out of the question. Do you understand?"

"Oh, I'm quite capable of that," Drew replied. "You, my dear boy, are about to make the most important decision in your life. And I'm going to see to it that you do so without Fiona's meddling."

"At our dinner, you told me that Fiona and I were the two most important people in your life," I said. "The next day, you told Townie how to blackmail Fiona and me. Why...why?" I was dizzy.

"You've got to get out from under her thumb and start making your own decisions."

"You don't understand," I yelled. "Fiona has made suggestions but doesn't tell me what to do. Furthermore, I haven't even discussed this with her. And Universal doesn't matter anymore because I just got fired. The blackmail was pointless, don't you see? Was it your anger? I understand the anger and the hatred, I do."

"I don't hate you or Fiona. I was distracting her." He stopped. "No, I was trying to frighten Fiona while you came to the proper decision. And frightening worked."

"When Fiona was caring for you and trying to reconcile? How outrageous."

Drew said, "Since you came back from Russia, Fiona has been focused on Townie. And we know why, don't we? What will happen to her precious social standing when word gets out that she seduced you when you were eighteen?"

"That wasn't the case."

"It was so obvious," Drew taunted. "When you never came to New York, I figured that Fiona had taken you to bed to humiliate me. You must know that Fiona is all about control; but since Fred died, I've been controlling her through Townie. And now you're going to take my business, whether Fiona likes it or not."

"You hate Fiona that much?"

"I don't hate Fiona, but I understand her," Drew said. "And I love you far more than I've ever loved Fiona."

"Drew, listen, Fiona doesn't know that you know about us. If you tell her, I'm out of your life forever. Is that clear?"

"Most certainly. However in exchange, you must come up here, immediately."

"I'm in no shape for a long drive."

"Oh, I know what you're up to. You're waiting for Fiona. So you both can retire to your intimate world to resume the deification of Tatiana?"

"Leave my mother out of this."

"My mother's involved, why shouldn't yours be? You must see your mother from the proper prospective." Drew paused. "Fiona hasn't told you about Tatiana's time in Paris, alone during the war?"

"I…I…I…"

"So it's up to me. Well, Tatiana collaborated…collaborated to the extent that she consorted with a German." He paused. "Moved in, as they say these days."

Silence.

"Alexander, still there?" Drew asked. "You and your father weren't close, know why? Come see me, and I'll tell you everything, which is far more than Fiona has done."

"I'm all through with you, Drew. All through."

"Don't you dare walk out on me again. Don't you dare." Drew screamed at me until the line went dead.

I poured a large drink and smoked a cigarette. Another drink, then nothing.

CHAPTER 23

SATURDAY, DECEMBER 27, 1986

SAN FRANCISCO

I spent the evening trying to talk to my mother. She sat in the chair next to my bed, studying her hands, perhaps pondering Drew's accusations. When I persisted, she turned away and went to the windows. I disgusted her—frustrating, so bewildering.

I pleaded with her. She came back to the chair, looked at me for an eternity before closing her eyes—ethereal, remote. Dawn was breaking; she was sitting on the end of the bed.

I said, "Skazhitye, pazhalsta." (Talk to me, please.) She turned to face me; I grabbed her.

"My God," Philippa said, "you startled me. How are you?"

"Don't know," I said. Her breath was on my face. My arms were around her waist. "Why are you here?"

Before she could answer, I kissed her. She kissed me back. We kissed again. My hands were under her blouse; hers under my shirt. I unhooked her bra and unzipped her skirt.

"Wait, please." She caught her breath. "What happens when we're finished?"

"Rest, then more?"

"Make a morning of it?"

"Sounds good to me."

"When we get out of bed, then what?" She gulped.

"Don't know."

"Everything will have changed. Risky, complicated. I depend on you."

"Got carried away."

"We both did," she said. "Unless we're going to proceed, we shouldn't stay like this." We let go of each other.

"How did I get here?" I was wearing boxer shorts and a T-shirt.

Philippa moved to the side of the bed and said, "I got the keys from Sally Roth and found you asleep on the sofa; the bloody shirt, blacked eyes, and bandaged nose frightened me. I couldn't wake you. Empty whiskey glass and a bottle of pills in your pocket, I assumed the worst. From the prescription, I rang up Dr. Sternberg, who dashed over. You should have read the prescription: no alcohol."

"I remember sitting on the sofa having a drink; that's all."

"Dr. Sternberg and I managed to move you."

"How serious?"

"Breathing was fine; pulse was slow. Dr. Sternberg asked me to watch you and said that you had been under a lot of stress and no sleep. From the pictures in your jacket and the Dictaphone recording, he wasn't understating. I'm in several of those pictures. Tell me everything, please." I did. Then Philippa said, "A bit dodgy, but explainable. Have you told Fiona?"

"I told her that everything was okay, all fixed up. But I didn't tell her about getting beaten up."

"One thing at a time, I guess." Philippa got off the bed and redid her clothes. "You should rest before driving to see Drew."

"Drew and I argued yesterday when I got home; he made terrible accusations about my mother."

"Accusations?"

"She spent World War II in Paris. Drew said that she was a collaborator."

"Many French collaborated."

"Drew said she lived with a German."

"Did she?"

"Don't know. Have to ask Fiona. Drew said she knows."

"I'm surprised that Fiona didn't tell you."

"So am I."

"You were calling for your mother last night, in Russian, I think." Philippa sat next to me. "You poor dear; it never ends, does it?"

"And it never will, never." I sat up; my mind bolted. "Insanity runs in families, certainly mine. My mother was as mad as a hatter; her brother must have been even crazier. He went back to Russia, with the Germans, the Nazis. What was he thinking? I'll never know. But I do know that I'll go as crazy as they did."

"Please don't do this to yourself."

"After all these years, I can't get the suicide reconciled, never could, never will. Doctors and Fiona told me that my mother was insane, like that explained everything. But it doesn't, not by a long shot. What did I have to do with her madness? Why did I disgust her? Well, it's finally sinking in: my mother was always crazy; she kept me close so that I couldn't stand back to see her as she really was."

"Alexander, please stop."

"When she went crazy, she let go of me; and for the first time I saw her as she really was. My realizing that she was barking mad, and always had been, that's what disgusted her."

"Steady," she said and pushed me back into the pillows. "Steady."

"Instead of running away, maybe I should have waited for the snakes to start slithering out of her head?"

"Don't attack Tatiana like that."

"My head must be full of the same snake eggs waiting to hatch."

"Alexander, this is so terribly destructive."

"And there's my father. Just who the hell was he? And there're so many things I don't know about my mother. Drew and Fiona know, but I don't. I don't trust them or anyone these days, not a soul." I tried sitting up, but Philippa pushed me back. "I trust you, of course. You're the only one."

"Why?" Philippa's voice was as soft as her eyes.

"You've never lied to me. But more importantly, I've never lied to you like I have to Drew and Fiona. I've lied to Fiona a lot recently.

Maybe that's why she lies to me."

"Relax," Philippa said, keeping her hand on my chest. "We'll never lie to each other, not after what we've been through. Will you trust me now?"

"Yes."

"I'm going to take you away from all of this."

"Are you going with me?"

"I'm going to help you on your way, but, no, I won't be accompanying you. You're going back to your parents as your memory held them before all of this. You must keep those memories as you learn more about them." She held my hand. "Now, close your eyes, and take your mind away from all of this: Fiona, Drew, and my problems. You're going back to France, when you were a boy. Where did you go for August vacations?"

"The Mediterranean: Cap Ferret or Juan les Pins. Les Pins, the Pines, was the best."

"I've been there," she said. "You're back in Les Pins. After a day at the beach, you and your parents walk up the mountain through the pines. Slightly sunburned, the three of you have supper: fish soup—garlicky and orange with saffron—then lamb grilled over grapevines and rosemary, and red wine. Now you're in bed, about to slumber off. Getting sleepy?"

I closed my eyes and could smell the thick salt air.

"A breeze off the sea rustles the trees. Heavy salt air mingling with clean pine. Freshly ironed sheets with a hint of lavender. It's heavenly. Your eyes are fluttering. Tatiana and your father are talking in the next room; Tatiana laughs, then your father. You love them and pray that they'll always be as happy as they are, in that room, just the other side of the wall." Philippa kissed my forehead.

**

I woke up and found my glasses on the side table; it was early in the afternoon. Philippa was sound asleep next to me on top of the covers. In the bathroom mirror I studied my face: swollen nose, both eyes purplish black. My nostrils were packed with dried blood that I removed only to start the bleeding again. Shaving, I tried to organize my thoughts but couldn't. In the shower, I put aside Drew and my mother. That left Fiona. I was angry that she had kept my mother's secret, but I'd worried that she was leaving me. Fiona told me that she wanted to go far away. A good idea, the best one of the morning. I dressed and went to the kitchen.

Philippa was brewing tea and asked, "How are you?"

"A hangover. Nose throbs. Couldn't find the pain pills."

"Last night, I put them away." She pointed to the kitchen counter. "They're over there."

"I'm not suicidal, but very upset."

"Upset? About this morning?"

"Gosh, I hope you're not," I said. "Not much thanks for staying with me last night."

Her smile was awkward. "We weren't thinking."

"You were; I wasn't. Ah, I don't know why I'm compelled to tell you this, but I've been faithful to Fiona."

"I'm sure you have," Philippa said. "If you wish, I'll explain those pictures to Fiona and tell her how we've become such good friends."

"Good friends?" Smiling hurt my nose. "Whatever we've become transcends friendship. Getting me calmed down this morning was very kind." Philippa shrugged like it didn't matter. "I don't know if, or how, I can ever repay you."

"Our relationship certainly transcends a banker's repayment schedule," she said. The toast popped up. She buttered it and arranged the pieces on a plate with lemon marmalade to the side. She poured the tea and handed me a cup after adding warm milk and one sugar. "Just the way you like it. Let's sit down and finish the pot."

We went to the living room; her luggage was by the front door. Philippa followed my gaze. "Don't leave," I said. "I'm thinking of driving down the coast for a few days, maybe Carmel or Big Sur. I can't leave it this way with Drew. And Fiona... I need time to think."

"So do I," she said. "I'd love to do it right here."

"That's settled. A good pot of tea isn't a panacea, but it's close."

"Serenity in a cup," Philippa said, lifting hers.

***

I packed and took a cab to the Union Square Garage to pick up my rental car. Taking Route 1 down to Carmel was on my mind. The highway cantilevered over California's coastline, but its switchbacks required more determination than I could muster. Maybe I'd head up north to the wine country: few tourists that time of year, good restaurants, and an easy drive through the undulating vineyards. Glancing at myself in the rearview mirror, I wasn't fit to be seen in public. There was Fiona's home; I had the keys.

At Fiona's, I couldn't decide which bedroom to use. Sleeping in Fiona's bed seemed presumptuous; I unpacked in my old room and went downstairs. My last real meal had been Christmas dinner two days ago. The kitchen was bare; I drove to a supermarket. Supper that evening was spaghetti with a sausage and mushroom sauce accompanied with a bottle of Barolo from Fiona's wine cellar.

I ate in the study in front of the television and dozed off during a situation comedy with mean kids tormenting their parents. Around midnight, I woke up and watched a John Wayne western to the end before falling asleep. The early-morning network shows were as bright as spring's first robin with handsome men and attractive women giggling at each other. I clicked it off and slept until the early afternoon.

With the exception of a trip downtown to see a specialist about my nose and visits to Safeway, I spent the rest of the year watching television and sleeping. I was treading time and decided that, after New Year's, I would settle things with Fiona and somehow come to terms with Drew. Then I would get my future employment sorted out. Accomplishing all of that required a no-nonsense business plan complete with timelines, decision trees, and quantifiable long- and short-term objectives. Pleased that my management skills would be employed, I opened a robust Zinfandel and ate a blue-cheese hamburger in front of the television before surrendering to a long nap.

CHAPTER 24

WEDNESDAY, DECEMBER 31, 1986

SAN FRANCISCO

Late New Year's Eve afternoon, I called Philippa to ask about her plans for the evening. "Where in the world are you?" she asked.

"Fiona's, on the other side of town."

"Honestly, it's as if you walked off the planet. A few days ago, Fiona called here from Lake Tahoe. I told her that you had gone away to think things over, but I didn't know where. She was just here looking for you and left about twenty minutes ago. She said that she was going home."

"You're angry? Fiona too?"

"No, I'm relieved. On the other hand, Fiona is most concerned—distraught, actually. Oh, I should have done better explaining to Fiona what's been going on. I'm afraid I was a tad slipshod with the photos."

I heard a cab pulling into the driveway and said good-bye. I met Fiona at the front door. She stood back for a moment before hugging me. I brought the luggage inside while she paid the driver.

"Good Lord, Alexander, where have you been?" she asked.

"Right here, sleeping and watching TV."

"I just left Philippa. Why didn't you tell me you had been fired, and that Townie had tried blackmailing you with those photos, and that you had taken a terrible beating?" She approached me. "You're leaving me?"

"Staying here is an odd way of going about it."

"But you're upset with me?" She took off her coat. "I should have told you about Tatiana years ago. Instead Drew told you in a fit of anger; he told me about your last phone conversation."

"What else did Drew say?"

"After talking to you, Drew had a seizure," Fiona said. "I went and stayed with him until this afternoon. He's somewhat better now, but it's a steep decline that's accelerating. Drew wants you to forgive him, but he's worried that you're finished with him." She started for the study. "I must tell him you're okay."

"Fiona, wait. I feel terrible about Drew. Both of us were angry, not thinking."

She turned back to me. "You were shocked and had a lot to be angry about. I don't blame you; neither does Drew. Your eyes and nose are healing properly?"

"Yes. Dr. Sternberg did an excellent job. What else did Drew say?"

"Drew's memory is tricky. At times it's all there, then it vanishes. Subjects start for no reason, go on and on, and then stop as abruptly as they started." She hurried to the study. "Speak with Drew and comfort him, please?"

"First, I'd like to know where things stand with you and Drew." I followed her.

Fiona was standing by her desk. "Several evenings ago, Drew and I sat down; he wanted to settle everything, once and for all. I made amends, actually apologized for being such an appalling mother. Drew replied with accusations and never got around to apologizing for his part—which, I guess, is all right. After all, I was the parent and Drew was just a boy when it all fell apart." She went to the French doors and looked out.

"What accusations did he make?"

"The usual: I was distant, cold. I didn't love him as I should have. And I sent him away to boarding school. Oh, and that I taunted him with my Scottish pictures. No one likes them, but I truly do. Anyway, he got it all out." She shrugged. "There were tears on my part, resignation on Drew's."

"As upsetting as it must have been, at least Drew doesn't know about us."

She leaned against the door frame with her head down. "That's best for the three of us." Fiona shook her head and went back to her desk. "Now I must phone Drew. If you don't mind, I'd love a very large Scotch." Fiona sat down at her desk and reached for the phone. Drew answered as soon as Fiona tapped the final number. She said, "Alexander is right here. He's fine. Here, talk to him." She handed me the phone and took the drink I had poured.

Drew said, "Where have you been?" I told him. "I suspect you have many things to settle with Fiona, but I'm too overwrought to remember exactly what. I need someone to watch over me. You'll do that?"

"I'll stay with you for as long as you'll have me. Ask the nurse to remind you that I'll be coming soon."

"I was so angry when I said those things. You'll forgive me?"

"I already have." We said good-bye.

Fiona had taken her drink to the sofa. After a long sip, she continued, "Right after Tatiana's death, you were in no condition to hear everything. So I put it off. As you grew stronger, I couldn't bear blemishing your memories of Tatiana. I told myself that keeping her secrets was an act of love; I still do. Question is, do you?"

"I do, Fiona, I do. But the last time we were together, when you left me standing in front of my place, I thought you were leaving me. Then on the phone, you were so unresponsive that I decided that you in fact were. Frankly, I was terrified."

"So was I. Even if the original deal with Townie and Chip had worked, our secret was out." Fiona sighed. "Rich old woman with a younger man. People will laugh. You have pride; I convinced myself that you wouldn't spend it on me."

"That's selling me short after all these years. Tell me that you're never going to leave me."

"I love you, Alexander. I don't know what more to say."

We held each other's eyes for a long time. "Fiona, why did Mother confide in Drew?"

Fiona's voice lowered. "Drew said that Tatiana told him most everything just before the suicide. Drew will fill in those details when you're with him." She paused. "Tatiana's imagination was her escape from the realities of her past. When her imagination deserted her, the past confronted her. Tatiana always loved you, you know that?"

"I wonder if I'll ever get her sorted out."

"I'm doing my best to do so," Fiona said.

"And my father?"

"You're the only son of Tatiana and Andre Romanovsky. You were born in a Paris hospital at noon on October 10, 1947, over three years after Paris was liberated. Your French papers were authentic and in order; I had that checked."

"By whom?"

"Richard. Dr. Sternberg. When he was visiting relatives in Germany that summer, I asked him to look up your birth records in Paris."

"That German?"

Fiona finished her drink and stood up. "The German's name was Joachim Haryett, descended from Huguenots who fled France and settled in Aachen, near the Dutch and Belgium borders. Tatiana called him Achim—Achim from Aachen. An army engineer, a full colonel, I think. He spoke excellent French and was an accomplished pianist. His family published art books. By 1943, Tatiana was destitute: no job, her brother had left, and her mother had died just after the war started, complications after surgery."

"What kind of surgery?" I asked.

"Back then, the term was 'female problems'—problems with the reproductive system. Back to Joachim Haryett, he was stationed in Calais, building fortifications for the expected Allied invasion. They met when she was working for the French construction company the German army employed. Reasoning that the Allies would prevail when they invaded, Haryett sent Tatiana to his family in Aachen."

"She went to Aachen?"

"I'll get to that." Fiona poured herself another drink. "Richard looked up the Haryetts that summer; they told him that Tatiana wasn't pregnant and didn't have a child."

"What doesn't Dr. Sternberg know about my mother and me?"

"He was trying to be helpful," Fiona replied.

"Mother going to Germany makes sense. Being a collaborator, she must have expected a rough retribution if she'd stayed in France."

"You're ashamed?"

"Realizing that, with the exception of my father, the rest of my family was on the wrong side of World War II is unsettling."

"There are other considerations." Fiona sat on the sofa's arm. "Both sides of your family were on the wrong side of the Russian Revolution and were slaughtered. Tatiana, her brother, and your paternal grandfather feared and hated the Communists far more than the Nazis. Furthermore, just because the history books say that something is over doesn't mean the people who were involved thought so."

"Fiona, you sent me to college."

Her eyes narrowed. "From what I've read, Stalin killed more people than Hitler."

"Stalin did, but most people in this country don't know that. Besides, Stalin was an American ally during the war, and it was the Red Army that literally decimated the Germans at Stalingrad and Kursk. Russian casualties were astronomical."

"Why so high-minded?"

"I'm trying to put things into an American context, the context I've been living in most of my life. More importantly, I am trying to see my mother as she actually was. I deserve to know that."

"You do indeed," Fiona replied with a placating smile. "Joachim Haryett was killed during the Normandy invasion. With nowhere to go, Tatiana stayed with his family."

"Wait a second, how did Haryett get her to Germany? I mean, even German colonels couldn't move a foreigner back to Germany without authorization."

"What are you getting at?"

"Did Haryett marry my mother? Getting his wife to Germany would have been easier than a stateless Russian refugee."

"No, not the case; Tatiana was not married to Haryett."

"How do you know?"

"The Haryetts confirmed to Richard that Joachim was not married to Tatiana."

"Then what happened?" I asked.

"There was a battle around Aachen. Afterwards the British put Tatiana in a displaced persons camp. Her papers from the League of Nations and France validated that she was born in Russia. Word got out that the British turned over all native-born Russians to the Red Army and certain death. Your father had returned to France and located Tatiana through the relief agencies. At the time Andre was attached to the Free French. He found Tatiana and had a British chaplain marry them on the spot. The British weren't going to turn over the wife of an Allied officer to the Red Army."

I said, "Andre Romanovsky was quite a man."

"He was." Fiona put her arms around my shoulders. "Philippa told me what you've done for her. She's most grateful and most fond of you. She made it clear your relationship is quite proper—reassuring from such an attractive woman," she said with a dry smile. "There's a lot of Andre in you; he would have been proud of you."

I had a lump in my throat. "I loved him. But as a boy, I thought I was Mother's, hers alone. And my father was this pleasant man who lived with us. I was jealous that he commanded mother's attention by stepping into the room. What a stupid, stupid boy I was."

"You were just a boy." She shook my shoulders.

"How did he seem to you?"

"Andre didn't seem like a mathematician. You know, way out there. A courtly man, always nicely dressed. And such wonderful manners. Women, myself included, liked being around him."

"Why?"

"Andre drew women out; we became alluring, captivating. You can do that, if you put your mind to it." She paused. "It was fortunate that Andre protected you and Tatiana before I tried."

I found a handkerchief and dried my eyes. "Why didn't you tell me all of this before?"

Fiona put her hands to my face. "After Tatiana, you needed love and stability. I've given you that." I put my arms around her. "I kept those secrets, thinking of you and Tatiana."

"Even as a boy, Mother was something of a mystery. I remember one time at dinner when we were still in Paris, I was asking her about the war and this big company she had worked for. She was evasive. I persisted but didn't realize how tense things had become until Father slapped me. I went to my room in tears. Later we had a long talk about their pasts."

"About what happened to Tatiana in the Civil War?" Fiona poured me a drink and returned to the sofa.

"No, mostly about his family."

"Tell me." She leaned forward.

I sat on the desk, facing her. "Oh, let's see. When the Revolution started, my father was a twelve-year-old prodigy studying university math in Petersburg. Adrian Romanovsky was stationed in Moscow. When the Reds started taking over Petersburg, he told his family to get out and join him. They left in two groups. Father went with the middle brother; they dressed as peasants and got a train to Moscow. The oldest son, a young officer, was to follow with his mother and sister. They vanished."

"Then what happened?"

"During the Civil War, Adrian Romanovsky became a staff officer for the White general, Peter Wrangel, in the Crimea. When the Whites were defeated, my grandfather and my father were on one of the last ships to leave Sevastopol for Turkey. From there they made their way to Paris."

Fiona said, "What happened to the middle brother who went with Andre?"

"His name was Konstantin; he died of typhus during the Civil War."

"So you understand why Andre's father went back to Russia?"

"Vengeance, or maybe he went back to look for his family. By then people like them had been killed or died in the gulags. I don't know about my uncle. He was a theatrical set designer, and I got the impression that he was unbalanced."

"Tatiana and her brother saw far too much when they were far too young," Fiona said. "Did Andre tell you about Tatiana and the German occupation?"

"A little: she was alone, and how rugged it had been for her. That's when I learned that my grandfather and my uncle had gone back to Russia. After that, Mother tried talking about her brother, but she always cried."

"The Russian Civil War must have been unimaginable," Fiona said. "As a young girl, Tatiana saw things, horrid things that no one should witness—let alone a little girl." She rested her head against the back of the sofa. "I'll tell you what I know about that, but later. I'm not up to it now."

"I don't know if I'll ever be."

"We'll see," Fiona whispered. "We'll see." She looked at me with tired resignation. "And you, dear man, will have to contend with my dotage."

"You contended with my adolescence."

"True."

"I was a difficult young man."

"Very," Fiona said. "I've read somewhere that women in their early forties are as sexually motivated as men in their early twenties. I guess I'm one of the few women who can attest to that. Sex was an escape for both of us; afterwards, talking was therapeutic. Guiding you into adulthood is the best thing I've done. Tatiana asked me to take care of you if anything happened to her." She blushed. "She couldn't have thought it would turn out this way."

Paraphrasing Philippa's thoughts, I said, "Mother and I had created a world of our own, and you were the only person we included. So it stands to reason that we found each other in the world my mother had left us."

Fiona blotted her eyes. "How do you feel now?"

"It's a wonder that she was as normal as she was."

"Are you okay?"

"I will be," I said. "I feel like I've intruded into an intimate part of my mother's life. I understand why you kept it from me."

"That's a relief," she said, "and we'll talk more." Looking at her watch, she added, "About six hours to New Year's. Let's have champagne and a lovely supper, here. Maybe you could rustle that up while I unpack, take a short nap, and bathe."

✳✳✳

Fiona was a marginal cook, and I did the cooking when we were together. I drove to the supermarket and was preparing dinner when she came downstairs in a silk dressing gown, looking fresh and smelling of soap. "Smells scrumptious, whatever it is," she said.

"Pâté is ready to go. The baguette slices are toasting. Champagne's in the freezer. Filet mignons in a cream and port sauce, roasted stick potatoes and sautéed mushrooms, and a salade verte. A bottle of Burgundy from my girlfriend's wine cellar is breathing."

"Your best girl." She laughed. "I moved your things into my bedroom. I doubt if we ever fooled my neighbors or yours." She handed me a slice of pâté on toast with a dab of mustard and sliced cornichon. I took the champagne out of the freezer and popped the cork. As we clicked glasses, she said, "Next year will be interesting, but we'll get through it, won't we?"

I agreed. Fiona loved me, and I was content.

We didn't wait for New Year's and went to bed after supper. At midnight, a honking horn woke me. "Happy New Year," Fiona said. "It's that obnoxious youngster a couple of houses over and his friends. Someone should phone the police."

"I dozed off, sorry."

Fiona rolled on her side to face me. "More sex or a cigarette?"

"Sex."

"Thought so," she said. "Ah, when Philippa was showing me Townie and Chip's photos, she had difficulty explaining a picture of Helen Jacobs."

"Helen does volunteer work for the San Francisco Opera. You've met her when you had volunteers here for dinner a few years ago."

"She looked familiar. Why is she in the picture?"

"Helen came to the Roths' Christmas party. Afterwards we had dinner and talked, that's all. Helen invited me to a dinner party on Christmas Day. The private detective Townie had following me phoned her apartment. I told Helen about us, and she asked me to leave. I haven't seen her since and don't expect to."

"Was she upset?"

"Very."

"So there was a connection, at least on Helen's part?"

"I guess so."

"And you?"

"Well, yes, sort of, I guess. She's going through a rough time, and I thought you were leaving me."

"Tatiana's son after all." With a smile, she asked, "Now where were we?"

"I was about to kiss you. But before we get to that, I was wondering about Dr. Sternberg. He told me that you trust only two people: him and me." Fiona nodded. "Do you trust Dr. Sternberg more?"

"I trust Richard differently." She tickled my ribs. "A soupçon of jealousy?" With a throaty chortle, she added, "You flatter me so. Mind if I tell Richard?"

"Go right ahead."

CHAPTER 25

NEW YEAR'S DAY 1987

SAN FRANCISCO

Rain against the window woke me. I rolled over and found the cool side of the pillow. Fiona was sleeping next to me; I fell asleep watching her. Waking again, I was alone, and there was the faintest smell of coffee. I found Fiona in the study on the sofa in a dressing gown with a blanket over her legs. She was reading a French novel and listening to Schumann's *Papillons*.

We kissed, and she said, "Lazy, rainy day. I haven't decided whether or not to get dressed. Snowing in the Sierras with a traveler's advisory; driving to Tahoe is out of the question. So it's New Year's Day and just the two of us."

"Answered prayers." I set a fire in the fireplace with plenty of paper and kindling; the fire took off faster than expected. We watched until the flames settled down before going to the kitchen. Fiona filled our coffee cups and handed me the pack of cigarettes I had left on the table.

"Smoke whenever you wish," she said. "I want you to quit but refuse to nag."

"I'm going to quit when things settle down." *After Drew's death,* I thought.

"Any thoughts about your next job?"

"I have the better part of a year to come up with something." I explained my severance package.

"Nice work," she said. "Drew wants you to take over his business. He told me that you've looked at the books and know about my loans; I'll do whatever you wish."

"If I don't take Drew's offer, how will you do?"

"I'll most likely recover the money I loaned Drew. My agreement with Drew states that in the event of his death, his estate will be liquidated and repay my loans." I didn't ask for the details. But she gave them. "I inherited Drew's home from my mother and leased it to him; his nominal monthly payments paid the taxes." Fiona's eyes clouded. "I knew when I loaned Drew the money that he'd never repay me," she said in her business voice. "I think he saw my loans as money I owed him for failing as a mother."

"I don't deserve Drew's offer."

"Some advice: put your guilt aside and follow your dreams; your innate talent will do the rest."

"Oh, I don't know."

"Please, Alexander, at least reconsider his offer."

"I will."

She shook her head and started back to the study.

"Fiona, something else has been on mind." She turned back. "You've always claimed that I seduced you when we first made love. I don't remember it that way."

"You didn't take much seducing." She blushed. "You were dumbfounded. After several nervous heartbeats of mine, you came around and participated."

"Why did you do that?"

"Before Tatiana's illness, you were a bright, engaging young man. Tatiana, you, and I spent hours talking about all sorts of things. I was quite fond of you. But when Tatiana became ill, you turned into a sarcastic knockoff of Drew. You were downright mean to me. Nevertheless, I wasn't about to let you go to New York."

"So you attacked me?"

"And in my arms I found Tatiana's child—lost, terrified, and about to make a profound mistake. You opened your heart to me. We made love, and I began falling in love with you."

"Didn't you think I was gay?"

"You have to be loved; it's your nature. Without Tatiana, you went to the first person who loved you, and that was Drew." I was about to rephrase my question. She put up her hand. "I was too absorbed with Tatiana to know what I was thinking about you and Drew. I may have thought it was a phase; sex among teenage boys isn't that uncommon. However, when you were younger, you were curious about women; I'd catch you looking at me and other women in that vaguely predatory sort of way that men have."

"All that was going through your mind?"

"Not really. One thought remains clear: I had promised Tatiana to look after you and was determined to keep that promise, no matter what it took. What would have happened if you'd gone to New York?"

"Drew would have figured everything out."

"In other words, you were going to turn your life over to Drew?"

"That's right."

"Did it cross your mind that Drew was manipulating you just like he did everyone else?"

"Not at the time."

Fiona nodded. "One more thing, Alexander: should I ever encounter Tatiana—let's say in the afterlife—I won't have a problem telling her about you and me. Tatiana would be proud of how you turned out. So would Andre. I certainly am."

"I was lucky to have found you."

"We're both lucky." She started back to the study. "Let's settle down and watch those football games." Neither of us had the slightest interest in sports.

"I'll run out and get some beer and a pizza."

"Always so thoughtful, Alexander."

Fiona went back to the sofa and picked up her book while I thumbed through a French magazine she had bought. When I turned to say something, she had fallen asleep with the book on her chest. I put the book aside, took off her reading glasses, and tucked the blanket around her. She said something I didn't understand and turned to her side.

Her book, a murder mystery set in a two-star restaurant in Aix-en-Provence, was very French with elaborate descriptions of the meals. I read until a chef carved a duck, then used a *canardier* (a duck presser) to extract the juices from the carcass. The renderings were swirled into butter, cognac, and Madeira to grace the medium-rare duck. My mouth watered. There was a whole chicken in the refrigerator I could roast along with potatoes, carrots, and pearl onions. Hardly pressed duck, but excellent for a rainy day. I was sliding the chicken into the oven when I heard the shower running.

"Roast chicken, perfect for a day like this," Fiona said, coming into the kitchen. She had put on lipstick, fixed her hair, and was dressed in slacks, a blouse, and a sweater. "Spending the day without getting dressed is decadent, or tacky, I can't decide which. Anyway..." She trailed off but refocused. "Drew accused me of putting my 'society friends,' as he called them, ahead of everything else. Do you think so?"

"No, but your friends are important to you. How will they react to us?"

"They'll laugh at me." Fiona sighed. "A man like Townie, with a younger wife, is revered for his prowess. An older woman with a younger man is pitied. The younger man is seen as...as..." She paused. "What's the French word I'm looking for?"

"Roturier?"

"You're hardly riffraff," Fiona said.

"We've been together longer than many of their marriages," I said. "And I don't care what people think of me."

"You're going to have to teach me how to do that." Fiona's smile was doubtful. "Things will change; getting to the resolution might be difficult. But we'll get there. On the bright side, family members are terrified. I'm not a vengeful woman, but, my Lord, watching them is enjoyable. That we've been together for this long dumbfounds them. They see the estate slipping away." She laughed. "I should have sprung this on them ages ago." Pointing to the wine cellar, she asked, "French or California?"

After lunch, Fiona went back to the sofa and her book while I stood in front of the television, clicking through the channels, past the football games, and came across a Matt Helm movie from the '60s. Dean

Martin was Matt Helm, America's tipsy answer to James Bond. The co-star, Ann-Margaret, at least seemed sober. The movie was shot on the French Riviera.

Watching Dean and Ann-Margaret smirk into the camera, Fiona put her book down and said, "They're not even trying to act and are tickled to get paid." After an aerial panorama of the Riviera, she added, "We should just pack up and go there. We could call ourselves Scott and Zelda."

"Or Dean and Ann-Margaret," I said, sitting next to her. "When I was a boy, we spent vacations around where that movie was shot. One afternoon, Mother and I dropped in on Somerset Maugham, you know, the writer?"

"I've heard of him," Fiona said with narrowed eyes.

"Of course you have." I patted her leg and turned off the television. "Anyway, it was our last summer in France; we were on the Riviera near Cap Ferret where Maugham lived up in the hills. Before lunch, Mother and I were walking up there when an enormous chauffeur-driven American car came around a corner and almost hit us. The couple in the back turned to look at us; Mother recognized them."

"Who were they?"

"I'm getting to that. Up the way, the car turned into an entrance-way. We followed and went through the opened iron gates of this grand home—two or three stories, white, wonderful garden. She introduced herself to the security people as Countess Romanovskaya, I was the young count, and we had been invited to lunch. Even though we arrived on foot looking like an ordinary French mother and son, one of the security men bowed and waved us through the front door."

Fiona said, "I've never heard this."

"So in we went; talk about nervous. In the foyer, Mother told a servant that she would have a whiskey and soda and orange juice for me. When the servant left, she winked at me. We looked at a group of fashionable people on the veranda listening to someone tell a story in English. They all laughed, then one, by one, by one, they turned to look at us."

"What did you do?"

"I wanted out; Mother grabbed my shoulder. An older man wearing espadrilles approached and asked in French what we wanted. He looked fierce but was polite, and he stammered. It was Somerset Maugham. Mother told him that one of his guests had almost run us over and she wanted an apology. About then our drinks arrived along with a man who was about my size back then. He spoke to Maugham in English."

"Okay, who was he?"

"The Duke of Windsor, King Edward VIII, who abdicated to marry the American divorcee, Wallis Simpson."

"You're kidding!"

"Not at all. Maugham translated; the duke apologized and offered Mother a cigarette. I remember his cigarette case, silver with engraved ostrich plums, the crest of the Prince of Wales. Mother said the cigarette was custom-made and delicious. That afternoon Mother was incredible; she had Maugham and the duke laughing with a story about a huge American car getting stuck in a medieval French town. The duke's wife joined us and was introduced as Her Royal Highness—an exquisite cobra Mother said later. Then lunch was announced, and we were invited. But we had to meet Father and were late as it was. The duke's chauffeur drove us."

"What did Andre say?"

"At first, he didn't believe us. Mother and I were always coming up with fantastic stories, but Mother had whiskey on her breath to prove it. And the chauffeur said that he worked for the Duc du Windsor, the old Prince de Galles."

Fiona got weepy.

I put my arm around her. "Sorry, not that amusing."

"I was just thinking about meeting you and Tatiana, and how we designed that home overlooking the Mediterranean." She began crying.

"Fiona, why not come with me tomorrow? Before I see Drew, I'll drive over to Reno and you can catch a plane back here. We'll be together another day. I'd like that."

"Why don't you drive that car to France," she said.

"Okay, let's go to France this spring. Spend a week or so in Paris. Then we'll rent a car and head south. No schedules, no plans. If we like some place, we'll stay until we're ready to leave. We'll end up on the Riviera and rent a place up in the mountains."

"The kitchen will have a view of the sea?" she asked with an unsteady voice.

"Of course. And we'll have meals out on the terrace and watch the shore lights shimmering off the water, just the two of us. We'll get a satellite hookup so you can watch baseball."

Fiona dried her eyes. "Is that a promise, Dean?"

"You can bet the farm on it, Ann-Margaret."

Chapter 26

Friday, January 2, 1987

San Francisco

The day after New Year's was cold and rainy, but the traveler's advisory for the Sierras had been cancelled.

I tried to convince Fiona to accompany me, but a new storm was expected in the Sierras that afternoon that might cancel flights from Reno. Fiona didn't want to risk being stranded in Reno and decided to stay. I called Drew's and told the nurse that I should arrive that evening, depending on the weather.

I stopped at my place to repack. Philippa was dressed for business and was going to meet Helen; I offered to drive her. In the car she said, "When I called Helen this morning, she seemed cool, not hostile, but cool. How was it left with her?"

I explained Christmas evening and said, "I was dishonest. But Helen offered you the favor, not me. She's honest, and I'd be surprised if she didn't keep her word. How does it stand with Universal?"

"I called in sick, terrible case of the flu. Did Fiona explain Drew's accusations?"

"We talked everything through. I'm the only son of Tatiana and Andre Romanovsky. I'll tell you the details later."

Looking out the window, Philippa started to speak but stopped. Approaching the Financial District, she said, "This is very personal, but I've actually prayed that your looking after Drew will…will…" She turned to look at me. "I hope caring for Drew will somehow loosen Tatiana's hold on you."

I parked in a loading zone across from the Growers and Ranchers building. Philippa was looking straight ahead. "Your prayers are important to me and so are you," I said.

"Please phone. Promise?"

"Promise. Helen is a kind woman. If this doesn't work, we'll think of something else."

***

I made good time to Sacramento. Through the foothills, the snow was light; it was drifting in the Sierras. At nightfall I saw the State Line casinos and realized that I had gone too far east. I backtracked and found the house I hadn't seen since that summer. Set on a forested hill, the half-timbered Swiss-inspired chalet was more imposing than I remembered. The steep driveway had been plowed; I put the car into its lowest gear and began the ascent.

The nurse, a no-nonsense Filipina, told me that she would wake Drew from his nap. The home's interior was rustic elegance: faded oriental carpets covered the pine plank floors; the living room ceiling was arched to about twelve feet; and a massive river-stone fireplace held a low fire that needed refreshing. Waiting for the new logs to catch, I noticed a photograph of Fiona's father on the mantel. Taken in the '30s or '40s, it shows him fly fishing in a three-piece suit and a homburg; chest waders were his only accommodation to the trout stream.

I heard Drew approaching.

"Fiona's father passed his dignity to her," he said, opening his arms. "I'm so very glad you're here." We embraced. Drew stood back. "Quite the Russian bear." I had purchased my boots, overcoat, and Astrakhan hat in Moscow.

Drew looked terrible. Weight loss had loosened the skin around his neck, his eyes were heavy with fatigue, and he spoke with a slight slur. Always vain, he was wearing a black-and-yellow silk foulard dressing gown that gentlemen wore "at home" around the turn of the century.

His pleated shirt was opened at the neck with a slim black ascot; formal trousers and men's pumps completed the picture.

"You look terribly smart," I said. "Right out of a British period-piece film."

"Flattery should only slightly exaggerate." Drew smiled. "My body is consuming itself." He touched my face. The blackness around my eyes was fading, but my nose was still taped. "Not a bear, a Russian raccoon? Are there raccoons in Russia?"

"I've seen them plundering garbage cans."

Drew began weaving. I led him to the wing chair by the fireplace. Motioning to the side table in the dining room, he said, "A glass of mineral water, if you please; it's in the wine bucket. I've had a supper prepared, but first let's talk while you help yourself to the Montrachet we drank when we were last up here that summer."

I gave Drew his mineral water, got out of my winter gear, and sat on the hearth, facing him. As I began uncorking the wine, Drew pressed a remote channel changer. "Your favorites, Rachmaninov's Second and Third Piano Concerti." We listened to the music's broad sweep that softened with an interlude of piano and violin.

"Very Russian," I said. "A snowy night deep in the forest, the evocative music; all we need is a pack of wolves outside howling."

"You like Rachmaninov, but I don't know. He's always struck me as a competent technician. Tchaikovsky, now there was an artist, the Russian sweep: the steppes, the broad river. The…what's that Russian river?"

"Plenty of them: the Don, Dnieper, and, of course, the Volga."

"Yes, the Volga. I see the Volga when I listen." He paused. "Who's that Russian?" I suggested Tchaikovsky, and Drew closed the subject. I poured a glass of the wine and tasted it. "Like you remembered it?" he asked.

"Lovely, just the same."

The music turned portentous. Drew shifted himself; the weight loss must have made sitting even in the padded wing chair uncomfortable. Snapping his fingers, he said, "Alexander, you really gave us a scare. Fiona spoke with the Englishwoman." He arched an eyebrow. "She's living in your place. Why?"

"She wanted to leave her apartment."

"She told Fiona that you were fired and the reasons why. What's her name?"

"Philippa."

"Yes, Philippa said that you had gone away, but she didn't know where. Fiona was beside herself but couldn't leave. You see, my last seizure was devastating." Drew tossed his head. "Oh, now don't blame yourself; the seizure was my fault. I was so terribly angry with you. But Fiona never lost her composure and kept her feelings as bottled up as ever." He put up his right hand and wiggled the fingers, strings tied around each of them. He extended his thumb. "This one reminded me not to tell Fiona that I've known about you two all along. The others are for us to talk about this evening, hopefully. We must get everything cleared up."

"Let's try."

Drew took the string from his thumb. "Of course, I didn't tell Fiona, although, I must admit, the thought of setting the record straight was tantalizing after all these years. But you told me not to." He tossed his head. "So it's as it's always been: you and Fiona, with me on the outside looking in."

"I owe you an explanation. I—"

"Tell me about Philippa. Is she the one you told me about when we had dinner?"

"No, she's not. Philippa has met Fiona. My relationship with Philippa is quite proper."

"Really?" Drew said, tenting his fingers. "Do I detect a certain ambiguity? You love Philippa?"

"I love Fiona much more."

He stood up and pointed to the string around his ring finger. "I must address my revelations about Tatiana, my lashing out. I was furious that you had discovered my efforts on your behalf. I still want you to take my business." Before I could answer, he added, "I was worried that you may have harmed yourself; so was Fiona." He paused. "Fiona watches you for signs of madness."

"Fiona told you that?"

"She let it slip," Drew said. "Fiona thinks you're…you're as fragile as Tatiana." He held on to the back of his chair. "Fragile? The Englishwoman's champion. Saving Fiona from Townie and Chip. You're quite intrepid."

"What did Fiona say about Townie and Chip?"

Drew continued in the same light tone, "Oh, she said that you advised her not to become involved in Chip's project. The Englishwoman told Fiona that you and Chip had come to blows. Looks like he worked you over quite thoroughly."

"Drew, Fiona has no idea that you encouraged Townie and Chip to blackmail her. I'll never tell her, and I've made sure that Townie, Chip, and Debra won't. So that'll remain between us."

He glanced at the strings. "But you'll tell her after I'm gone?"

"No, I won't, I swear it."

"Why?" Drew demanded.

"Fiona would be devastated; I won't let that happen."

"I hope you're being truthful," he said, "I don't want her thinking that jealousy, or revenge, or anything like that motivated me. I was thinking of you, only you." As he looked off into the fireplace, Drew's breathing was ragged.

I ventured, "There are a couple of things you should understand about Fiona and me."

He went ashen. "Understand? I understand plenty. Fiona was always cold and indifferent to me—me, her only son. When you and Tatiana took Fiona into that private world of yours, she grew more remote."

Seeing he was about to topple over, I took his arm. "Drew, calm down." He pulled away. "When my mother and I met Fiona, you were playing Fiona off against your father. Later you told me that you hated Fiona."

"She would have you believe that."

"I'm repeating what you told me back then."

"I loved Fiona, but what could I do?" Drew shouted. "You and Tatiana took Fiona away from me; then Fiona took you from me. I was left, all alone. Alone. Do you understand what that's like?"

I grabbed the lapels of his dressing gown before he fell. The nurse ran out of her room.

Drew waved her away, but she didn't leave. He pushed my hands away. "You've never been walked out on, have you? Never given your love, unconditionally, only to have it scorned? Ignominy, what do you know of that?"

"What do you think my mother did?" I said, helping him back in the chair.

"That's different," Drew hissed. "Not the same, not the love we had. Our spirits had joined." The nurse hurried to the kitchen and returned with a glass of water and several pills. Drew downed the pills; the three of us were quiet until he said, "I went through a lot of men, looking for you. But I forced them to leave. Know why?"

The nurse went to her room just off the living room and left the door opened. A tranquilizer was working; the tension in his shoulders subsided. I sat on the arm of his chair and took his hand.

Drew leaned back. "Know why?"

"So you could walk out on them before they walked out on you?"

"How did you learn that?" he asked.

"A person I knew briefly drew the same conclusion."

Drew continued, "I only wish you had told me about Fiona when it started. Eventually, I'd have understood. Instead you just left me hanging, alone." He pulled his hand from mine.

I stood up. "Our last dinner was very personal; why didn't you tell me that you had it figured out then? Maybe we could have avoided Townie and Chip and kept it between the two of us."

"Better put—the three of us," Drew said. "We all had secrets to keep. You and Fiona would have looked utterly ridiculous: you with a mother substitute and Fiona keeping a man half her age. I believe the eminently upright Fiona Sinclair was your legal guardian when she first took you to bed? Risking her measured life to recapture her youth? Or was it an effort to raise a son whom she loved and who loved her?"

"Despite some uncomfortable truths—"

"I see; love above all." Drew glared. "What about me and my mortifying secrets? Not so long ago, I was so attractive that men and women looked at me. And yes, quite amusing. Enchanting, I dare say. One might have assumed that everything was going my way, but there was the tiniest fly in the ointment: the man I loved ran off with my mother, a cold, arrogant woman. Having that get out would have made me an unbelievable laughingstock. Have you ever thought of that? Has Fiona?"

"Yes, we have. Look—"

"No, you look," Drew said. "Telling Townie about you and Fiona, I put my very soul on the line to help you. That's the sacrifice I made; that's how much I've always loved you."

"I know that, and that's why I'm here. I never gave you an honest explanation because I couldn't bring myself to do so. I prayed that you would never find out; so did Fiona. The humiliation would have been horrendous for the three of us, but more for you and Fiona. With the least to lose, I took the easy way and waited until now."

"Until I was dying," Drew said.

"That's right. When Fiona and I came together, we thought about you, but we thought of ourselves more."

"Really, you included *me*?" he asked with grave sarcasm.

"Yes, of course."

He looked into the fire. "Ours was a very consuming relationship. I've never been that close with anyone else. Fred was close, but…"

"Drew, it wasn't going to last; I'm not gay."

"You had *me* fooled." His laugh had some tranquilizer in it.

"Well, that's not discounting youthful enthusiasm. But you're the only man I've ever gone to bed with. Since you, the thought of another man has no appeal whatsoever."

"And Fiona the only woman?" Drew asked.

"That's right. Not much of a sex life by today's standards."

"But you don't have AIDS. You love Fiona?"

"Very much."

Drew nodded, glanced at the strings before closing his eyes. I drank some wine and watched him; he was so still that I thought he had fallen asleep and was about to get the nurse when he said, "Fiona must know that I know."

Caught off guard, I managed, "I'm sure she doesn't. Thank you for not telling her." There was a question in Drew's eye. "And Fiona will never know."

"Swear to me that she won't."

"I swear that too."

"So now you know all the secrets," Drew said.

"I'm pretty good at keeping them."

"All of us are," he added. "I've always wondered what would have become of us if you had come to New York." Looking at the strings, he continued, "You could have gone to art school; I would have secured the money from Fiona or my father."

"You've always had money. Back then I was living off of Fiona's largess."

He nodded. "That's how it started with you two, didn't it? Fiona's money?"

"Maybe the money was a consideration."

"It's so very clear. Fiona paid for Stanford and got you the job at Universal. So you've used her—just like everyone else in the family."

"Unlike everyone else in her family, I love Fiona."

"In my own way, I love Fiona, sure I do. And she loves me. We've been telling each other that since I came up here. Alex, you have talent; it's in your genes. And what did you do? You let Fiona throw it away. Scattered it to the winds, a triumph of comfort over innate talent." With fluttering hands, he continued, "Pathetic, so pathetic."

"I've seen artistic talent; my mother was gifted; so are you," I said. "In college I realized that I had a flare for design, an interest in art, but that was it."

"So you became a banker, a man who finds fulfillment in a book of accounts. How very common." His tone was supercilious; that summer, we spoke that way.

"My, my, so bourgeois," I said with an indolent wave. "Back in college, I pictured myself owning a shop on Union Street. I might have called the enterprise Count Romanovsky's, an appealing cachet for the bourgeois. Bitching at my customers, those arrivistes, I'd hate myself for stooping to take their money. Frankly, that frightened me."

"Making fun of me and my clients?" Drew asked.

"I envy what you've accomplished."

He shifted in the chair and winced. "What if I don't give you what you want? Will you run away, leave me here alone?"

"No, I won't."

"You could witness my suicide."

"I pray that you don't."

"Couldn't take it, could you?"

"Probably not."

"Then what?"

"I'd probably go as crazy as my mother. That's what you want?"

Drew was quite cool. "Floundering in self-hatred, Fiona would pity you once again; and you two could start over, but this time without the distraction of me around." I started toward the dining room. "Leaving?" he asked.

"Rachmaninov and this lovely wine isn't working," I said. "Need something that packs a wallop; warm vodka should do it. Liquor still in the kitchen?"

"So dismally Slavic," Drew said. "After all your duplicity, I was hoping for truthfulness. Fiona managed that, in her fashion, and I was hoping you would." His voice rose. "But instead you're going to swill vodka and continue spinning fatuous mea culpas. Well, go right ahead; you've got a captive audience after all."

"Drew, I came up here to ask for your forgiveness and to be with you. You said that Fiona and I were the two most important people in your life; well, you and Fiona are the most important people in mine. But Fiona's not up to this; so it's just the two of us." I took his shoulders. "You're angry with me and have every reason to be after what I've put you through. I'm not defending myself, only explaining. I won't be driven away. I refuse to let you die alone."

"Because of Tatiana?"

"In some part. But you see, I won't lie to you anymore."

He looked past me.

I was on the hearth facing him. "Drew, look at me, please."

His eyes were tearing.

"I have no idea what you're going through. But I was terrified, and you found me and loved me. And I repaid you with deceit. Now I must redeem myself."

"One of those Catholic things. A penance?" Drew asked with a sob.

"It's a confession, as honest as I can make it. They're no good otherwise. My mother told me that people aren't really gone until they're forgotten, and I'll never forget you, Drew, never."

"I wanted to make it nice," he said, wiping his eyes. "The music, the wine, roasted chicken, and warm French potato salad—your favorites.

I didn't want to put you through this, but I had to hear it all. Now our time together will be meaningful, I promise." He looked at the strings. "I realize that you won't take my business. Fiona doesn't think so either."

"Did she say why?"

"No." Drew wiggled his forefinger at me. "But I know why."

"I don't deserve it, not after how I've treated you."

"Quite a penance," he said. "I don't know about such things, but denying God's gift is a sin, if you ask me."

I couldn't talk.

"One more thing: Why did you become a banker?"

I wiped my eyes. "I liked wearing three-piece suits and being pompous."

He looked baffled.

"I was trying to lighten this up a little."

Drew smiled. "I want to tell you about my last conversation with Tatiana." He read my face. "No, no, nothing to worry about. I've told Fiona, and she asked me to tell you." He got up. "Give me your arm and walk me into the kitchen." He continued, "Just before we came up here that summer, Fiona asked me to watch Tatiana while she and the nurse did errands; you were out some place. Tatiana was lucid that day. When I told her that you and I were going to take a trip, she started in French—the wars in Russia, the Germans in France, the German officer. She…she knew. And the Russian internment camp in Germany. She begged me to take you away because she was afraid all that might spill out."

"Why didn't you tell me before?"

"Like Fiona, I wouldn't damage your memories of Tatiana," Drew said, leaning against the kitchen counter. "Tatiana must have decided on suicide and wanted to get to it; Fred was the same. I can only assume that Tatiana wanted to spare you witnessing her death or stumbling on its aftermath. She loved you too much to risk that."

"Oh my God!"

"Alexander, I'm dying and want to get to it, but I won't end this miserable existence of mine—my gift to you, the only one you'll take." He held up his hand and untied the strings, except the index finger that he wiggled at me. "To remind myself everything is forgiven and settled; I promise." It was a promise he couldn't keep.

CHAPTER 27

MARCH 9, 1987

LAKE TAHOE

I slept on a trundle bed next to Drew's. Preparing for the night's sleep, I would read while he watched the evening news. Some evenings, he would sleep through the night. But often early in the morning, he would awake, screaming from nightmares. He was confused and didn't know who I was or where we were; getting him back to sleep required sleeping pills.

With the sleeping pills, Drew's nightmares were replaced with a kind of sleepwalking. Drew would wake up and announce that he had been dreaming of me. In a sullen temper, he marshaled his accumulated resentments.

His preparation reminded me of artillery drills in the National Guard. The guns were unlimbered; range and elevation were checked and rechecked. Once the target was acquired, shells were slammed into the breeches and the lanyards pulled. His barrage commenced with my duplicity, Fiona's deceit, our wickedness, Fiona's security, the indolence that Fiona's security imbued. Then desultory volleys of invective followed: clinging, weak, slothful, childish. The ordnance exhausted, Drew fell into a sweaty sleep.

One morning, Drew woke up looking somewhat refreshed. "Sleep well?" he asked.

"Okay."

"Then why do you look so dreadful?"

I got up to make tea. "Did you dream of me before I arrived?"

"Good Lord, my dreams aren't always dreams. I mean, sometimes I'm kind of awake."

"That's right."

He swung his emaciated legs out of bed and started to get up but sat down. "And I hurl the most awful invectives." He fell back into the bed. "What to do?"

The dark had always frightened Drew. To end his nighttime terrors, we started dozing during the days and talked through the nights. That worked; perhaps his anger had run its course, or perhaps he had become too weak to continue. His nightmares had given way to hushed scenes of sinister birds and foggy landscapes. He thought his dreams were those of a man awaiting death.

About three months after I arrived, I was sitting next to Drew in bed, reading aloud from *Alice in Wonderland*. He loved the story, and it was up to him whether I read in French, Russian, or English. That morning, it was French. Alice was about to slumber off when Le Lapin Blanc in a waistcoat ran, stopped, looked at his pocket watch, and ran away. Alice followed him into the rabbit hole and floated down to a small door in a garden wall that led to Wonderland.

The sun rose from the Nevada basin over the Sierras, filling the room with thin winter light, its pale radiance trailing mist from the great purple lake below. Drew tugged my sleeve and called me; I held him as the light left his eyes. I closed his eyes, untied the last string from his index finger, and pulled the sheet over his face.

***

Drew had asked that his funeral be limited to his closest friends. Fiona contacted Drew's father, who was incapacitated and could not attend. The service was held at the Presbyterian church that Fiona attended. From the unadorned altar, the forthright minister went to the matter at hand: the contemplation of Drew's life and memorializing his death—efficient and swift.

At the interment, the minister led final prayers as mourners placed flowers on Drew's casket. Fiona would be buried between her parents and Drew. If I wished, I would rest next to my mother. Drew thought my mother and I had come between Fiona and him; but in death Drew would be next to Fiona while my mother and I would be at the edge of the family plot. Maybe it should have always been that way.

Drew's funeral was on a Monday. The following Thursday afternoon, Philippa phoned and said, "Not calling too early, I hope. How are you and Fiona?"

"Oh, we're doing okay," I said. "I was thinking of calling you and getting together for a drink. Maybe today after work?"

"Love to. Oh, take a look at the newspaper…the business section."

We agreed to meet at the Growers and Ranchers Bank's main entrance.

After I went to Tahoe, Philippa decided to return to England in the near future; I suggested that she leave her dingy apartment and stay in my flat until she left. Helen found Philippa a job in the bank's revolving secretarial pool; a month later, Philippa became Helen's administrative assistant. From what Philippa told me, they got along.

I was smoking a cigarette outside Growers and Ranchers when Helen approached.

"Philippa asked me to tell you that she's running about ten minutes late." Helen closed her eyes. "A month without a cigarette, and they're still on my mind. I dream of the damned things: I'm sitting in an empty room smoking one Marlboro after another, holding the smoke down before exhaling—delicious."

"One month," I said. "You've got the physical addiction whipped; now it's the mental part." I took a final drag and flipped the cigarette into the street.

Helen's eyes turned envious as the butt bounced onto the cable car tracks. "Easy for you to say. Philippa told me that you were with Drew. How are you doing?"

"I'm okay, I guess. And you?"

"Okay," she said. "I'm sorry about Drew, not that I ever knew him. I mean, it's that, well, AIDS…" She paused. "Being there, dealing with that must have been difficult. Horrendous, I imagine. Drew was lucky to have had you there."

"Nice of you to say, but I don't know. Thinking about it, Drew would have been happier if I had stayed in France."

Helen grimaced.

"Sorry. Right now, everything is bubbling up and splashing around, even on your kind intentions."

"I know, I know; it's tough going. These things take time." With a sad smile, she asked, "Are you taking Drew's business?"

"Too much baggage."

"Too much to carry and run a business?"

"That's right."

"None of my business, none whatsoever," she said. "But you might want to consider this: the mind usually overrules the heart; guilt trumps both of them. And…" Helen looked down the street.

"Helen, about Christmas…"

She turned to me.

"I apologize; the phone call at your place was frightening. I was dishonest and apologize for that as well."

"Philippa told me a little about all that. What a terrible family Fiona Sinclair must have."

"They are, but I still feel badly."

"No need to be," Helen said. "I've thought about it: we had dinner, talked a lot, and went to a cocktail party. Two people at loose ends getting through a lonely Christmas. I called you names, I regret that."

"You called me dishonest; it fit."

"Well, as it turned out, it doesn't matter," she said with a dismissive wave.

"That's one way of looking at it."

"That's the way *I* look at it," she replied. "I'm just full of useful insights this afternoon. Before I run out, got to hop, festivities this evening."

"Well, enjoy yourself."

She then looked back. "Just wondering: if I asked you for a cigarette, would you give me one?"

"No, you'd just have to quit again."

"Certainly don't want to go through that." Helen hurried down the street.

About five minutes later, Philippa met me, and we started walking up California Street.

"Sorry, last-second call that went longer than I thought," she said. "How are you doing…really?"

"Getting through it. The desolation comes in waves."

"The waves get smaller," she said. "Why don't you and Fiona spend the summer on the Riviera? Sun and saltwater, along with French food and wine, mends the soul. As for me, it's TTG."

"TTG?"

"Time To Go Home. Everything has come together rather quickly."

"Oh dear, what are you going to do?"

"An uncle found me a job at Lloyds, the insurance people."

"I've heard of them."

She laughed. "It's a job while I figure out how to do what I want to do. Did you read the newspaper?"

"I did. Wow."

"What do you think?"

"Neville's all through," I said. Andrew Neville lost the race for Universal's CEO; the winner announced that Neville would be President of Universal's new investment banking operation in New York. "He's been put on a shelf. A commercial banker masquerading as an investment banker never works. People at Universal are probably distancing themselves from Neville."

"Helen said the same thing. What will happen to him?"

"Do you care?"

"Not at all," Philippa said.

"How did you leave it with Neville?"

"His ruthlessness begot mine," she replied. "After the General Loan Committee meetings on Fridays, Andrew and the Committee members would go to his office for lunch. I gave them time to settle in and marched past that officious secretary of his. Andrew reached for the phone. I told him that would look bloody marvelous: uniformed security turfing his ex-mistress out of his office. Everyone just sat there. Then I told Andrew that it was time to settle up, and to my satisfaction. The other men left. And, I suspect, with them went Andrew's chances at CEO."

"That took courage."

"We English are at our best with our backs against the wall. I told Andrew that I would hire the smarmiest lawyer in San Francisco and sue him—some ground-breaking palimony sort of thing. Andrew said that the case would be thrown out of court. Fine with me; it was the publicity I wanted. Salacious publicity? Neither Andrew nor Universal's board had considered that."

"How did he take it?"

"Furious, incredulous, until it sunk in. I told him that in exchange for half a million dollars, I'd be out of his life and return home. I gave him the name of my London bankers and told him that if the money wasn't there in ten business days, I would commence legal action and grant interviews to the press or anyone whose interest may have been piqued."

"And?"

"The money was there in eight days," Philippa said. "I think Universal's board wondered how Andrew could run that enormous bank if he couldn't manage me."

"That's probably right."

"I allowed Andrew to look into my soul, but I didn't look into his that well. I never imagined he'd cheapen me, betray me." She looked me in the eyes. "You don't approve, do you?"

"It's just that, well, betrayal has been on my mind," I said.

"Drew? You certainly repaid Drew for whatever you may have done to him. You understand that, don't you?"

"And I understand my mother more. Drew said that before the suicide, she asked him to take me away, probably because she didn't want me there when she killed herself."

Philippa's eyes were shiny. "Tatiana's love for you transcended even insanity. You can live with that?"

"I'll have to."

"I wanted to see you this afternoon to tell you about Andrew and to thank you…and for this." She handed me a cashier's check for the money I had loaned her. "You safeguarded my dignity until I could reclaim it. Now tell me, why did you help me in the first place?"

"You were desperate, but no more desperate than I became."

"Partly right, but you're missing the important part: you're a kind man—that's why."

"Philippa, you never flinched when I was at my very worst. And your phone calls were heaven sent." We had called each other two or three times a week when I was with Drew.

"Back to what I did to Andrew. What's the American term? A shakedown? It's rather like what happened to you and Fiona?" Her eyes were wary.

I put my hands on her shoulders, "Andrew Neville knew you were defenseless because you loved him."

"That's not actually the point," she said.

"To a large degree it is. Neville didn't think he'd get pushed back, real hard. He never saw that coming, and executives get the big bucks for anticipating the unexpected."

"Sure, there's that," she said. "Helen put it right when she said that Andrew Neville measured me against his ambitions, and it was no contest." Her eyes were misting.

"Sacrificing you for anything I can think of is just plain nuts."

Several blocks behind us on Universal Bank's executive floor, Andrew Neville might have been looking out across the Bay; perhaps as forlorn as Philippa had been that evening I went to her apartment. Rush-hour pedestrians were brushing past us.

"You're a courageous woman," I said. "You've made it and are going home, on your terms."

"No, Alexander, we made it. I'll never forget you." She brushed tears from her eyes. "My British phlegm is foundering." Looking at her watch, she said, "Helen is having a bon-voyage party for me with people from the office. She asked me to invite you but didn't think you'd come."

"Oh, please thank Helen, but I've got to get going."

We continued walking, and Philippa said, "I've gotten to know

Helen. There was some magic between you two?"

"Helen is a nice woman, and I, ah, well…"

"That's precisely what Helen says: 'Alexander is a nice man, and I, ah, well…' Never finishes and blushes like you are." She took my arm, "Just an observation. I leave Saturday morning and want to take you out tomorrow night. Will Fiona mind?"

"No, she has an Opera Alliance meeting."

"Well, think of it as interest on the money I borrowed. We'll do it up proper: vintage champagne, the works."

"Champagne, I love it."

"It makes me happy," she said.

"Me too."

***

Friday night, Philippa and I were meandering our way down Powell Street. It was the champagne: Philippa ordered a bottle of Bollinger '83 to go with the caviar and blini; we had a bottle of Burgundy with our entrées; Clicquot '82 was dessert. We were heading to the St. Francis Hotel, where she had moved after leaving my flat.

"Haven't had this much fun in ages," I said. "Tight as an owl, full of good food and great champagne. My Lord, champagne hangovers are the worst. I'm going to pay for this tomorrow."

Philippa smiled. "All I have to do is sit on a plane and deal with the dehydration." She turned around, looking at the skyline. "Good-bye, fair and misty city. Hopefully my memories of you will improve."

"I'll drive you to the airport."

"Can't abide airport scenes. We'll say good-bye here when we're happier than we ever thought possible last Christmas."

Walking into the hotel lobby, Philippa said, "Have you ever wondered how it might have been if we had met under more conventional circumstances? Let's say, we were vacationing in the south of France, Juan les Pins. After a day at the beach, we might have met while having aperitifs on the terrace, or maybe split a bottle of champagne before supper. A perfect night overlooking the Mediterranean, we would have talked about this and that. And I would have wondered if all

Russian men were so handsome and charming."

"It wouldn't have worked," I said. "If I had stayed in France, my English would have been terrible. And I would have told myself that all English women, especially the beautiful ones, are cold and snotty."

With a sad smile, she said, "But you've considered it?"

"I have. We would have been at a grand dinner party. I would have been in white tie; you would have been radiant and serene—a perfect English rose. I would have been your dinner partner and worried sick about saying something so fatuous that you'd have dismissed me with an indifferent nod. But I'd have pulled myself together for a clever observation; you'd have replied with a heavenly smile."

"How divine," Philippa said. "And I dare say, you and I would have had a delightful life."

"We'll keep in touch, really in touch. We're too close to end it this way."

"Oh, there will be phone calls, then letters, later Christmas cards." She put her hands to my face. "Whatever the correspondence, Alexander Andreivich Romanovsky, we are special people—not many of us left. And I love you so very much, as much as I know you love me."

We put our arms around each other and kissed. Philippa turned and walked to the elevator without looking back.

CHAPTER 28

JUNE 1987

SAN FRANCISCO

Fiona and I were weary. *Le grand ennui*, as she called it.

When Fiona went to Los Angeles on business, we drove instead of flying. Stopping over in Carmel and Santa Barbara, we stretched a one-day drive to three or four. Back to San Francisco was even slower. Before one of her meetings, I found an ad for available cabins on a cruise ship from Los Angeles to Puerto Vallarta, where we stayed a week. We were always together as Fiona withdrew from her family, and her friends distanced themselves.

Fiona's family had expected Drew's death, but not me; they assumed I would be the principal heir. After learning that I was unemployed, their fear became dread. Fiona categorized their reactions: outrage was greed masquerading as scandalized propriety; sycophancy, greed dressed as concern; and disbelief, greed looking for a costume.

Aggressive family members insisted that Fiona distribute the estate "while everyone could enjoy the benefits." The less gracious threatened to contest her competence with the implied threat that a judge would examine the history of our relationship. Fiona withdrew behind a phalanx of lawyers and severed contact with all but a few relatives. Friends were different.

Fiona's friends had erected a bridge and expected her to cross in an acceptable manner. Fiona decided that we'd cross together; her friends didn't concur. The suppers we hosted were grueling: conversations were uneven, departures were early, the good-byes a reprieve. After one such supper, Fiona declined the few invitations she received. She claimed that she didn't mind, but I knew that she did. A counterpoint was the summer opera season that opened in June with *The Flying Dutchman.*

The opera's season openings were an important event on San Francisco's social calendar: women in evening gowns, men in white or black tie. Wagner's *The Flying Dutchman* was tiresome; but, as far as Fiona was concerned, Wagner was better than no opera at all.

During intermission, I watched Townie and his wife engaging a group of Opera Alliance luminaries while Fiona chatted with an old friend. When I joined Fiona, her friend broke off the conversation in midsentence and left Fiona foundering.

"That remarkable woman approaching us looks familiar." Fiona said.

"That's Helen Jacobs. After introductions, I'm going outside for a cigarette."

"Better not." Fiona elbowed me.

Helen was a study in red: Titian-red gown, pendant earrings with blood-red stones, and crimson lipstick. Her hair was pulled back like a ballerina's, and she wasn't wearing glasses. Making the introductions, I reminded them that they had met at an Opera Alliance dinner that Fiona had hosted. Helen recalled the evening as delightful; the compliment buoyed Fiona.

Helen was effervescent and said, "Adolf Hitler loved Wagner, and that makes me wonder about Wagner devotees." Helen stammered, "Having said that, you probably love Wagner?"

"Wasn't it Mark Twain who said that Wagner's music is better than it sounds?" Fiona replied.

We laughed.

Helen and Fiona began discussing the year's opera schedule: the forthcoming productions, performers, and directors. Sprinkled into the conversation were bouncy Italian phrases—*opera buffa, aria cantabile*—along with the German *Gesamtkunstwerk*, whatever that means. I pretended to follow the conversation while gazing at Fiona and Helen.

Fiona, always understated, was in a muted sapphire ensemble with pearls; her cool bearing counterpointed Helen's sunny exuberance.

As the lights dimmed, Helen said to Fiona, "I've enjoyed reconnecting. I'm having friends, true devotees, over for a late supper. Care to join us?"

"Well, thanks—" I began.

Fiona interrupted. "We'll be happy to."

Going back to our seats, I said, "I don't think that's good idea."

"What could be the harm?"

Helen had invited two other couples: John and Kay Widmer, old friends from college, and Sy and Greta Frank. Greta, erupting out of an expensive mauve gown, was uneasy; Sy, in white tie and looking even more like Leonard Bernstein, was cool towards me.

We were standing by the front windows overlooking the Civic Center and the Opera House, and Sy pronounced the evening's performance as excellent and began a monologue on Wagnerian operas. Helen asked me to see to the first drinks from the impromptu bar in the living room while she and Greta checked with the caterers in the kitchen. When I served the drinks, Sy was still holding court.

Fiona disagreed with Sy on a point and asked the Widmers for their thoughts; they disagreed as well. An actual conversation ensued and turned to the Italian composers who would dominate the opera season. Center stage with insights that engaged the others, Fiona sparkled. Supper conversation was more of the same, and Helen asked Fiona which was her favorite opera.

"Oh my goodness!" Fiona said. "I'm quite fond of Mozart's. My favorite is *The Marriage of Figaro*—wit, grace, a perfect opera." Reflecting for a moment, she added, "Figaro was my first opera. I was twelve. Mummy and I studied the opera and the class struggle that propels the story. Afterwards, Daddy took us to his club for supper and an adult discussion of the performance. An indelible memory. Thank you, Helen."

Helen said, "When I was fourteen, Daddy introduced me to opera; his introduction meant so much to me." She didn't explain and asked Sy, "Opera recollections you'd care to share?"

Sy smiled. "We were just married, and Greta squirreled away

enough money for good seats at *La Bohème*. As newlyweds in a dingy apartment on Russian Hill, we identified with the characters and their aspirations." He raised his glass. "To Greta, for introducing a young man from the wrong side of LA to life's more civilized pursuits." A blush bloomed from Greta's décolletage as we raised our glasses.

The Widmers described their introduction to opera. I would be next and caught Fiona's eye and grimaced; she grimaced back. Helen saw us. The Widmers finished with an amusing anecdote; Helen asked the caterers to serve the salad, then said, "You know, most people dismiss opera as overupholstered singers singing in languages they don't understand. That's too bad, isn't it, Fiona?"

Fiona agreed and described the Opera Alliance's outreach programs; but there wasn't much interest, and the conversation turned back to opera itself.

I was trying to look attentive when Sy asked me, "Isn't there an annoying nationalism running through Russian opera?"

"Sorry, I don't know—"

"I mean, early Russians composers focused on nationalistic fairy tales, like *Boris Godunov* and *Prince Igor*."

Fiona interjected, "Opera bores Alexander, but there's no accounting for taste."

"How in the world could opera bore anyone?" Sy asked.

"That people find baseball exciting mystifies me," Fiona replied.

Helen stood up and suggested that we move to the living room for coffee and dessert. Helen and Sy stayed behind, whispering before joining us. By 2:00 a.m., the evening's comfortable intensity was lagging; Fiona motioned to me that it was time to go and said to Helen, "A most enjoyable evening that's catching up with me."

Sy stood up. "With her good manners, Helen would let this opportunity pass, but I won't." Helen looked anxious. He continued, "Fiona, rumors have it that you're leaving the Opera Alliance board. And Helen wants to become more involved; she knows opera and is a capable executive who'd be a stellar addition to any of the organization's worker-bee committees. Perhaps you could introduce Helen to the right people?"

The silence was awkward.

Fiona realized that her influence rather than her company had prompted Helen's invitation. "I'll see what I can do," she said.

I went to the bedroom for our coats.

Helen followed. "I asked Sy not to do that, but that's Sy for you. He's quite something, a real…"

"Jerk," I said. "A pompous, overbearing poseur with no manners."

"Sy doesn't like you. You made a fool of Julian."

"Julian humiliated you," I said. "Should Julian grow up, I imagine he'll be like Sy, only a lot cuter. Nice friends you've got."

"Fiona intimidates Sy. Sy is an opera buff, but Fiona's knowledge is encyclopedic."

"So for that, Sy put down Fiona in front of people she had just met?"

"Shush. He'll hear."

I picked up our coats. "I was polite while Sy tried to embarrass me. But I'm not feeling so polite right now and am going to tell Sy what I think of him."

Helen stood in front of the door. "Please, no scenes. I didn't mean for this to happen. During supper, I decided to approach you before asking Fiona. I didn't want to upset you or her. I told Sy that, but he's bullheaded."

"Excuse me, I'm leaving."

"Fiona is delightful; I see why you love her."

"Helen, if you want something from Fiona, ask her and you'll get a direct answer. You know, earlier this evening, Fiona was happier than I've seen her in a long time. Now she's out there mortified. And I'm really angry."

"True, I wanted something from Fiona, but not this way, so graceless. Fiona should lecture on opera. I could listen to her forever."

"Helen, you're on your own with Fiona. And you're in my way." She stepped aside.

Sy was staring out the window, Greta was in the kitchen, and the Widmers looked sheepish. Fiona stood by the sofa. We said good-bye to the Widmers. Speaking to his back, Fiona said, "Good evening, Sy."

Sy didn't move.

"Sy," I said, "Fiona wished you a good evening."

Sy bowed. "Good evening, Fiona."

Fiona led me to the front door. She was polite and thanked Helen; Helen guided Fiona down the hall. I passed them on the way to the elevator. Helen was speaking; Fiona responded with a burgeoning smile. About five minutes later, they parted with a hug. Helen wished me a good evening.

Walking back to the car, I said, "I told you so."

Fiona took my hand. "Sy wasn't Helen's doing; she was embarrassed and apologized. Helen's the real article and quite knowledgeable. Do you mind if I introduce her around?"

"Go ahead. About leaving the Alliance, perhaps more thought?" I opened the car door.

"I've grown tired of it, and it of me," she said as I got in. "I know that Debra is waiting for me to leave so she can make her move." Fiona looked out the passenger window. "I might try poisoning Debra's aspirations but have neither the influence nor inclination." She turned to me. "What suasion I have left might be better spent on Helen?"

"Sure," I said. "Have you heard anything about Chip Morgan?"

"Oh, meaning to tell you…Chip got into terrible trouble with the district attorney. Something about a complicated arrangement with AIDS victims and condos in Marin County. I wasn't involved, thanks to you."

"You're leaving the Alliance, thanks to me. Thanks to me, your friends slight you. Your family ties are severed, thanks to me. And that jerk Sy humiliates you. I've put up with those people, but I'm really fed up. And—"

"And," Fiona said, "I told you this was coming. Now that it's here, I don't mind as much as I thought. Petty humiliations are annoying for their sheer malice." I watched her silhouette, trying to determine her mood. She winked at me. "You shouldn't fret so."

"You're upset with me about Helen?"

"No, you were candid about her, weren't you?"

"Of course," I said, waiting for a stoplight. "This evening, that's bothering you, or something else?"

"Oh, nothing really." She shrugged. "Thinking of Drew. And Tatiana. And you and me." She was still for several blocks. "Tatiana's grave seems so lonely."

"I think about that too and wish…I wish, oh, I don't know."

Fiona said, "We should get away."

"Let's hop on the first plane to France."

Fiona brightened. "I've got a few things to do, but soon."

Early that morning, I got up to go downstairs for a cigarette when Fiona sat up.

"I can't sleep either," she said, looking at the clock. "Quarter to five. Come back to bed. We'll talk, like we did in the old days." On our sides, facing each other, Fiona asked, "Out with it. What's bothering you?"

"Everything, it seems. All the reminiscing at Helen's about parents passing on their interests, passions; I had nothing to say."

"Tatiana's gift is too intimate to share with strangers." Fiona moved closer.

"You think I should have taken Drew's offer?"

She ran her fingers through my hair. "I understand why you didn't, I do. I also understand that guilt saturates your life. I pray you'll be rid of it." She paused. "I was hoping that during this nebulous time you'd consider other options."

"Meaning?"

"Tatiana," she said, putting her finger to my lips. "You refuse to see yourself as you are, as you could be. That's what Drew thought. Philippa told me that too. I agree with them. Three distinct individuals have come to the same conclusion. Why not accept Tatiana's gift, your innate talent?"

"I've got to start looking for a job when we get back from France."

"I hope you'll consider what I've said. We'll talk about this more, when you're not so grumpy," Fiona said.

"It's too late to start over again. Anyway, why didn't we talk about all of this a long time ago?"

"We did. After your sophomore year when you announced that you were going to major in economics, I tried convincing you to stick with art history; but you were determined to put all of that behind you. 'All of that' being Tatiana and Drew." Fiona kissed me and moved closer. "We have nothing to do tomorrow."

"Sorry I'm so crabby," I said, taking Fiona in my arms. "This is kind of like the old days."

CHAPTER 29

AUGUST 1987

SAN FRANCISCO

As summer progressed, Fiona became evasive about France while I pointed out that there was nothing to keep her in San Francisco. She agreed but procrastinated and concentrated on business matters that her lawyers could have handled. I started a job search.

I prepared resumes and was searching the financial press when I found an ad for a position with the multinational consortium constructing an oil and gas pipeline from the Soviet Union to Western Europe. The consortium was looking for an assistant treasurer who spoke fluent English and Russian; French and/or German were pluses. I sent my resume to the headhunter in New York.

The headhunter called and explained the position's responsibilities, then pointed out that the job would require working with the Soviet Bank for Foreign Trade. He wanted to meet before the consortium's senior management was in New York to interview potential candidates in a few weeks.

I tracked down Boris Izmailov by phone and described the position I wanted. Boris asked me to phone back the next day when he'd have his boss on the line. The three of us talked for over an hour; both men were frank, although the call must have been monitored.

Five days later, through the San Francisco Soviet Counsel General, the bank invited me for meetings in Moscow. Domestic flights were my expense; New York–Moscow–New York flights were on Aeroflot and their account. I spent three days in Moscow and left with the Soviet bank's strong recommendation. Boris had gone from black-mailer to valuable friend.

References from Universal Bank would be a problem, and I started with my old manager from Syndications, who had just been promoted to Senior Vice President, International Correspondent Banking. He promised a good recommendation, and we spent lunch gossiping about Universal's new CEO. He had eliminated an entire layer of senior and executive vice presidents who had allied themselves with Andrew Neville: outright firings, forced resignations, and early retirements.

Anton "Jesus" Kleist had replaced my old boss as European Division Executive. While Anton and I got along, I left two messages before he got back to me late on a Friday afternoon and suggested getting together at a bistro near the Presidio Gates, where he lived. After catching up and a glass of wine, Anton got down to my reference.

Anton was concerned that I might direct future pipeline business away from Universal Bank if I had the consortium job. I told him that any hard feelings were about Andrew Neville, not Universal Bank; and new business would be decided according to the best deal competing banks offered. Another problem: Universal's officer handling the pipeline project was a lady who had reported to me. No problem—she was a good banker, and we had worked well together. Still uneasy, Anton handed me a letter of recommendation. Blunt, it stated that I had worked with him, not for him, and he attested to my honesty and diligence. About what I had expected.

We were leaving when Anton said, "Wait, tell the headhunters or the consortium management to phone me if your termination becomes an issue. I'll tell them what happened." Tearing up his letter, he said, "This stinks. Worse, it's cowardly. I'll tell them everything: Andrew Neville, Philippa, your getting fired. But putting that on paper is…"

"Is airing Universal's dirty laundry."

He ordered two iced Russian vodkas.

"Anton, thanks, that's perfect."

"Neville was a bad man," he said, lifting his glass. "To Philippa Tate-Palmer, who singlehandedly sank Andrew Neville. She had more guts than any man in the bank. Do you keep in touch?"

"I do. I'll send your regards."

"Send Philippa my deepest respect."

We downed the vodka; I bought the next round.

***

I was hired in early October, two days before my fortieth birthday, and was scheduled for orientation in Frankfurt a week later with the Chief Financial Officer, a German who spoke colloquial English. When he offered me the job, we agreed that I would work in Paris. Since France and Germany would take the Russian oil and gas, financial teams in both countries made sense; and communications and transportation between Paris and Frankfurt were excellent. On top of that, he loved French food.

During the interview process, Fiona was supportive. When I received the job offer, she was excited and wondered how the French would react to us. I ventured that Parisians were, in general, less judgmental about a person's private life than most Americans, even the laid-back San Francisco variety. I tried convincing her that Paris offered us unimaginable freedom and a fresh start, away from her family and the friends she once had.

The day before I left, Fiona was studying a map of Paris and its twenty arrondissements (districts). She had been to Paris twice, once on her honeymoon, and later on a tour of Europe's great opera houses. She had been studying Paris. She swept her hand across the map. "Where did you grow up?"

"We lived in the nineteenth, around the Parc des Buttes Chaumont, out of the way and kind of bohemian. We were the only Russians in the neighborhood."

"Where did most of the Russians live?"

"Right after the Revolution, most of them settled on the west side, in the fifteenth and the seventeenth, where I went to Russian school."

"Russian school?"

"Sure, like the Chinese schools here. After regular school, we were taught Russian grammar, vocabulary, stuff like that. There were cultural and social studies too. Best of all, the older boys taught us how to swear in Russian."

"How lovely," she said.

"Fiona, you've got to lighten up."

We had settled on a plan: I would find a temporary apartment while Fiona concluded business and would join me before Christmas. After New Year's, Fiona would begin looking in earnest for a more permanent arrangement. I said, "So you're really going to do this? No more dithering around?"

"I wasn't dithering," she scoffed.

"I know dithering when I see it; you were dithering up a storm."

"I don't dither, never have. Well, I may have been dithering a little, but just a little."

"If we don't like it, when the pipeline finishes, we can come back here or try somewhere else. But I'm pretty sure we'll stay in France."

"This will be great. I know it will."

I left San Francisco in mid-October, and Fiona had put her home up for sale; we decided that we'd use my flat when we were back in San Francisco. Her lawyers were given more latitude, and what business Fiona had to conduct would be done via fax and phone with trips to San Francisco if needed. By late November, I had found a one-bedroom apartment in the eighth arrondissement's eastern side between the Champs Elysée and the Place de la Madeleine. Fiona had booked a flight and would be in Paris the morning of December 19, a Saturday that year.

Early in December, I was in Frankfurt for meetings when Dr. Sternberg tracked me down by phone to tell me that Fiona had been killed in a car accident.

CHAPTER 30

FRIDAY, NOVEMBER 27, 1987

SAN FRANCISCO

Fiona had been walking out of a parking garage in downtown San Francisco late one afternoon when a car hit her. The interior neon lighting and setting sun blinded the driver; it was ruled an accident. Fiona was pronounced dead at San Francisco General from a fractured skull—"severe cranial trauma" as Dr. Sternberg phrased it. He said that death was instantaneous.

The funeral would be three days later. Although I had just started, the pipeline's Chief Financial Officer said to take as long as I needed. I left Frankfurt that afternoon, returned to Paris, and managed to get an early-morning flight to Chicago with a connecting flight to San Francisco.

Fiona's favorite cousin met me at the arrival gate and described the preliminary funeral arrangements. The service would be held in the same Presbyterian church as Drew's. The cousin assumed it would be flooded with family, some of whom had threatened Fiona, and friends, some of whom had snubbed her.

The service was as austere as Drew's; the plainspoken minister reflected upon Fiona's accomplishments and generosity. I sat with the cousin and his family; behind us the extended Sinclair family filled several pews. Afterwards a sympathetic gauntlet gathered at the front of the church to comfort relatives making their way to the waiting limousines. People I may have met but didn't remember shook my hand, patted my shoulders, and murmured condolences.

I saw Helen in the crowd; we waved and began edging toward each other. "I appreciate your coming," I said.

Helen was just keeping the tears back. "Sorry, funerals tear me up. I'll miss Fiona, such a kind, gracious woman."

"She was quite fond of you," I said as two of Fiona's nephews jostled their way next to me. "Sorry, I've got to go." The interment was limited to family and selected others; I was one of the others.

"Be brave. Write when you get back to Paris, promise?" Helen said as a nephew guided me toward the limousines.

"I promise." We kept eye contact as I was shepherded away.

I accompanied Fiona's cousin and his family in a limousine for the journey along the windswept Pacific Coast to the Sinclair family plot in Colma, south of San Francisco. The minister led prayers over Fiona's casket as it was lowered into the grave. As the crowd began the hushed walk down the low hill to the waiting cars, I took a bouquet of roses from Fiona's and placed them on my mother's grave.

I heard the limousines leaving and sat on the stone wall beside my mother's grave. I hoped Fiona's last days were buoyed by thoughts of Paris. My childhood came to mind: the excitement of coming to America and my outlandish expectations made me smile; junior high brought a scowl; my mother's garden a lump in my throat. In front of me were buried the people I loved.

I was alone. Poignant reflection was preferable to commiserating with people I didn't care for any more than they cared for me. I walked over the hill, wondering about a cab to San Francisco, and saw Fiona's cousin waiting for me next to the last limousine. He would have waited as long as I took. A kind man, he was unique in Fiona's family.

We were driven to a relative's home in St. Francis Woods, an expensive neighborhood in San Francisco's southwest, for canapés and drinks. A clear day with a gusty wind, many people had gone to the dining room overlooking the garden. I had a drink or two and a couple of cucumber sandwiches before saying good-bye. A limousine took me home. I went to straight to bed. A deep sleep with dreams of my mother followed: far away and hurrying toward me. She was worried.

The next morning, I was depressed and jet-lagged. A pale slumber took me until the phone began ringing around noon. The first call was Dr. Sternberg; he invited me to dinner that evening. One of Fiona's lawyers, Hopkins Browning, called and apologized for the timing. He wanted me to execute a limited power of attorney, allowing him to represent my interests in the estate's settlement. I agreed.

***

The evening before I returned to Paris, I had dinner with Sally and Bert Roth. They knew Fiona. The four of us had run into each other over the years. While we had exchanged pleasantries, I assumed that Sally and Bert had drawn the right conclusions about Fiona and me. Sally did know that Drew was an old friend I had cared for before he died.

Sally asked about my immediate plans. I would return to work and deal with the sorrow as best I could. Sally noted that dealing with two deaths in a short time might prove difficult and suggested that I watch for signs of depression: changes in diet, sleep disorders, and abnormal mood swings.

After dinner, I went back to my flat and dozed off on the sofa. I wasn't alone.

"Zdrazdvitye? Gdye vi?" *(Hello? Where are you?)*

"Ya zdyes, Sandro." *(I'm here, Sandro.)*

My mother was standing by the family pictures with her back to me. Turning to me with wide eyes, she said, "Sandro, I worry about you."

"I'll get through it."

Wringing her hands, she continued, "Sandro, Sandro, dangerous times."

I woke up with a start and looked at the pictures; I was alone and went to bed.

I wondered what the dream meant and if more would come. As I feared, they became more frequent in Paris and were always the same:

my mother worrying about me as she stared at the family pictures I had left in San Francisco. I made a deduction: Fiona's fears that I couldn't bear being alone were manifesting themselves in the dreams.

Some days were more desolate than others. Imagining how Fiona would have loved Paris was heartbreaking. Wanting to tell Fiona something and realizing I never could was disorienting. I refused to think about the house my mother, Fiona, and I had designed with a kitchen overlooking the Mediterranean. Unlike my mother's death, sadness rather than guilt fueled the initial grief.

I tried resisting, but the personal recriminations did begin. Secrets didn't belong in such a relationship as intimate as ours; I should have been more honest with Fiona but lacked the courage. As memories of Fiona became more conflicted, the dream of my mother became more frequent, leading me to think the secrets and the dreams were somehow intertwined. I threw myself into work.

I hired two English-speaking French assistants: a young man, an Alsatian, who was fresh out of business school and spoke fluent German and an attractive young woman from an émigré family who had banking experience and spoke outdated Russian like mine. Quick studies, they were able to run the office when I was in Moscow, which was far too often.

The Soviet bureaucracy had a terrible reputation; The iron-headed bureaucrats issued conflicting regulations with no warning. Complying with the regulations could shut down construction. So could noncompliance. Arguing was pointless; the apparatchiks would walk away. Going above a functionary was useless, because no one wanted to make a decision when they could issue regulations.

I tried outlining what I thought were their objectives so we could work within their overall strategy. My attempt was met with blank incredulity and profound mistrust. So I went back to obtaining special permits, then waivers for the onerous sections of the special permits.

Returning to Paris was a reprieve; attending Philippa's wedding in London was joyful. Philippa returned to London and took a job with Lloyds while she figured out how to enter the business of raising and training racehorses. During her search, she had met and fallen in love with her future husband. His family had been raising horses for generations. The understated morning wedding was followed by an elaborate brunch that was centered around lobster and champagne. Philippa was radiant and serene.

Paris is a walking city, and the eighth arrondissement included the touristy Champs Elysée. On nice days, I strolled home and often took an aperitif outside a café and watched the tourists. There was the simple pleasure of sitting outside a café, drinking milky coffee accompanied by a warm croissant and sweet butter while reading an entire newspaper without being bothered.

My apartment faced west and was sunlit and cheerful. French doors to the back opened to a walled garden. The neighborhood's buildings were sturdy, its parks were leafy and tidy, and the upper-middle-class denizens were as distant as the French are with foreigners, even those who of us who spoke French with a Parisian accent.

I was correct and kept my distance while going about day-to-day routines. The sardonic shop owners were fun, more so after my becoming a regular. Almost rude at first, their thoughtfulness became touching: a special cut of meat they saved for me; a strong cheese they knew I would like; the particular wines for their better customers.

As I began fitting in, the local bistro's surly waiters turned somewhat courteous, then even considerate. The crowd at the bar ignored me for weeks before we began talking; later we bought each other drinks. I was referred to as the American, later the Russian, which I took as a promotion of sorts. Given enough time, I would become one of them.

***

Almost a year after Fiona's death on November 25, 1987, I returned to San Francisco to work on financing for a liquefied natural gas (LNG) terminal on the Soviet Baltic coast near Riga. Universal Bank managed the loans that were syndicated among a group of American, German, and French banks. I arrived on a Wednesday; Sally and Bert invited me for supper that Friday.

Sally's Crab Louis was a meal I dreamed of in Russia: an incredible amount of fresh crab and homemade mayonnaise with the slightest hint of horse radish. The masterpiece was served with French Chablis that I brought. The Roth twins didn't care for crab and opted for canned spaghetti with chopped-up hot dogs. After dinner, Bert was putting the girls to bed while Sally and I finished the wine.

Sally was a small woman with large sapphire eyes and an easy laugh. Refilling our glasses, she said, "Doctor Roth, fabulous chef and pretty good head-shrinker, is in. How are you doing?" Tapping her head, she added, "Up here."

"Okay, I guess. Keeping busy . . . traveling a lot. But there's a problem: recurring dreams of my mother that started right after Fiona's death. I'm concerned, kind of worried actually."

"Really?" She put her glass down. "Do you dream of your mother often?"

"I do, but these are different: vivid, a couple of times a week."

"Tell me." Her eyes twinkled with wine and curiosity.

"She's looking at family photos upstairs. Especially one: it's my parents' engagement party in Paris just before the Germans invaded France. She's worried about me being alone."

"Tell me about your mother and the people in the picture."

"There are five people: my mother, her mother and her brother were the only members of their family left after the Revolution; the other two are my father and his father. Of those people, only my parents survived the war. My father was evacuated to England when France fell, and my mother was alone in Paris during the German occupation."

"Hold on." She snapped her fingers. "The similarities with your Paris and your mother's?"

"I don't understand."

"Your mother was alone in Paris after her family had perished; you're alone after Fiona's death and your friend Drew's. Plausible?"

"I hadn't thought of it that way."

"Any other similarities?"

"Well, during World War II, my mother worked for a French construction company the German authorities utilized. Part of my job involves working with French construction companies. The man I report to is German."

Sally's eyebrows arched. "Anything else comes to mind?"

"I never thought of it that way. And then there's…" It was so obvious: I was translating Russian regulations to my French and German associates; my mother had translated German and French orders to the Russian laborers.

"What else were you going to say?"

"Oh, nothing. Just a thought." My voice tightened.

"Not ready for prime time?" Sally made a pensive face. "Difficult?"

"Complicated. Don't know where to start."

"Perhaps you've subconsciously put yourself in an updated version of your mother's past?"

"I don't know about that. I was qualified for the job and wanted to live in Paris with Fiona. That was the extent of my thinking."

"You and your mother, reasonable relationship?"

"We were close, too close, I think."

Cocking her head, she asked, "How close?"

"Nothing sexual or anything like that." I blushed. "I was a mother's boy; that's what I meant."

"This is all very informal, and we've had a fair amount of wine." Sally refilled our glasses. "But maybe there's something going on way down deep, something unfinished with your mother? Maybe an appointment or two with me?" Looking around the dining room, she said, "I've got an office, no children around, no wine, professional. After a couple of sessions, I could recommend you to a psychologist who might help."

"Sally, I appreciate this, I do, but let me think about it."

"Well, let me know," she said. "Oh, the complicated information of yours, have you told anyone?"

"Fiona knew. So did Philippa."

"Why did you tell Philippa?"

"We stumbled into each other's personal lives and ended up trusting each other."

"You're fond of her?" Sally smiled.

"Yes, why do you ask?"

She laughed. "You've got to trust people before opening up?"

"I guess so. I like you and Bert."

"And we like you, but you're reticent?"

"I must have gotten that from Fiona. You're very insightful, aren't you?"

"Hey, it's how I make a living."

CHAPTER 31

SATURDAY, DECEMBER 3, 1988

SAN FRANCISCO

A week later, the hectic Friday started at 5:00 a.m. at Universal with calls to the bankers in Paris and Frankfurt about last-minute problems with the LNG deal. Those problems wrapped up, we met with Universal's Project Finance team ironing out details that always plague large loans. Later in the afternoon, two New York banks called to finalize issues that had popped up at their end. It was pitch-dark when I left the Universal building, looking for a cab.

At home I flopped on the sofa, thinking about supper, but a heavy sleep overtook me. Hours later, I got up and went to bed. No dreams, but the next morning, I woke up in front of the picture that fascinated my mother.

So clear, so obvious, everything meshed: her make-believe, my disgusting her, the secrets fueling her insanity. I may have known all these years, but it was down too deep inside and beyond my rational mind. Assumptions joined: Fiona must have known my mother's last secret; since Fiona told Dr. Sternberg everything, he must know as well.

I called Dr. Sternberg's office and asked an answering service to have him call back at once. When he called about ten minutes later, I told him about my dreams. Words jumbled. I couldn't come up with an English term and tried French—then I was speaking French. He said that he'd be right over.

I found an old photo album and was leafing through it when Dr. Sternberg rang. I buzzed him in and ran down to meet him. He stared at me; I was wearing a T-shirt and boxer shorts. "I'll get dressed in a second," I said. "But first let me show you these." I pointed to several pictures of myself. Handing him the picture of my parents' engagement, I said, "Now look at the younger fellow with the glasses." He glanced at the photos without answering and led me upstairs. Inside, I said, "Those pictures were taken at the same point of our lives—our mid-twenties. Tell me what you think."

Dr. Sternberg studied the photos. "Well, you made it through the seventies without sideburns or a ridiculous moustache." He was watching my eyes.

"My uncle and I are identical. Same hair, same eyes and mouth. Even our rounded horn-rimmed glasses match. We hold our heads the same; we stand with our hands behind our backs. That man, Alexander Trepoff, he's not only my uncle—he's my father too? I was born in 1942, after he left for Russia, wasn't I?"

"Wait a second," he said.

"Unable to bear his great sin, he fled to Russia, didn't he?"

"It's complicated. I'll—"

"I want the truth." I grabbed his jacket lapels. "Out with it."

"I've never lied to you." Dr. Sternberg tried to break free.

"That's slicing the baloney pretty thin." I pulled him closer. "But you've withheld information. Don't tell me you haven't."

"Now . . . now, calm down. You've got a violent side, I know you do." He managed a nervous laugh.

"You think this is funny? Funny?" I couldn't catch my breath and let him go.

He stepped back. "You're verging on hysterics. You must settle down; then we'll discuss this…reasonably."

"Are you going to answer my question?"

"In a minute, yes." He went to his satchel and took two small pills from a bottle.

I backed away.

"I'm your doctor and would do nothing to harm you."

I swallowed the pills. "Okay, is Alexander Trepoff my father?"

"No, he's not, definitely not. Why do you think so?"

"I've been having these dreams of my mother looking at that family picture. Those dreams were my suspicions of what drove her crazy; what will drive me crazy." I flinched. "Crazy? I'm already crazy. I knew it, I knew this would happen. So did Fiona. With a gene pool as shallow as mine, she kept me around so I wouldn't go out and father a pack of congenital idiots."

"That's not the case." He took my shoulders. "According to Fiona—"

"What didn't Fiona tell you about me and my mother?"

His shoulders slumped. "Suicide often runs in families. And after Tatiana's suicide, you were verging on a mental breakdown. That's what Fiona and I were worried about." He took a deep breath. "If you were born in 1942, you're five years older than you think you are, correct?"

"I must be."

"What are your first memories of time? What year it was? Think about it."

I had to think about that. "Mother was teaching me how to read calendars before my fourth birthday. The year was 1951."

"Ten years after Alexander Trepoff went to Russia. Am I right?"

"You are. Nevertheless, you and Fiona were hiding something, weren't you?"

"Yes. But first, I want you to sit down."

I stumbled to the sofa. "You withheld information from Fiona," he said. "You told me you'd never tell Fiona that Drew knew about you two from the start." He sat on the coffee table, seeming to wait for me.

"Okay, Drew admitted to me that it was his idea to blackmail Fiona into a lousy real estate deal that fell through. I never told Fiona that either."

"You did the right thing, you know that?"

"I don't know that."

"I haven't told my wife certain things that are too upsetting." Dr. Sternberg looked guilty. "The point I'm making is that Fiona did the same for you."

"Go on."

"Brother-sister pregnancies often abort naturally; the recessive genes are too much. You were born about six years after Alexander Trepoff went to his death in Russia. Andre Romanovsky was your father. I have no doubt. If you want children, have them. They're blessings."

"Then what are you hiding?"

"I want to tell you a story," he said. "No, two stories, both true. I was nineteen at the Normandy landings. A first lieutenant, Fred Kellerman, and I were translators. Going forward to interrogate prisoners, German artillery opened up—those damned 88s. A shell fragment caught Kellerman; I was splattered with blood and brain matter." Touching a small scar on his right cheek, he said, "One of Kellerman's teeth." Dr. Sternberg stopped. "The memory is vivid; I still dream of it. Tatiana and her brother witnessed far worse, as children."

I stood up. "I'm not up for this right now."

"Then when?"

"I, ah, don't know. Maybe later, when I'm feeling better."

"You can't leave it this way—unfinished," he said. "I must tell you what happened. You'd better sit down."

"All right, all right."

Dr. Sternberg began pacing. "Tatiana was four or five, I think, when Red Army Cossacks attacked her family's home, somewhere in Russia, out in the country, in the south, I believe. Tatiana and her brother were outside with a nanny, and their father ran to them. Two Cossacks rode after him, laughing, egging each other on. One pulled ahead, stood in the stirrups, and swung a saber—down, through her father's head. Only feet from Tatiana and her brother."

"My God."

"The Cossacks went on a killing frenzy—family, servants, even the pets. Tatiana's mother…" He closed his eyes. "Tatiana said the Cossacks *abused* her. Tatiana and her brother were put in a closet while that went on. How much they saw or heard, Tatiana refused to say." He studied me. "How are you doing?"

"Shocked, kind of sick."

"Understandable," he said. "I don't think Tatiana had much use for reality after that."

"Do you know what happened afterwards?"

"Bits and pieces," he said. "Someone got them to a nearby town, where a doctor took them in and cared for your grandmother." Dr. Sternberg began pacing again. "I doubt if a provincial doctor could have properly treated her. Sexually transmitted diseases must have been rampant. No antibiotics, of course. Tatiana said that her mother was more or less ill for the rest of her life. Hard to imagine how the woman held together mentally. Anyway, the doctor got them to Kiev, where the Bolsheviks *recruited* your grandmother to appraise confiscated art. Later they were sent to Leningrad before they were allowed to leave. That's all I know."

"Fiona said that my grandmother died after an operation for female problems."

"It's no wonder, the poor woman."

"Tell me what you know about this German, Haryett."

"After your father died," he replied, "Tatiana started rambling about Paris and Joachim Haryett. Haryett had sent Tatiana to Aachen before the Allied invasion. Fiona asked me to visit his family when I was visiting mine in Germany. They were called 'good Germans' after the war."

"Did you find out if my mother was married to Joachim Haryett?"

"What did Fiona say?"

"Fiona said that they weren't. I think she was lying."

"They were married. Tatiana's papers, such as they were, identified her as the wife of Joachim Haryett, a Wehrmacht colonel. Tatiana and the Haryetts were notified of Haryett's death at Normandy. That's as much as I know about that." He paused—seeming to steel himself. "Shortly before the suicide, Tatiana told Fiona that your father was her brother. Alexander was his name too. I heard the story from Tatiana with Fiona translating. Tatiana was terribly confused, but not about the incest."

"Did she even know where she was?"

"Tatiana was ricocheting in time—unsure of time, people, and places. Fiona said that Tatiana was confusing you with her brother. Once after you had spoken to her in Russian, she told Fiona that her brother had returned from Russia and had talked to her. But towards the end, she was terrified of her brother—you, I should say."

"So that's why she sent me away?"

"Did you tell Fiona that Tatiana had sent you away?" he asked.

"I did, a long time ago, after my mother's suicide. Fiona and I had been arguing. The circumstances were, well, they were very confused. Anyway, my assumptions and dreams weren't so far off the mark?"

"They weren't," Dr. Sternberg said, looking past me with sad eyes. "Maybe Tatiana should have been hospitalized, but Fiona and I thought that would have terrified her even more. I'll never understand why the poor woman had to suffer so."

"I should have helped her more."

"Stop it," he yelled.

"Sorry." I put my hands up.

"No, I'm sorry. You couldn't have done anything. None of us could. Tatiana was determined to kill herself. After France fell, Tatiana and her brother were all alone facing hostile soldiers, but Germans instead of Cossacks. Given their childhood traumas, they were unstable and on the thinnest edge. They clung together like they did that horrible day in Russia. Trouble was, they clung too tightly. Tatiana's guilt must have become unbearable. She had to tell someone—Fiona and me."

"Do you think my father knew?"

"Fiona was sure that he didn't." Dr. Sternberg sat at the other end of the sofa. "But I'm not sure. At a Christmas party, Andre had been drinking—not drunk, not sober either—and was telling me about the Civil War and fleeing Russia with his father."

"I've heard those stories."

"I asked Andre if he had seen too much as a youngster. He said that Tatiana had seen far worse and told me that God had given him Tatiana to look after while she watched over you. Andre knew she was delicate. But how much he knew, I don't know."

"Drew knew," I said. "That secret was the last string around his finger when he died."

"I knew too," Dr. Sternberg said in the softest voice. "Put yourself in Fiona's position. Then mine. And Drew's. Ask yourself what you would have done?"

Stifling a sob, Dr. Sternberg went to the kitchen before I could answer, poured a glass of water, and took a long time drinking it. He returned and said, "Some people are driven insane. That was Tatiana's case—demons breeding the demons that destroyed her. That she kept going was a testament to how much she loved you." With a wan smile, he added, "You may have trouble sleeping, but sleep can be therapeutic. I'll give you a prescription."

"Worried that I might take too many?"

"Should I?"

"No."

"No alcohol like the last time," he said. "Grief, and shocks like this notwithstanding, I told Fiona that, thanks to her, you're mentally far more resilient than, than…" He closed his eyes. "Than Tatiana ever was."

"I owe that to Fiona."

"I couldn't believe it when Fiona…when Fiona decided that you needed love if you were to survive. Her decision was just that simple. And you two fell in love, really in love. I didn't take that well. To be frank, I was jealous—me, a married man. I had lunch with Fiona a few days before she died. She was so happy. Paris and Fiona would have been perfect."

"Please stop or I'll start crying."

"Russians . . . so tough, so emotional." Dr. Sternberg went to the front windows, studying the living room. "This is quite elegant; you have talent." He took a business card from his wallet and handed it to me. "I've dealt with this man, Hopkins Browning, one of Fiona's lawyers. Fiona passed on to me her opera recordings and books, priceless to an opera lover like me. You should see this Browning fellow."

"I've met him. He's on my list of things to do."

Dr. Sternberg drew himself to attention. "My wife tells me that I tend to lecture; it's a German trait." With a click of his heels, he said, "If it's not too late to learn the truth about Tatiana, then it cannot be too late to reorder your life according to your talents?" He put his hand up. "End of lecture."

"I'll give it some thought."

Gathering his satchel and handing me a prescription, he said, "I hope I'm still your doctor. However, if you wish, I'll recommend another."

"That's not necessary."

"I'm going to call to see how you're doing. Talking to a psychologist may be helpful."

"I have one in mind."

Dr. Sternberg made that rigid German bow: arms tight to his sides with an abrupt drop of the head. "I hope you forgive me. But, if I had to do it over again, I'd do the same. That's as honest as I can make it."

I walked him to the door.

He was hesitant. "Do I have your understanding?"

"Not only that, you have my eternal gratitude for helping my mother and putting up with me back then."

Dr. Sternberg dropped the satchel and put his hands over his eyes. He was about to fall down the stairs; I put my arms around him. "This has been too much," he stammered. "My wife thinks I'm too emotional. I shouldn't drive." Drying his eyes with his sleeve, he asked, "Will you drive me home?"

"I'll get you a glass of water, and we'll get going."

He sat on the sofa and loosened his tie. "You may wish to dress first."

Chapter 32

Late that afternoon, I walked to the local drug store and had Dr. Sternberg's prescription filled. The pharmacist suggested taking the sleeping pill on a full stomach. I bought a small pizza on the way home and took a pill after an evening of dreadful television.

After a deep, uneventful sleep, I woke up late. Drinking coffee while looking out the front window, I saw Sally Roth and Arnie, the Roth's dachshund, heading out for their daily walk to the Marina Green. I rapped the window and motioned that I was coming down.

Sally was wearing jeans, a crew-neck sweater, and a trench coat. She pointed at Arnie. "Have you seen his commercials?"

"I did last night. Bert gave me a heads-up and told me the ads were his idea." The television commercial had Arnie wearing dark glasses with a black leather jacket over his narrow shoulders while he pitched a high-fiber dog food. The voice-over was just like Arnold Swartzenegger doing the Terminator.

"I worry about Arnie turning into just another dog star, but so far he's handling it," Sally said. "The young boys around here are crazy about him."

"So, Arnie, how's show biz?" He wagged his tail while I leaned down and patted his head. "Don't forget your fans; we're keeping you in doggie treats."

Arnie gave my hand a good sniffing and tugged on the leash. The day was brisk and windy with ill-tempered clouds to the north.

"I heard you pacing around last night," Sally said. "I couldn't sleep either. TV was awful, wasn't it?"

"Except for Sissy."

"Phone-sex Sissy." Sally grinned. "Bert always runs into her when he's channel surfing."

"She's pretty much like I expected."

Sally stumbled from Arnie's pulling. "You phoned Sissy?" She tried to make Arnie heel.

"Stretched out in that leopard bikini, on a white fur rug in front of a fireplace with a low fire—what's a guy to do?"

"Lonely night, lonely guy, and Sissy. Yeah, it figures."

"Sissy's kind of, oh, what's the word I'm looking for?"

"Mercenary?"

"Let's say businesslike. The credit card authorization doesn't enhance the romance."

"I don't think Sissy's one for long walks on the beach," Sally said. We turned north and headed for the Marina Green as Sally got Arnie to heel again. "I sense you want to talk to me professionally. The dreams?"

"It's more than the dreams. My mother always seemed a little, well… I loved her, of course. But she was kind of mysterious."

"People often think their parents are somewhat mysterious. But before we get to that… Sissy?"

"I didn't phone Sissy, but I don't change channels when she's on."

"Well, your male hormones are percolating," Sally said. "Your dreams? More? Worse?"

"I figured them out yesterday morning. But now my thoughts are bouncing around."

"The subconscious is sloppy. The conscious wants to analyze the information it receives. When the subconscious sends up too much, the circuits often start popping. That's your case?"

"The dreams of my mother started after Fiona's death. I thought they were somehow connected. Yesterday morning, I discovered they were. My mother went mad. Is that word still used?"

"It's been replaced for the most part."

"I figured out that Fiona lied to me about my mother's past, which led to her suicide."

"Suicide," Sally said. "I wish you'd told me. The endless what-ifs, the lingering guilt and residual anger. Did you witness the suicide or discover the scene?"

"She made certain I wouldn't, thank God."

"Thank God indeed," she said. "Suicides are devastating. Survivors are left with questions the suicide rendered unanswerable. Where should we start?"

"Shouldn't we have an arrangement? Fees?"

"Later." She pulled Arnie away from a shrub he was inspecting. "Did you see a psychologist or psychiatrist after the suicide?"

"The psychologist told me I was suffering from acute depression and tried convincing me that my mother's mental illness caused the suicide. But that was incomplete. Fiona lied to me to make sure it stayed incomplete. So did Drew. Drew was her son."

"I thought Drew was a friend of yours." Sally's eyes widened. "We'll get back to him, go on."

"My mother was evasive, like there was something I shouldn't know. Maybe I didn't want to know, or maybe I did. Maybe my misgivings triggered the dreams that led to the lies that led to the truth. Sounds plausible?"

"There's very little implausible with the human psyche. I know you were born in France. Should we start there?"

"No, everything started in Russia."

I took over two hours recounting my mother's life and mine as we circled the Marian Green time and again. About halfway into it, Sally phoned Bert from a pay phone to let him know she was talking to me professionally and would be late. Other than a few questions to clarify events and people, she let me continue with the timeline that ended the previous morning. We found a bench where we sat for a long time without talking. Arnie was on my lap dozing, and I said, "Sally, my story is peculiar. Better put, it's weird, isn't it?"

"It's unique and quite layered."

"May I ask questions?"

"The doctor is in."

"Do you think I'm gay…or bisexual…or maybe a repressed homosexual?"

"Are you concerned that you are?"

"Not really. I was attracted to Drew. But since Fiona, men haven't interested me sexually."

"Why were you attracted to Drew?" Sally asked.

"Drew was attractive, and he flattered me."

"How so?"

"Drew said that we were messengers of a brilliant dawn: I would become an interior designer of breathtaking originality; Drew would become an iconoclastic art dealer. Overheated fantasies?"

"Like the imaginary worlds you and your mother created?"

"Somewhat, I guess."

"Anything else?"

"He'd tell me that I was an elegant Russian of impeccable breeding."

"Are you?"

"Don't you think I'm elegant?"

"You're always well groomed and nicely dressed." Sally smiled. "This breeding of yours?"

"My mother's father was a Russian nobleman, a prince. My mother and I were proud of our lineage, although it wasn't worth a dime. But the pretense didn't last."

"Why?"

"It was like my mother took away my identity when she killed herself. Can people do that, take away another person's identity?"

"If Tatiana formed your identity, couldn't she take it with her?"

"Sounds like a Russian soul," I said.

Sally looked puzzled.

"Russians used to believe that an individual's soul can be bought, sold, given, stolen—and, of course, lost."

"You were lost and Drew found you?" Sally asked.

"I tried becoming like Drew. But he was far more sophisticated, smarter, and better educated."

"Have you ever thought that Drew used you?"

"Drew asked me. I told him no."

"Then why did he ask?"

"Maybe he thought he had, but he had it all wrong. I had been using him. Years after I broke off our relationship, Drew invited me back into his life."

"Physically?"

"No."

"Then why?"

"He loved me."

"What was in it for you?"

"I loved his gallery showings with the flamboyant artists and the Bay Area's glitterati. While I'm not naturally engaging, I was—at those showings. Drew actually said that I effervesced. Anyway, I must have been teasing him, subconsciously."

"You teased him consciously?"

"Of course not. Later when I told Drew that I had been teasing him, he told me that wasn't the case."

We got up from the bench and started in the general direction of home. "Why did you care for Drew while he was dying?" she asked.

"In some part, to atone for running away from my mother before the suicide."

"Hold on, Alexander. You told me that Tatiana sent you away. Now you're telling me that you ran. Which is it?"

"When she sent me away, I ran. To Drew."

"And your caring for Drew was atoning for the way you had treated him?"

"Yes, I was the only person Drew wanted to be with."

"So your feelings for Drew?"

"I couldn't let him die that way, alone and unloved. I repented for treating him so terribly. It was a good confession, even by Russian Orthodox standards."

"Back to Drew offering you his business . . ." Sally cocked her head. "Refusing his gift was a penance?"

"Yes."

"Did you want his gift?"

"I didn't deserve it, couldn't take it."

"You didn't answer my question."

"I didn't want it."

"The truth?" Sally asked.

"I'll rephrase: I wanted it."

"Leaving Drew for his mother was another reason you refused it?"

"Fiona and I humiliated him; we let him stew in that indignity until he died."

"I know nothing about Russian Orthodox confessions, but are they subject to conditions? You vowed to keep Drew's secrets from Fiona in exchange for his absolution?"

"Well, not exactly."

She arched an eyebrow. "You kept Drew's secrets from Fiona because neither you nor Drew wanted Fiona to know them?"

"Right."

"Your promises to Drew?"

"Were unconditional. I thought Drew and I had come to resolution, complete with tears and assurances. That wasn't the case. Drew withheld my mother's secrets. I thought Fiona had explained some of the mysterious parts of my mother's life. Afterwards, when I asked Fiona if there was anything else I should know, she said we'd discuss that later. But later never came, and, I guess, I was fine with that. But I know why both of them lied."

"Why?"

"I was too weak."

"I see," Sally replied with a level gaze. "If you had it to do over again, would you have kept Drew's secrets from Fiona?"

"I would have told her the truth."

"Your feelings if you had?"

"Noble."

"How do you feel now?" she asked.

"Stupid."

"Why?"

"You caught me lying. You're quite good at that, aren't you?"

"I'm very good," she said with a smile. "Lied to whom?"

"I didn't have the courage to tell Fiona."

"Was it courage…or something else?"

"The truth would have devastated Fiona. I couldn't do that."

"In Fiona's place, would you have kept Tatiana's secrets?"

"Yes."

"Do you see the irony?" Sally said. "You took it upon yourself to keep of all the secrets only to find out that Fiona—and Drew—had been keeping Tatiana's secret, the secret that held the others. You've embraced the guilt. Why?"

"I deserved it."

"You're grappling with Fiona and Drew's dishonesty as well as yours. What was the underlying motivation for that dishonesty?"

"For starters: fear, sex, embarrassment, jealousy, cowardice, greed—and I'm just getting started."

"Those are negative motivations. Are there positives?"

"Nothing comes to mind."

"You're resisting. You told me that you loved Fiona and Drew. Fiona kept Tatiana's secret not to harm your memories; you kept Drew's secrets from Fiona for much the same reason. Drew and Fiona took Tatiana's secret to their graves because they loved you. You may wish to keep their motivations in mind, and yours too, the next time you start tearing yourself down."

"It's critical analysis."

"Alexander, that summer you were an unstable young man—a 'selfish, conniving nitwit' was your description. Nevertheless, that desperate boy survived, matured, and grew to a reasonable adult. Why not accept the decent man you've become?"

"Doctor's orders?"

"This doctor's fondest hope."

"You're going to recommend another shrink?"

"No, I'm not. According to professional protocols, I should. But I want to help you, as a friend. One more thing: this friend doesn't charge for assistance rendered."

"Sally, now, I'll never get to raise your rent."

She laughed. "If friends can't be useful, what's the point in having them?" We approached the yacht club.

Sally, Arnie, and I stood on the breakwater, looking across the Bay toward the Berkeley hills. The earlier clouds had broken, and a heavy fog loomed outside of the Golden Gate. The wake from a passing ship lapped against the moorings as a Strauss waltz from a reception at the yacht club drifted on the breeze. Arnie's ears were flapping.

Sally said, "You might want to take a new look at Tatiana's garden. Despite her problems, or perhaps because of them, she created an unbelievable world of beauty and art where she escaped and you escaped from junior high. I would have sold my young soul for that."

"Why do I feel so odd?"

"The suicide is a wound that's never properly healed and has been reopened," she replied. "You've got to apply the sutures to finally heal it." She tugged my elbow. "Let's head home." After a couple of silent blocks, she stopped and turned to me. "Sally to Alexander, some feedback?"

"I feel strange, almost like when my mother told me to leave her. If that's progress, it's most unsettling."

"That's remarkable," Sally said. "Maybe you're getting ready to say good-bye to the Tatiana you knew as a boy and accept all of her. Don't worry, but don't fight it."

Two young boys ran toward us making motorcycle sounds while Arnie strained on the leash. One said with an Austrian accent, "I lied." Paying no attention to Sally or me, the boys stooped over Arnie, who rolled on his back. The boys squatted, patted his belly, and talked to him like Arnold. Arnie got up and licked their faces. Ready to leave, one boy said, "Hasta la vista, baby." The other said, "I'll be back." Arnie wagged his tail as they kick-started their Harleys.

Sally's sapphire eyes were merry. "With Arnie's help, those boys turned themselves into Arnold Swartzenegger for a few moments."

"My mother and I could do that."

"You told me." Sally smiled. "You're going back to Paris soon. That's why I've been pressing you. Let's try and fit in as many sessions as we can?" I agreed. "Oh, and another thing: I believe in journals. Your journal will record your progress. Nothing structured, just free-form it. Back to Tatiana. She's the fulcrum balancing your past and your future. Time to come to terms with her?"

"I've done that. No matter what happened to her or what she may have done, I love her as I always have and always will."

"Keep those thoughts," Sally replied.

CHAPTER 33

TUESDAY, DECEMBER 6, 1988

SAN FRANCISCO

After our walk on the Marina Green, Sally and I had scheduled a session at her office the following Tuesday after work. But meetings forced me to break the appointment. I was paying the cab driver later that evening when Sally appeared at the front door with her arms crossed—inauspicious female body language.

"Sorry, Sally, couldn't get away: last-second snags on the loans I'm working on, which boils down to our lawyers arguing with their lawyers so they can run their meters."

"Come in. Eaten yet?"

"A sloppy Joe with chips from the cafeteria was dinner." I entered the living room and stepped around a dollhouse. "I'm not ducking you, but my boss wants me back to Paris as soon as possible. I've got to take care of a personal matter and hop on a plane."

"We have even less time than I thought," Sally said, motioning me to the sofa as she sat in a chair facing me. "Bert's in New York and the girls are in bed. We won't be bothered." Looking past me, she said, "Here comes Arnie. He spends most of his time with the girls and me and needs some guy company." Arnie stood in front of me, wagging his tail. "He wants to sit with you."

I patted the sofa. Arnie jumped and curled up while I scratched his ears.

Sally took a notebook from a side table and clicked her pen. "So how's it been going since our talk?"

"My thoughts seem to spin and spin off to irrelevance. Today, my grandfather crossed my mind. That my grandfather was hanged as a war criminal is disturbing. But, getting down to it, what I can do about him? Nothing, that's what."

"How do you feel about him?"

"I understand his motives and sympathize to a degree, but that's it. Then my mother's brother popped up, and I decided that wondering about him is a waste of time too."

"So, that's that for them?"

"Yes," I said and pointed to the ceiling near the front windows. "Weren't you going to have that crack repaired and deduct it from your rent?"

"Bert's hopeless around the house, and scheduling a repairman is a hassle. But I'll get it fixed, promise. You're in a funny mood. What's going on?"

"If other things need fixing—leaky faucets, drafty windows—get them done too." I stood up to get a better perspective. "While you're at it, why not think about repainting?"

"Yellowish walls might brighten the place up," Sally said. "You seem apprehensive?"

"I've been jumpy all day."

"Your intuition is pretty good. What's it telling you?"

"Something momentous is boiling up, and I don't think it's very good."

Sally nodded. "What else is going on?"

"Now that I know everything about my relatives, none of it seems to matter." I sat down. "Except for my mother, of course. We were so close in so many ways. I only hope I don't end up in the loony bin, where she belonged."

"Look, Alexander, Tatiana's suicide… It's that, I mean…" She clicked her pen several times. "What I'm trying to say is that it's time to address the suicide's residue. I think you're strong enough to do that."

"I can thank Fiona for that. I wish I had known everything before she and Drew died."

"Why?"

"If I'd known the burdens they carried for me, I'd have done more for them."

"What more could you have done?" Sally asked.

"Oh, I don't know, but I should have done something."

"Sounds like you've got a bad case of Jewish guilt. Catholic guilt is never getting it right. Jewish guilt is never doing enough. One's as bad as the other; the recipients are on the hook." Sally seemed more composed. "When a Jewish friend of mine became a psychologist, her mother expressed her not-so-subtle disappointment that she hadn't become a psychiatrist."

I laughed. "What are you telling me?"

"Time to get off the hook?"

"Exactly." I snapped my fingers. "That's what I've been doing. When I wake up at night thinking about all of this, I remind myself that they're dead and gone, all of them. Then I think of my mother and can't get back to sleep. But she's gone too, so losing sleep over her seems pointless."

"You've drawn a lot of conclusions." Sally made some notes. "Closing most everything down, are you?"

"I refuse to wallow in pointless speculation. The past can't be altered, and there's not a thing I can do about those people and what they may have done, or should have done, or didn't do. That's not to say I don't appreciate what you've done."

"Gee, thanks," Sally said with a tight smile. "Any loose ends you want to cover before we wrap this up?"

"Do you think I have an Oedipus complex…or something like that?"

"Applying labels is too easy. When they're overused, they don't mean much. Your relationship with Fiona, what was in it for her?"

"We knew what the other was going through, which was comforting."

"And for you?"

"At first, Fiona held me close to protect me."

"From whom?"

"Myself."

"I know you were depressed back then, but suicidal?"

"Fiona thought I was very fragile and about to fall apart like my mother had."

"But you didn't. Are you fragile now?"

"I guess so."

"I'm not so sure," Sally said. "You protected Fiona and took a beating when she was blackmailed. You witnessed Drew's death. When Philippa was living upstairs, we had her down for dinner a couple of times. And she told me what you had done for her at Universal. Fragile?" She made a puzzled face. "Maybe I'm missing something?"

"Fiona said that I had inherited some of my father's attributes. The man was a genuine hero: commissioned a Free French officer. Later, he put up with my foolishness and my mother's oddities. I wish I had known him better. But, I guess, I could only idolize one parent at a time."

"You rarely mention him," Sally replied. "Back to you and Fiona. What was in it for you?"

"Well, sex with a woman was new. Fiona and I were breaking taboos. That enhanced the sex. But more than that, I craved Fiona's security. So I dumped Drew and went for the big bucks."

"Alexander, that's so self-deprecating. What I saw of you and Fiona, you were happy together and persevered despite blackmail and Fiona's social humiliation. A testimony to your love for each other?"

"It is," I said. "Fiona treated me as an adult. She could be sarcastic but seldom used it on me, even when she'd lost her formidable temper. Fiona's sense of order was what I needed; she reassembled me after the suicide."

"Reassembled?"

"Fiona raised me, settled me down, and sent me to college. Sure, my mother's make-believe was fun, but I had to grow up. In short, Fiona saved me from my mother's crazy influence. And now I'm much like Fiona: guarded, aloof, and a bit frosty."

Arnie was stretched out on his back sound asleep. "If he starts snoring, tug his collar." Sally folded her hands. "Go on."

"I've been thinking a lot about Fiona; I'm pretty sure that she and Drew discovered that they each knew my mother's last secret when they were at Tahoe. But that's just one more thing I'll never know for sure."

"And that's that," Sally said, jotting a few notes before closing her notebook. "Got all that settled quicker than I thought. Before we finish, I'm curious: when you and Fiona were arguing about your going to New York, she attacked you. Then you made love. You said that Fiona instigated the sex. Why?"

"My mother had asked Fiona to take care of me if anything happened to her."

"Like that?"

"No, of course not." I felt myself blush. "A day or so afterwards, I asked Fiona what was going to happen to me when she left me. She told me not to worry—that she'd always take care of me. And she did until she died."

"What was Fiona like before Tatiana became ill?"

"Fiona, my mother, and I talked about all manner of things. Fiona was like an aunt I never had. But after the suicide, she stood between Drew and me. So I started treating her like Drew did. Drew got everything he wanted; I got a beating."

"Followed by sex and a lasting relationship," Sally said. "Perhaps Fiona was determined that you weren't going to become the mistake she'd made raising Drew?"

"I don't know about that. But I do know I'm a better Alexander Romanovsky than a knockoff of Andrew Faircloth. Do you have more thoughts along those lines?"

"I do. You told me that Fiona watched you for signs of insanity. Could Fiona have seen the parallels with you and Tatiana's brother? Two unstable young men facing profound shame? Your uncle fled to Russia and his destruction. You ignored the suicide and repressed your guilt and were about to flee to New York. Could Fiona have decided to stop you from following your uncle's path?"

"Possible, I guess. Fiona knew more about my family that I did at the time. One more thing before we close: You seem to know how I'll answer your questions before you ask them. Frankly, that's annoying."

"Sometimes I can make pretty good guesses. Alexander, you asked for my help, and I'm happy to provide it. To do so, I need your unvarnished honesty, which requires the courage I know you have. Earlier, you tried slipping around me with housekeeping details. Now I sense you're wrapping up bothersome issues for another day. That day is here. I doubt it will ever return."

"Okay, if it's honesty you want… I'm sure that Fiona didn't think I was following my uncle's footsteps. No, I was following my mother's. She clung to people: her mother, her brother, a German colonel, and my father. When my father died, she snapped. Fiona thought that I'd inherited my mother's fear of being alone."

"Go on."

"When I thought Fiona was leaving me, I started clinging to women. Philippa refused my advances. Around the same time, another woman recognized my dishonesty and broke things off. So you see, I'm indeed my mother's child."

"And?"

"I'm frightened."

"Did you start a journal?"

"It's a study of a mother's boy, a sissy."

"You don't come across that way," Sally said.

"I throw a baseball like a girl."

"I'm sensing anger?"

"Edgy, that's all." Arnie woke up and shook himself before heading to the kitchen.

"I see," Sally said, watching Arnie. "How is this mother's boy doing on his own?"

"At work all I do is talk to people, so the time alone is a break."

"Are you seeing if you can bear being alone, unloved?"

"That's right."

"Sounds cloistered?" Sally countered.

"Some cloister—apartments in Paris and San Francisco."

"What about sex?"

"Cloistered and celibate."

"Does the prospect of a relationship concern you? Worried you'll fall for the first reasonable, or unreasonable, woman? Worried you'll have to explain your family? And Tatiana? And maybe you'll resort to lying?"

"Yes, all of that. Frankly, my mother embarrasses me, and I'm embarrassed about being embarrassed."

"Sounds like you're stuck. Because of the unanswerable questions Tatiana left: 'How could she leave me this way? Wasn't I more compelling than death?'" Sally paused. "Tatiana left you holding the bag, didn't she?"

"You don't understand my mother. She was magical. We stood with Dante as he watched Beatrice walk along the banks of the Arno. We went to the ballet with Degas, and Spain with Goya. Mother could have inspired me to things of beauty instead of a stupid pipeline. She fashioned my identity only to let it shatter like dropped crystal when she slashed her wrists. Thank God, Fiona was there to put the pieces back together. To answer your next question: I'm not suicidal, but I'm not that crazy yet."

"Okay, okay, hold on." Sally paused. "What are your plans when you get back to Paris?"

"The pipeline will take years to complete. By then, I'll know how to make big bucks greasing trade between Russia and the West. In essence, starting over."

"Starting over?" Sally shook her head. "Gosh, how many people have come to San Francisco with just that in mind? Are you looking for anyone?"

"I don't understand."

"Tatiana?"

"Sally, don't be silly."

"Remember my Crab Louie dinner when we discussed the similarities between Tatiana's time in Paris and yours?"

"Coincidence, that's all."

"Easy, easy, calm down, sit back." She leaned forward. "You're looking for Tatiana, aren't you?"

"No."

"Level with me, level with yourself. What do you want from her?"

"Forgiveness."

"She killed herself."

"I know that."

"Why so angry?"

"Isn't it obvious? Me, I'm angry at me. I should have prevented the suicide."

"What else?"

"She left me."

"You're angry with Tatiana?"

"I'm not angry, I'm livid. Fiona and Drew lied all these years to hide the mess—me—that my mother dropped in their laps. Thank you, Tatiana. And may God damn you."

"Alexander, calm down."

"Oh my God! What have I done?" I closed my eyes for the longest time until I felt Arnie's nose on my hand.

"Dogs understand us better than we think," Sally said. "Arnie knew you were upset and left. Now he thinks you need comforting that only a wet nose can provide. Look, I realize this was somewhat graceless. When we first talked, I hoped your insights and conclusions would arise over several sessions, but time doesn't permit that."

"Is my anger the feeling that something momentous was coming at me?"

"What do you think?"

"I think it was."

"So do I," Sally said. "When you talk about Tatiana, you range from tender idealization to the harshest invective. Anger isn't uncommon with suicide survivors. Survivors often try to ignore it, like you did right after the suicide. Or replace it with guilt as you've been doing for years."

"What now?"

"You might try reconciling your humanity, all of it: your dishonesty, the anger and shame, the embarrassment, your problem with a baseball. The appealing aspects too: your essential decency, courage and compassion, and your Russian toughness."

I laughed. "Toughness."

"I mean that. You've come through to the other end in relatively good shape. And you're brave enough to have come to me and confronted your deepest feelings. If you're going to forgive yourself, you may have to start by forgiving Tatiana."

"That sounds very tidy," I said.

"Not at all. It's messy and time consuming, but you're up to it."

"I'm worried that I'm like my mother."

Sally said, "While you've inherited many of your mother's characteristics, you've led a far different life than Tatiana's with far different results. Perhaps it's time you decided what to keep?" Her eyes turned troubled.

"You've been touched by a suicide?"

"You'd have made a pretty good shrink." She closed her eyes. "That morning, my mother and I had a nasty argument about cleaning up my room. That afternoon, I came home from school and found my mother in the garage, in her car with the motor running. She had killed herself. I still can't believe she did that to me." She opened her eyes. "Long story short, I started acting out and was sent to a psychologist who'd gone through her father's suicide. Our experiences are different, but there are similarities: the guilt, unworthiness, and the anger."

"My God, Sally, I'm sorry."

"Don't be. We have a bond; we're survivors."

"Does the suicide still bother you?"

"It always will. I watch myself for cycles of depression and have taken steps. I married Bert. He's kind and gets me out of depressions. He and the girls, I'd never do to them what my mother did to me. Of course, there's my Russian landlord of impeccable breeding."

"And Arnie?"

"And Arnie too."

"Your mother, do you love her now?"

"Always have," Sally said. "But, like I said, it took work and time."

"Still angry?"

"A little," she replied. "That she allowed me, a girl of fourteen, to find her… that she didn't think of me is, well, you know how it goes."

"Don't know what to say."

"We've both said enough for one session."

CHAPTER 34

WEDNESDAY, DECEMBER 7, 1988

SAN FRANCISCO

I met with one of Fiona's lawyers, Hopkins Browning, whose specialty was estate law. When we first met in his office, I suspected he was an anglophile based on the décor: dark wood paneling adorned with paintings of British manor houses, muted oriental carpets, and Georgian furniture. Plump and in his late fifties, Browning was a study in pink with a London-tailored gray suit with a faint pink stripe, pink shirt, and forest-green bow tie with reddish tea roses.

Standing next to his antique Sheraton desk, Browning shook my hand and said, "I'd hoped we'd have this conversation somewhat earlier, but Fiona instructed me not to press you." He spoke with an accent I couldn't quite place.

Fiona's will forgave my mortgage and passed on her wine cellar and the Scottish paintings that were in my garage waiting for me to gather the courage to sell them. Fiona thought more generosity might target me for legal action when her family began dragging each other into court. I didn't know if the estate was being litigated and wasn't about to ask.

"I thought everything had been settled," I said, sitting down in the perfect Queen Anne chair next to his desk.

"Fiona added a codicil that she hadn't discussed with you. She asked me to do this in person. Otherwise you'd refuse." He leafed through the file. "Oh, I'm to make sure you're in a tranquil state of mind." Looking over the half crescents of his reading glasses, he asked, "Are you?"

"I guess so."

"Depression?"

"Sadness."

"Takes time, doesn't it?" Dropping his voice, he continued, "Fiona was concerned about your adjustment in the event of her death, but you appear to be doing rather well?" His purling vowels delivered with a slightly clenched jaw were the products of a New England boarding school, perhaps the same one Drew attended.

"It's a work in progress, but I'm as sound as a Yankee dollar."

"Gosh, that's good to hear." Browning took a document from a file. "Fiona's proposal. I'd appreciate your thoughts."

Fiona proposed to establish a trust that would support me while I took courses in interior design, attained the necessary certifications, and set myself up in business.

"This is Drew's money, isn't it?" I asked.

"Drew and Fiona were my clients," Browning replied. "When Fiona added this codicil, Drew was still alive and I hadn't liquidated his estate. Therefore, one may presume those funds were Fiona's."

"As I'm sure you know, money is fungible. Besides, I told Fiona my taking Drew's business was out of the question."

"Fiona said you'd be difficult." He cleaned his glasses with a hand-kerchief.

"Sorry." I stood up. "I'm leaving."

"Hear me out, please. I'm obliged to proceed." Browning motioned me back to the chair. "It's quite straightforward: I disburse funds for your living expenses and studies; you'll find that I'm amiability person-ified. Why don't you, at least, consider this?"

"You haven't answered my original question: Whose funds are these?"

"Fiona didn't say, and it never occurred to me to ask."

"This is Fiona acting for Drew."

"Where she obtained these particular funds, I can't say. After all, money is 'fungible,' as you reminded me, and Fiona was quite wealthy. She did tell me that you weren't prepared to explore your real talents when this was executed." He chuckled. "I believe she planned convincing you to explore your talents but wanted this arrangement in the event of her death."

"I do appreciate your efforts, however—"

"You see, I'm in something of a pickle." Tenting his fingers, he said, "This bequest will tempt those...those..." After a gasp, he continued, "That Fiona, such a civilized woman, was related to those grasping hyenas confounds me." He stood to face me. "Should you decline, the funds will be disbursed to Fiona's family."

"I can't help that. I told Drew that I couldn't take his offer and why. And I've taken far too much from Fiona to take any more."

"Your mother's name was Tatiana?"

"What does *she* have to do with this?"

"Correspondence from Fiona." He handed me an unsealed envelope and turned toward the window.

Dearest Alexander,

If Hopkins has given you this, my life has ended.

I pray that you accept Tatiana's legacy. Drew and I are but the vessel; the talent Tatiana gave you will flourish with nurturing, we have no doubt. Then, Alexander, you will be at peace with yourself as Tatiana would have wished and Drew and I had hoped. Speaking for the three of us, I regret being denied the beauty you'll create and the joy that will be yours. Perhaps we will be together again somewhere, sometime, and you'll tell me about it.

Please pray for Drew and me as you pray for Tatiana.

Fiona

Browning looked over his shoulder. "Your mother's gift, my good man."

"Don't know what to say."

"Unsettling, I know." He patted my shoulder. "I have an appointment that will take the remainder of the day. Stay here as long as you wish." He shook my hand.

"I'll get back to you soon."

"There's a good fellow."

CHAPTER 35

APRIL 1989

SAN FRANCISCO

If you're going to forgive yourself, you may have to start by forgiving Tatiana. That's what Sally told me.

I stopped grappling head-on with my mother's revelations. My initial momentum faltered as I became angry with myself for being angry with my mother. Sally suggested a solitary introspection about the new, uneasy relationship with my mother.

After several weeks, I asked myself: Forgive my mother for what? For defying incipient insanity for most of her life and passing on many of her gifts to me? And being a most unique mother? Those questions were the momentum.

Doing the week's shopping on Saturday morning at Safeway, I ran across white endive, one of my mother's favorites that she prepared with ham and a cheese sauce with white pepper. Tatiana emerged from the dimness where I had relegated her. My thoughts turned to Dr. Sternberg. He said that demons breeding demons drove the insanity, but it was the wolves. The Russian wolves had stalked her since that terrible day in Russia that had forever marked her. She was a valiant Russian who held the wolves at bay for as long as she could.

I returned to that terrible summer and watched her retreating into her past but always returning to San Francisco, only to flee again to

Russia and her family's destruction. On to Paris, her mother's death, the German occupation, Alexander Trepoff and Colonel Haryett, and the displaced-persons' camp awaiting the Red Army's mercies.

Happier times in Berkeley? Yes.

San Francisco at Fiona's? No.

Who was I? Alexander Romanovsky? Alexander Trepoff? Or a hideous hybrid she and her brother had created? Beholding her—as she was, as she became—I loved her as I had before that terrible summer.

What to keep? What to cast aside?

Going home, I pulled into the Marina Green parking lot and walked to the sea wall. It was a warm summer day. I looked east to Berkeley and could just make out the university. Behind Cal were the hills where my parents had been their happiest, in our home with its garden overlooking the Bay. I would revisit the garden to see if Mother's magic lingered. But I had always carried her magic: our trips to museums where she encouraged me to embrace art; the vacations on the Mediterranean; dropping in on Somerset Maugham; cheeseburgers and milkshakes in California. Pleasant memories, but not entirely.

I would visit my father's grave that I had neglected. A kind man I didn't know well, I accepted his love without returning much and was left with the hope that he saw through my indifference. Mother and I were blessed that he had watched over us until Fiona took us.

If we hadn't met Fiona, my mother and I wouldn't have survived. The fact that Fiona kept my mother's secrets had to be measured against her love for my mother and me. And she guided me to a somewhat reasonable adult. Fiona and I fell in love and became best friends—a testament to Fiona's forbearance and humanity.

I found a bench on the Marina Green and looked at Drew's home. After his death, Fiona had sold it to a shipping mogul from Hong Kong whose extensive remodeling resulted in a fussy Tuscan exterior. *Fussy Tuscan.* Drew might have found that amusing. Drew said that taking his business would allow me to dream again. He was right; my dreaming now consisted of actual plans to be implemented.

Behind Drew's home, San Francisco sparkled. The fog had lifted, taking away the previous night's transgressions. Once again, the City was starting afresh that morning. Starting over, that's what brought many of us to San Francisco. I was starting over too, not only professionally but ethically. When Drew was dying, I came as the penitent to confess my duplicity—and was forgiven. However, contrition requires a vow to renounce forgiven sins. Mine was dishonesty, an untested obligation.

People on the Marina Green were walking dogs or letting them run. By the Yacht Club, small sailboats bobbed in anticipation; the starter's pistol cracked; sails popped as the tiny vessels skimmed over the running green swells. A knot of joggers huffed passed; a bicycle rider staring at a beautiful woman almost ran into her; a boy launched his Daffy Duck kite. Daffy danced on the wind, sticking his tongue out at me.

I always liked that duck. He kept going. No matter what, exploding cigars or running through walls, Daffy waddled on with truculent resolve. Resolve, a wonderful attribute for ducks and people.

***

I saw Sally and Arnie approaching. "I think I heard you getting in last night?" Sally said as we exchanged a polite hug. Sally and I sat down, and Arnie hopped up on my lap. "How did it go in Russia?" she asked.

"Most everyone is waiting for the system's last gasp."

"What do you think will replace it?"

"At best it'll be mildly authoritarian. If things get out of control, I suspect the army and the security services will step in. My friend, Boris Izmailov, thinks there's a lot of money to be made in oil and gas."

When I resigned from the pipeline consortium, I suggested that they have my two assistants run the Paris office and hire Boris to work out of Moscow. Boris leaped at the opportunity. The pipeline consortium paid for the week I spent in Russia showing him around the agencies that I had come to know. A clever man, Boris would become one of Russia's richest men—oligarchs, they would be called.

Sally asked, "How's the job search going?"

"Just before I left for Russia, I received an offer after an interview that didn't seem to go well. Long hours, lousy pay, and the owner is a tyrannical bundle of insecurities. But it's a first job."

"How about you and Tatiana?"

"Better, far better."

"You've settled the problems?"

"Yes, I think I have. My relationship with my mother is much like your relationship with your mother."

"Way to go," Sally said with a proud smile. "And Fiona and Drew?"

"They're resting peacefully now."

"Your anger?"

"Small controllable eruptions, but I'm getting there."

"Let's talk later. If you've come this far, we'll make sure you make it the rest of the way." Sally glanced at her watch. "Any movement on the lonely-guy front?"

"*Hey, foxy lady, my name is Alex and I'm a Libra.* Does that still work?"

"I don't think it ever did."

"You know, I've got zero dating skills. One of the few dates I've ever had was a couple of years ago. You met her at your Christmas party."

"The tall, striking woman?"

"We exchanged letters when I was in Paris, but those fizzled. Long story short, she doesn't trust me."

"Why don't you contact her? The worst she can do is say no."

"She shops at the Marina Safeway. I've spent way too much time there hoping to run into her. Anyway, she's probably moved on. So should I, I guess."

"That sounds like a lonely guy explaining why he's a lonely guy. Take some of Tatiana's advice: Do what you have to do." Sally checked her watch again and stood up. "I've still got time to shop. We're going to celebrate tonight."

"Celebrate what?"

"Your progress." Sally's sapphire eyes sparkled. "I'll do my Crab Louis. You bring the wine?"

"That's a great dish. We'll start with French champagne."

"It makes me happy," Sally said.

"Me too."

CHAPTER 36

FRIDAY EVENING, DECEMBER 1, 1989

SAN FRANCISCO

Through Dr. Sternberg I managed to get a seat behind the orchestra for the opening of *Tristan und Isolde.* I thought of arriving at the intermission, but I opted for arriving on time. The lady next to me was nice enough to elbow me when I fell sound asleep during the first act. With intermission approaching, I tried coming up with a clever critique, but I had always left that to Fiona.

I went to the great hall where Fiona had liked to stand and looked around. My eyes met Townie's, and we nodded. True to his word, Townie had apologized to Fiona after Drew died. Fiona accepted, and that was the end of it. Watching Townie feigning interest while listening to opera enthusiasts discussing the performance, I did empathize. Debra recognized me with a frosty smile and drew Townie back into the Opera Alliance's luminaries.

Looking for Dr. Sternberg and his wife, I saw Helen Jacobs standing with another group. I caught her eye and waved; she waved back. After thanking the Sternbergs for my ticket, I drifted back toward Helen.

"Looking for me?" She tapped my shoulder.

"Yes, I am," I replied, turning to face her. "Gosh, you look lovely. Life must be going well." She wore a black gown with long gloves, her hair was sleek and drawn back, and her eyes were a violet shade from contacts.

Helen accepted my compliment with an encouraging smile. "Life was going great for a while, job-wise." She sighed. "Several months ago, I was promoted to Senior Vice President, Human Relations—Northern California. Then Universal announced its tender offer for Growers and Ranchers. It's a done deal. Staff positions like mine will get axed first. So it'll be wham, bam, thank you, Ms., and step lively because there're plenty more behind you."

"Oh dear, I haven't been following that. What are you going to do?"

"Thank God, an offer turned up before the desperation." She waved away the subject. "Have you and Philippa talked lately?"

"We spoke around Thanksgiving; she seemed fine. We try to talk every several months; I'll phone her after New Year's. Why do you ask?"

"About a week ago, Philippa phoned and asked if she could suggest that you get in touch with me. She's concerned about you."

"I can't imagine why."

"Philippa thinks you're becoming a recluse, a monomaniacal dullard." Helen laughed, "Hey, just paraphrasing."

"A 'monomaniacal dullard.' Wow." I noticed a man in Helen's group staring at us. "What did you say?"

"I told her that I was more than a little annoyed with you."

"Annoyed? Why?"

"Oh, several things."

As I had promised at Fiona's funeral, I wrote Helen a longish letter when I returned to Paris. Helen had answered my first letter and told me how she missed Fiona and how helpful she had been introducing her to Opera Alliance members and other key people in San Francisco's opera world. I wrote back, and we exchanged several letters. Then after a long letter of mine, she stopped writing.

"I appreciated your letters, Helen. They were thoughtful and a delight to read. I wish you'd kept writing. Why did you stop?" She shrugged without answering. "When you stopped, I thought you were upset, or something else was going on. I thought my letters were pleasant enough. I did write several letters asking you what was wrong, but they seemed whiney and I tossed them."

"In my letters I asked you, several times, how you were getting along after Fiona's death . . . coping . . . feeling."

"Oh, there were rough spots, you know. So I threw myself into work. There was a lot of traveling."

"That's what I meant," Helen said. "I asked you personal questions; you gave me a travelogue: Russian weather reports, the crappy Russian food—riveting stuff like that. Reading between the lines, I realized that you were telling me to stop meddling. If you had mailed one of the whiney letters, I'd have gladly kept writing."

"Why didn't you say so? I would have at least tried to be more..." *Touchy-feely* came to mind but wouldn't have worked. I managed, "More open, more candid."

"I didn't want to pry more than I already had."

"I see. From our letters, I'd hoped we could get together when I was back here on business. When you stopped writing, I put that idea on hold until I could...until I could think of another approach. Which took until now."

"Why didn't you tell me that the grief was too devastating to write about?" Helen frowned. "Putting that to paper wouldn't have been so difficult?"

"Oh, I don't know."

"Men are such stoics: going off by themselves, brooding like some Wagnerian character."

"I wasn't brooding."

"Brooding, no. That's not you." After a moment's consideration, she continued, "You're reticent, restrained. Yes, that's it."

"I may be somewhat reserved until I get to know people. Look, instead of going into all of that, I was wondering if we could get together, maybe this evening after the performance. A drink, a bite to eat?"

"Why didn't you phone me?"

"After Fiona, I had to straighten out some delicate issues... Problems, I should say. And I was worried about fouling things up with you, a recurring theme that's repeating itself now." Helen seemed on the verge of replying but didn't. The man in Helen's group hadn't stopped looking at us. "Anyway, I hoped we'd run into each other at the Marina Safeway, but neither serendipity nor you showed up." Helen laughed. Although she was laughing at me, I detected a shard of sympathy. "So I got off the dime and phoned your office and tricked your secretary into telling me that you'd be here tonight."

"I'm flattered. As far as tonight goes, I'm committed. Sy and Grets are hosting a supper. Doubt if you're up for another evening with Sy."

"Maybe tomorrow? But no, that won't work. I've got to be in LA tomorrow afternoon and don't know when I'll get back. And that fellow in your group hasn't stopped looking at you and me. I've never get it right with you, never. And this isn't going the way I had planned... or hoped...or... Anyway, it was nice seeing you again. I better get back to my seat."

"Don't want to miss any Wagner," Helen said. "I haven't been exactly waiting for you by the phone."

"No, of course not. Anyway, I hope you... Actually, I had hoped that we..." I paused. "Ah, good luck with the merger. Then again, I guess it doesn't matter." A deep breath. "Anyway, this isn't working. Well, so, anyway, I'll get going. Anyway..."

"Anyway," she said. "Anyway, you sat through Wagner, which I know you hate, so that you could *run* into me?"

Glancing at the handsome man trying to catch Helen's eye, I said, "You know, after all these years, I still don't know a good opera from a bad one."

"This one is so-so," Helen said, turning to the man. "That's Richard. He lives in my building and is a huge opera fan. Charles, his partner, hates opera. So Richard escorts me and takes his responsibilities seriously." She smiled at Richard and motioned that everything was okay.

"So you're not seeing anyone?"

"I see whomever I please." She tossed her head as the lights dimmed.

"Of course you do, of course. Honestly, I wanted to see you earlier, but I didn't know how you'd react."

Helen's expression was hard to read. Then she said, "Philippa told me that you spent a Christmas with her. How's she doing?" The lights dimmed for the last time and people were brushing past us.

"She's great, just great. I was finishing up in Europe and spent Christmas and Boxing Day with Philippa and her husband, Edmund, and a house full of family and guests. She and Edmund raise those big English racehorses that jump over hedges, from the looks of it quite successfully. Edmund adores Philippa, and she radiates, even in muddy riding gear."

"What's her husband like?"

"Nice guy, terribly British, somewhat older than Philippa. Comes from old money, I think. Served in the army and was a captain in a fashionable cavalry regiment, the same one as Philippa's father."

"You get along with him?"

"Getting through the Britishness takes time. We got along okay, but after a couple of days, he was getting edgy. It was time to go anyway."

"You love Philippa, don't you?"

"We went through a lot together. She's the closest friend I have."

"I see." An usher asked if we were going to our seats, and Helen said, "Oh, I've had enough Wagner this evening." Nodding at me, she added, "And he's had more than enough for a lifetime. We'll stay out here."

After a silent moment, we started talking at the same time and laughed. "This new job of yours?" I asked.

"Thanks to Fiona, I'll be starting a job with the San Francisco Opera early next year. Problem is, it's personally rewarding *and* artistically enriching, but not much money. My lifestyle will take a huge hit." Her expression turned nostalgic. "When you were in Europe, Fiona and I often had dinner—delightful evenings. Did Fiona tell you about helping me?"

"Yes, and how much she enjoyed doing so. She was quite fond of you."

"Fiona was one of the kindest people I've known," Helen said with her eyes glistening. "I told Fiona that I had to follow my passion. Bless her soul, she took it to heart and introduced me to most everyone who had anything to do with opera. Now I'm making my move. Thrilled, but sad that I took so long."

I thought about Fiona and Drew. He once told me that he was a Good Samaritan, and he was. So was Fiona. If relatives had approached Fiona as Helen had, she would have gone to great lengths.

Helen cleared her throat. "You miss her, don't you?"

"I do."

"Philippa told me that you were happy, deservedly so, after some personal issues." Helen put up her hand. "Philippa was discretion itself. She did say that you had changed careers but didn't elaborate."

"Fiona left me funds to tide me over while I studied interior design and got situated—a job, that is."

"You told me there was too much baggage to take Drew's business?"

"Fiona and Drew rewrapped the gift so that I couldn't refuse. I'm glad they did."

"So, tell me about it," Helen said.

"I started taking courses. But it's like swimming. At some point you've got to jump in. So I went around to every interior decorator in the Bay Area trying to get that first job with no experience. Talk about rejection. You know, that business is full of jerks."

"Who'd have thought?" Helen smiled.

"Then it dawned on me: most decorators have no business sense, none whatsoever. Their initial estimates aren't right, and the cost overruns drive clients right up their fabulous wallpaper. To make the money, they jerk around the contractors and beat up their suppliers. So I tried another approach: I'd cost out the projects, deal with the suppliers and the contractors, do the accounting, and make sure that everyone got paid. That worked, in that I got hired. Trouble is, I'm working for the biggest ninny west of the Rockies—pompous, tyrannical, and bitchy. Considering my hours, I'm making less than minimum wage."

"You're talented?" she asked.

"I can get clients to visualize the finished project without relying on mock-ups and drawings. Right now, we're finishing a big job in Los Angeles. I've been running flat-out since Labor Day. Erratic clients, awful schedule, completion before Christmas. There's a chance it'll be featured in one of the slick magazines. The project is mine: my ideas, my planning. If it keeps going well, we'll make a pot full of money."

"Sounds exciting," Helen said.

"We're both starting over, aren't we?"

"A good thing, I guess," she replied with less enthusiasm.

Something had changed. The more I tried engaging her, the more she withdrew. The final applause from the theater was perfunctory, and I asked, "What about getting together around Christmas when I'm finished in LA?"

"Oh, I don't know. Leaving the bank, new job, and all of that. Maybe after the first of the year. But, no, that won't work. Later, sometime later."

"What's wrong?"

"I've been thinking." Helen crossed her arms. "Philippa said there was magic between us. There was, but it's unraveled. Besides, you're in love with Philippa. And Philippa's husband knows that too?"

"Philippa's my best friend. Should she ever need my help, I'd be on the first plane to England. But I doubt I'll ever be taking that trip because Philippa and her husband are in love. That's as honest as I can make it."

"Philippa is taken. I deserve more than that."

"Philippa wasn't taken; she became happily married." Out of the corner of my eye, I saw Sy and Helen's escort approaching. Helen motioned to Sy that she would be coming.

"There's more to it than that?"

"Yes, there is," Helen said, stepping back. "I'm not beautiful like Philippa. And Fiona was not only kind but intelligent and attractive. You should find someone like them."

"Helen, don't belittle yourself."

"Yes, yes, you're right about that." She hesitated. "Since Philippa called, I've given you a lot of thought. Seeing you again, it's all come together. You…you lied to me from the get-go. Since I don't trust you, getting together is quite pointless because I'd never know whether or not you're telling the truth, shading it, or withholding something. Not much to base even a casual relationship on, is it?"

"I've never lied to you."

"Oh, far worse." She flushed with anger. "When we first met, you let me believe that I had legitimate reasons to keep seeing you. What's more, I felt secure enough to tell you personal things. Thinking about it, I'd rather be lied to than deceived."

Sy came up and said, "Helen, we've got to go. Greta will have a fit if we're late."

"Helen, why did you even bother even talking to me tonight?"

"Hadn't thought it through. Must have been feeling sorry, but I didn't know for whom. Still don't, not that it matters." Sy took her elbow. "Good-bye, Alexander."

I watched her walk away, hoping she'd look back. Of course, she didn't.

I reclaimed my coat and started the long walk home. I should have started by telling Helen that I had vowed to become an honest man. Perhaps too dramatic for a crowded intermission, but that bold step might have worked. Then I should have told her that I wanted to see her sooner but was too consumed sorting through my past. But I hadn't been as forthright as I should have, and turning over a new leaf doesn't turn away the past.

I thought of trying again, but running into her at Safeway, she'd walk away; at her office, she'd call security; at her apartment building, the doorman. If I phoned her, she'd hang up.

CHAPTER 37

CHRISTMAS EVE 1989

SAN FRANCISCO

Christmas Eve that year was on a Sunday, and I caught an early-Sunday-evening flight from Los Angeles. With delays and heavy rain in both cities, I got home around nine o'clock. My raincoat was soaked through, and water was running down the back of my shirt. In the foyer, Sally was saying good-bye to a group of her guests. I stood aside as they left.

"Hey, jingle, jingle." Sally giggled.

"Jingle, jingle yourself. I'm going to get out of these wet clothes and crash."

"There's still plenty to eat and drink. How did it go in Tinsel Town?"

"Couldn't have gone better. Finished on time. Check's in the mail."

"Come in, I've saved some lamb chops."

I left my coat and luggage and followed Sally into the living room. The party was breaking up, and two couples were involved in an intense conversation while Helen sat on the sofa, listening. She looked much like she had when we met in Denver. "Helen—oh dear! How does she seem?" I asked.

"Go see while I get you a glass of wine. Red or white?"

"Red. How do you know Helen?"

"You introduced us a few years ago, remember? Once someone

comes to a Roth party, they always return."

I approached Helen. "Mind if I sit down?"

She made room. "Looks like you've had a long day."

"Long and wet. I know you're upset with me. And I don't blame you."

She smiled. "A confession: I've come to these parties hoping we might reconnect. But you weren't around or had just returned to Europe. I asked Sally not to tell you. Did she?"

"No. Ah, sorting out my personal issues took longer than I thought."

"And you've sorted out those issues quite thoroughly."

"What I did wasn't fair."

"Not at all." She laughed.

"I hoped and hoped that you hadn't found someone else," I said. "Then I prayed and offered up a deal: if I could see you again, I'd never lie or mislead you, withhold information, or any of that."

Helen shook her head. "Deal prayers don't work."

"I know. At the opera, I was honest, but not enough. Something had to be done, but I was out of ideas until I realized that every shred of honesty I could muster was in the journal Sally told me to keep. So I pulled it up on the computer, hit Print, and mailed it. Presumptuous?"

"Very—and one of the bravest acts I've encountered," she said. "You don't know much about me."

"I know your hopes, dreams, fears, and regrets. And I know you're honest."

"I've lied and probably will again, but not to you. There's virtually nothing I don't know about you, your mother, or your family, and the rest."

"And?"

"The first reading was unnerving," she said. "But after you opened up so completely, I wanted to talk to you, in person, but you were in LA. So I called Philippa, around midnight her time, and scared her half to death. Very, very long conversation. My nickel, the bill's out of sight. When I told her what you had done, she asked about your mother, if I knew everything. Philippa said that you told her when you spent a Christmas with her and her husband."

"As you probably know, Philippa and I stumbled into each other's personal life. And I—"

"I know," Helen interrupted. "Philippa asked about your family. Why Alexander Trepoff went back to Russia, we'll never know. Your mother and her brother, they were so damaged. In Paris, with no one to turn to, they might have fallen into an intimate survivor's syndrome. Or maybe..." She looked away. "I don't know. Couldn't possibly imagine. And Adrian Romanovsky certainly paid for whatever sins he committed." She seemed deep into her thoughts, then reemerged with a conflicted smile and said, "Reading it was breathtaking too. The daring and profound trust."

"When I'm stressed, I still think of cigarettes," I said.

"I don't think about them anymore. Are you nervous?"

"I'm relieved, but still..."

"You confronted your dishonesty and atoned. You can't do more than that," Helen said. "I got to know Fiona fairly well. She'd never tell me such a thing, but I sensed you were her special accomplishment. You have many of Fiona's best qualities."

"I don't know about that."

"I do," Helen said. "Philippa said there was magic between us, and she was right." I laughed. "You don't believe in magic?"

"I do, I do, but sometimes it's difficult to recognize."

"Sometimes magic is too magical to understand. Have you gone back to Berkeley, to Tatiana's garden?"

"I did. It was smaller than I remembered, but the trees are much larger. The owners, a nice young couple, were going away for the day and let me spend the afternoon. The memories are quite vivid."

"You said that you and Tatiana walked into paintings and talked to the people."

"That was a long time ago."

"That magic could return." Helen took my hand. "I want to visit Tatiana's garden and thank her for giving me the man I've fallen in love with."

"Really?"

"Really. Always a kind man, now you're an honest one. Oh, and very handsome too."

"Think so?"

"Know so. Did you ever talk to Sally about me?"

"I told her I was spending far too much time at Safeway, hoping to run into you."

"What did she say?"

"Sally told me to follow my mother's advice: 'Do what you have to do.'"

"And so you did." Helen squeezed my hand. "You told me once that I'm exotic?"

"Oh, you are, like a movie star—one of the Italians, Sophia Loren. Especially your smile." We were close. Other than a couple of polite hugs, it was our closest physical contact.

"Sophia Loren," Helen said, laughing like Sophia Loren, head back, unrestrained.

We were alone. The lights had dimmed; lamb chops and wine were on the coffee table in front of me. Sally and Bert were cleaning up in the kitchen and talking. Bert dropped a pan that sounded wet. Sally laughed; they both laughed.

"Time gets funny when I'm with you," I said. "Kind of grainy: faster than lightning at the opera, slower than melting snow—hoping to see you again. It has something to do with how time moves and Einstein's theory of relativity."

"Einstein?" She laughed out loud.

"I say the stupidest things when I'm nervous. Fact of the matter is: I love you, and regret it's taken this long to tell you."

"That's wonderful," she said. "Why don't you tell me all about Los Angeles while I fix supper? Upscale hamburgers with gorgonzola—they're pretty good."

We said good-bye to the Roths and went to Helen's. We didn't get around to the hamburgers that evening and stayed in bed well into Christmas Day.

Sy and Greta were hosting their Christmas dinner party, and Helen talked me into going. We ran into Julian and managed a short, polite conversation. Sy and Greta were gracious, past unpleasantries forgotten.

EPILOGUE

The following summer just before dawn, my mother visited me. "Sandro, gdye Elena? *(Sandro, where's Helen?)*

"Doma, San Francisco." *(Home, San Francisco.)*

Going to the window and looking out, she asked, "Where are we?"

"Los Angeles. A magazine is taking pictures of work I did last year before Christmas."

"Ah, you'll be famous?"

"Becoming recognized."

She sat on the end of the bed. "You're marrying Helen?"

"This December."

"Problems? Religion? Helen's converting, or you?"

"Neither of us; it's how we connect with the people who've gone before us."

"That's right," she said with glistening eyes. "More problems?"

"Helen works for the San Francisco Opera."

"I detest opera," she said. "Dear boy, you'll never get away from it." Her voice dropped a register. "Other problems?"

"Helen's mother doesn't care for me: I'm Christian. Worse, Orthodox. Far worse, Russian. And starting a new career later in life—the complaints are endless."

With that distinctive Russian sigh of resignation with the faintest glimmer of hope, she asked, "What mother likes her daughter's husband?" She smiled. "You and Helen like each other?"

"Remarkably well after such terrible starts. When I'm not with Helen, she's on my mind."

"You love her?"

"Yes, I'm lucky to have found her." We held each other's eyes. "Oh,

meaning to tell you, Helen and I went back to our garden in Berkeley. We hosted a picnic for the new owners. The magic you planted is still there."

"We were happiest in Berkeley, weren't we?"

"We were. I thought of asking her about the Russian wolves... But I decided they had returned to Russia where they belonged.

Mother had always asked if I loved anyone more than her; she wouldn't ask this time. Leaning over me, she said, "Sandro, opera, such a small price."

"Will I see you again?"

Without taking her eyes from me, she backed to the window, illuminated in the brilliant morning light. "Sandro, I've always loved you, always. You know that?"

"I do."

She was ethereal, shimmering radiance, then light itself. "Sandro, remember me?"

"Always."

I dream of her. We're in the garden having tea, and I watch a young boy clutching his mother's enchantment. I pray for her.